Rebecca Benson's War

Also by Patti R. Albaugh

Treat Gently This Gentle Man: A Daughter's Prayers

The Ups and Downs of Miss Margaret Landings

Rebecca Benson's War

A Novel

Patti R. Albaugh

Rudin Press
Tucson, Arizona

Printed in the United States of America

First Printing, 2021

Cover Image from Dreamstime.com

ISBN: 978-0-9895530-4-9

Library of Congress Control Number: 2021919452

Rudin Press

Tucson, Arizona

DEDICATION

With humility and caution that only a writer of perilous times can experience, I dedicate this story to men and women everywhere who have struggled with, and perhaps died for, the meaning of patriotism.

TRUTHS

There are three truths: My truth, Your truth, and The Truth

Chinese Proverb

PART ONE

I am more and more convinced that man is a dangerous creature and that power, whether vested in many or a few, is ever grasping, and like the grave, cries, 'Give, give.'

Abigail Adams

Prologue

Sometime in 1943.

On a blood-soaked French battlefield under a gun-metal gray sky, a forgotten arm with a magic tattoo lay in the mud. The tattoo would never again comfort a little girl back in Ohio, but it would haunt the woman she became.

A young Rebecca looked at her sleeping father, dressed in his uniform—colorful ribbons and shiny bars pinned to his jacket. She waited for the steady up and down of his chest, but he lay still.

She stood on her toes and tentatively reached toward the arm she knew had a blue tattoo. The tattoo had her name written across an American flag, and it was magic. If she were crying, her father would take her on his lap and let her kiss the flag on his arm. When she kissed the tattoo, he would give her a big hug and say, "See. Everything's going to be okay."

His stillness bothered her, and her curiosity was motivation to reach for the magic tattoo. "Daddy, Daddy, wake up!" She shook his arm and tugged on his gloved hand. Instead of feeling an arm, her fingers grabbed softness like one of her stuffed animals. She pulled up his sleeve and down on his glove. His arm came out of the sleeve in one long cottony log with the gloved cotton hand at the end. She froze and tried to make sense of what she saw.

"Where's Daddy's arm?" Rebecca screamed. "Where's Daddy's arm?"

Her scream pushed aside the people around her, and her mother appeared, white-faced and bug-eyed.

"Oh, Rebecca, what did you do?" Her mother tried to put the arm back in the sleeve, but the batting was too thick, and she couldn't return it to its formerly crafted position. Her shaking hands only served to make a mess of the cotton, and soon the box was filled with clouds of soft billows.

A man came over and gently led Rebecca and her mother into the next room where refreshments sat waiting. "We'll take care of it, Mrs. Herman." He ushered the rest of the people in, too. He went back into the viewing room and closed the big wooden doors.

Rebecca sat, numb, on a folding chair. She looked down at her dress, which had bits of cotton stuck here and there. She shivered, remembering where the cotton had been. Her red bow tie was wet with her tears, and it had stained the white collar her mother had so carefully ironed that morning. Even the blue skirt had some red that her hand had smeared from the bow.

She shivered again. Her stomach hurt.

Her mother knelt beside her and cupped Rebecca's chin with her hand. Her face had that "Rebecca's been bad" wrinkle. "You shouldn't have done that, Rebecca. You have to respect your daddy and let him sleep in peace."

"I don't want Daddy mad at me," Rebecca said through her sobs. "I wanted to kiss the magic tattoo.

Where's his arm?" She put her face in her hands and cried with long, high pitched wails.

Her mother sat in the next chair, pulled Rebecca onto her lap and rocked her. "It's okay, Darling. Your Daddy isn't angry with you."

She nodded, and her sobs settled into quiet irregular gulps.

"He's dead, isn't he, like the rabbit in our yard?"

"Yes, dear, but he's asleep. He'll wake up in Heaven. Rabbits don't wake up in Heaven." Her mother paused while she stroked Rebecca's hair.

"Your Daddy was a hero, darling. He fought in a war to protect us. When you grow up and have children of your own, you can tell them about their brave grandfather."

"Wars put daddies to sleep."

"You don't really think that, do you Sweetie? Now, what are you going to tell your children when you're a mommy?"

Rebecca folded her arms and scowled. Big tears fell on the already soaked bow.

"Say, 'my Daddy fought in the war and he was a hero.'"

Rebecca looked down and mumbled, "My Daddy was a hero."

"That's a good girl. Now go on over to the refreshments and get yourself a cookie."

Rebecca slipped off her mother's lap and looked back at the casket where her daddy lay, visible through the reopened doors. She wanted to climb into the box with him, even if he didn't have an arm. She wanted to ask why the tattoo wasn't magic for him. She wished she had a magic tattoo he could kiss to make things better.

The red, white, and blue dress she wore screamed out from the sea of black clothing around her. She scratched where the wet bow touched her skin. She was glad her dress was ruined.

"You look just like an American flag," a woman had said to her. "Your daddy would be so proud to see his little girl look so pretty and patriotic."

She had wanted to wear the yellow sundress, so she could be Daddy's sunshine. She missed his deep voice and large, soft hands. The deep voice would sing the sunshine song. "You are my sunshine, my only sunshine," he would sing as he rocked her, and his large soft hands would hold her so securely that the most gigantic tornado could not blow her away. She hadn't heard the sunshine song in a long time. She thought for sure she would hear it today. Instead she learned what "dead" really meant.

She went back to her mother and leaned into her. She fought the soft sobs that welled in her throat.

"Why is Daddy dead?"

"He was hurt when he was fighting to keep us safe from the dangerous people."

"I thought fighting was bad."

"Not when dangerous people threaten us."

"Where's his arm?"

Her mother looked at her. "I don't know."

Her mother turned to a friend who came up to her. Rebecca watched her mother—standing and talking—and looked at her daddy—lying down and silent. The room twirled around her in a swirl of red, white, and blue flags. She ripped off the itchy red bow at her neck and ran back to her daddy. She lifted the drape of the casket, and looking around to check no one was watching, climbed into a dark cocoon underneath the casket where there were no flags or flowers or tearful people. She curled tightly into a ball so monsters and bad people would mistake her for a rock and go away. She was no longer a colorful dwarf among black skirts and purses, black slacks, and shiny black shoes. In her cocoon the sweet relief of drowsiness pulled her away from the darkness of a world without magic tattoos.

1

July 1965.

Far away from the rice paddies where American boys were losing limbs, lives, and naiveté, the houses in Liberty, Ohio, displayed their owners' patriotism. American flags, posted for the upcoming July 4th parade, graced the railings of homes built in various colonial architecture of Greek columns and Georgian verandas. Spacious front porches gave residents front row seats for the bands, marchers, and floats. An All-American town Liberty was. But the copious waving of the stars and stripes couldn't dispel whispers that all was not well nor going to be well. Most residents hardly noticed the creeping presence of change.

On Elm Street, named after the stately elm trees that had once draped the avenue with their long and leafy branches, a mailman waved and smiled his way up each sidewalk to the mailboxes mounted on front porches; he was as regular on his route as Old Faithful was in its timely spewing of heated water; in fact, people called him that—Old Faithful.

The mailman shouted a hearty hello to Mr. Jackson, a World War I vet, who kept a straight bearing as he clipped the shrubs in front of his well-kept and modest house. He had a nickname too, Old Man Jackson. Like Old Faithful, he was steady and unchanging. When Old

Man Jackson altered his routine, talk in the neighborhood likened it to an omen of things to come.

A couple of doors north of Mr. Jackson's house, ladies were gathering for a meeting of the Daughters of the American Revolution. Women, dressed in some fashion of shirtwaist dresses, paraded down the sidewalk. Ribbons studded with gold pins adorned the shoulders of some. They greeted each other as longtime friends.

One house, across from Mr. Jackson, was a particularly typical small-town home—white clapboard siding, green roof, green shutters and a matching front door. The house projected the American Dream—cozy , well-kept, and white as the stripes in the American flag. Except this house had no flag flying from its porch.

The front door opened on the no-flag house. Rebecca Benson and her Springer Spaniel dog, Clipper, stepped out for a walk to the city park. Rebecca, wife of police officer Adam Benson, could have been a Donna Reed double except for her ample calves which shown below the hem of her orange capris. Reddish brown hair touched the collar of her white shirt, wrinkled a bit and showing some remnants of a fast breakfast. She had a *New York Times* tucked under an arm.

Mr. Jackson waved. "Beautiful day, isn't it?" he shouted to her across the street.

Without a smile, she waved in return. She glanced toward Mr. Jackson's house and saw the painting crew who were covering the barely peeling white clapboard with soft yellow. Change.

Mr. Jackson gave a snappy salute to her. He grinned and shouted, "Where's your flag, Missy?"

"Still can't find it." She had hidden the flag, and she smiled to think how impossible it would be for Adam to find it. She liked the little bit of control she had over unadulterated patriotism.

"Well, you and your handsome husband ought to look harder for it. Gotta show pride in our country, you know."

She cast her eyes down and gave a thumbs up.

At the city park, Rebecca sat on a bench under a large maple tree. She reached over to read the headline on the front page of the *New York Times*: "Viet Cong Assault on Da Nang." Photos showed Marines making a landing on some pristine Vietnamese beach. Another article announced plans for protests around the country. "Why do you care what the world is doing?" her husband, her mother, high school classmates, and bridge club women had said over time. "Leave it to the politicians." Liberty, Ohio, was her hometown, but it was not always a place where she felt at home.

A Korean War veteran, her husband had promised not to re-up in the Marines, but she wondered whether or not she could believe him.

"I'm too old for war, Becky," he said, "being a police officer is all the excitement I need. Korea was my last war."

He said he would not soldier again, but she saw an intensity in his face as he watched the reports of the war on television—-his soldier eyes scanning the black and white images for ways he could lead men better than what he was witnessing.

A young boy toddled up to her. His mother frantically tried to catch up with him.

"Hello, young man," Rebecca said.

"Hi." He looked at the dog at her feet. He glanced from Rebecca to the dog and back again. He held out a tentative hand.

"Do you want to pet Clipper?" Rebecca smiled and looked at his approaching mother. "He would like to meet you. Let's make sure it's alright with your mom."

The little boy looked back at his mother, who had finally caught up to her son. She nodded.

"Go ahead, honey," she said to her son. "Just a little pat and then we need to go."

The little boy extended a plump little hand and gave Clipper a soft pat on his head and looked up at his mother.

"Good job."

I wonder if his mother knows how lucky she is, Rebecca thought.

They both smiled at Rebecca and walked away.

Rebecca heard a baby babbling and turned to see a young mother with a wispy haired baby in the stroller. When she held up her baby, Rebecca saw a little girl with ruby bowed lips, rosy plump cheeks, dark hair. Maybe between three and five months. Another child to long for. The park was a temptress of hope.

Adam was adamant about not having children. Didn't have the patience, he said. And Rebecca was okay with that...at first. When they met, she was relieved that she had found a man who didn't reject her because of her barrenness—thanks to a misguided surgeon who robbed her of her ability to have children. Unnecessary hysterectomy, another doctor said.

The trees funneled the cacophony of children's voices

directly to her—stabbing her with childish screams of glee and giggling. The stabs of regret reminded her of a short-sighted eagerness to please Adam. And as time went on, she was not sure Adam was being totally truthful about his reason for not having children. Just a feeling, but one she didn't have the courage to pursue. Both of his parents were gone, and he barely spoke of them. He didn't talk about the past. Wouldn't even explain the scar on his back. What guy is not proud of his scars? He was a live-in-the-moment kind of guy. He had double bolted the door to his past.

Rebecca watched the children on the swings. The rhythmic to and fro was like the endless arguments she and Adam had about adopting—his view, her view, his wants, her wants. "You're all I need," he would say, finishing the conversation by a pat on her head and a kiss on her cheek, a gesture that made her feel more like a pet than a wife.

She admitted to herself that she loved him more than could be put into words. When they walked, her small hand fit perfectly into his large and protective hand. His smiling and whistling when doing the dishes or taking out the garbage sounded like a domestic symphony.

"How did I luck out to get a woman like you?!" he would ask.

A dog's devotion and a loving husband were not enough. As much as she tried to quell the storm of grief within her, she could not forget that she was childless. Bridge, church work, Clipper, friends...nice, but not enough.

"Pretty heavy reading, there." A passerby pointed to the *New York Times* in Rebecca's hands. No one was safe from an opinion in a small town like Liberty.

"I beg your pardon?"

"You know. Those protestors are such cowards. They're too scared to be men, to do their patriotic duty. The government knows more than we do. We need to trust them." A sigh displayed her impatience and disapproval. "My son is over there, defending our freedom."

Rebecca opened her mouth to answer, but the woman clucked her tongue and kept moving down the path.

She stood, put the paper under her arm, and took Clipper's leash. "Sorry I upset you," she muttered to the disappearing woman.

Rebecca and Clipper walked down the wide tree-lined avenue toward home. Clipper had a characteristic lope as would any dog who anticipated the sights and smells of a walk. She pulled on his leash to slow their momentum. Pretty cheeky of that woman, she thought. Her next thought was about her unwillingness to confront her. Coward.

Flags flew from the front porches of many of the houses she walked by. But the red, white, and blue symbols of freedom only evoked anger. War, death, and power hid behind the happily waving flags. *Defending freedom? Whose freedom?*

The mile between the park and her house offered Clipper numerous watering opportunities and offered familiar sights of insurance offices, the post office, and a newsstand.

She noticed a new business office on Main Street—Shriver's Adoption Services. She had read about it in the local paper and had told Adam.

"Rebecca, we've talked about that. We are not

adopting," he had said during one of their many arguments about children.

She stopped, and Clipper looked up at her like he was trying to understand the sudden disruption. Standing in front of the office window, her reflection was next to the painted likeness of a young boy. The image in the glass window made a family—a young child looking up with love and gratitude, Clipper sitting at the boy's feet. She placed Adam's likeness in the reflected portrait. *What would it hurt to check it out?*

2

The bell on the door tinkled when Rebecca walked in. The fresh paint and the orange vinyl of new furniture announced the newness of the office. The walls held crisp posters of happy families.

"May I help you?" A grandmotherly woman appeared out of nowhere. Her gray hair was pulled into a bun at the nape of her neck. She reminded Rebecca of her favorite grandmother, Mimi, who had the carriage of an aging queen and the lap and arms of a Southern nanny. The very thought of her made her feel loved.

"We were walking by and I saw your sign." She pointed to Clipper, who sat dutifully at her feet. "May I bring him in?" The woman nodded a warm invitation.

"I have some questions."

"Oh?"

"I'm worried my husband and I are too old to adopt."

"Please have a seat." The woman smiled and pointed to a chair next to the main desk. "My name is Mrs. Lucey. And you are?"

"Rebecca Benson. My husband is Adam."

"Oh, Officer Benson. Such a nice man. A Korean War hero too. You must be so proud."

Rebecca smiled.

Mrs. Lucey took out a legal pad and a pencil. "Now ask me your question again."

Rebecca sat and directed Clipper to lie at her feet. She

crossed her legs at her ankles, placed her hands in her lap.

"I'm thirty and my husband is thirty-nine. Are we too old?"

"Tell me why you are thinking of adoption now? Have you been trying to have a baby all this time?"

"Well, no. I'm not able to have children, and my husband and I have thought we would be fine with just the two of us, but now we realize what we are missing." She put her hand to her throat and hoped she sounded convincing.

"I see. Would you like to make an appointment for both of you to come in and talk?"

Rebecca cleared her throat. "Could I take home some brochures so we could be better informed? Then I could call for an appointment."

"Of course, dear."

Rebecca left the adoption agency with a pocketful of brochures illustrating the endless love of families who open their hearts to homeless children. She walked down the tree-lined sidewalk with Clipper, patted the brochures, and smiled to herself.

This won't be like the last I brought up adoption. His stubbornness, her tears, the slammed door, the packed suitcase that never made it to the car. This time I have Mrs. Lucey on my side.

The call of a raven interrupted her thoughts of that horrible night their marriage survived. How could it hurt to try again?

3

Home. Rebecca looked at the clock and realized how soon Adam would arrive. Usually when he came home after work, he would grab her and plant his ritual afternoon kiss. They would hug with Clipper whining for his turn. His arms were strong, safe, and ready to save her from the bad guy. She loved playing the adoring housewife—fresh lipstick, Courageous Coral, of course, a spritz of Chanel No. 5 cologne, and hair—brushed into a Mary Tyler Moore smooth flip. Clipper always approved her looks by wagging his tail. He gets me as I am, she thought.

The back door squeaked, and Clipper barked his happy greeting. Rebecca watched Adam enter—even at a distance, his uniform smelled of the drunks he reined in during his shift as a police officer. She avoided his gaze.

He went to the sink and poured a cup of coffee from the percolator she always had ready for him. He sat at the table, and his attention locked onto the display of pamphlets from the adoption agency.

"Oh, Rebecca, not again."

She crossed her arms and squeezed her elbows. "I'm not your focus now, Adam, the police department is, and the shooting club, and your poker group…and I'm lonely."

"You're lonely when I'm not here, and you're restless when I am here. I don't think a child will fix things."

"How can you say that? You don't have the emptiness I have."

"That need, Rebecca, can't be filled by a baby or by me. I see it all the time in my work—people blaming what's happening on the outside instead of looking inside." He set down his coffee cup and studied something in there that kept his eyes on the coffee rather than on his wife.

Feeling insignificant and out-maneuvered again, Rebecca turned from him, arms still crossed. "If I'm so flawed, why did you marry me?"

He came over to her chair and gently pulled on her arms so she stood facing him. "Because you are the most loving and accepting person I have ever known. So why can't you accept this?"

She stared back at him.

"I'm saying it, and I don't want to say it again. I don't want children. Period."

"Why?"

"I've told you before. I'm too old, I'm not a patient person. I want to focus on us. Besides, I was an only child. I wouldn't know what to do with kids."

"I don't think you're being honest with me. There's something else. You're so wonderful with me and my mother, but you never talk about your childhood. Did something happen to make you afraid of having children?"

Adam gave her a look that she had only seen once or twice when he had been challenged by a colleague—eyes hard, jaw tightened, his hands clenched. He frightened her.

"You have no idea what you're talking about. You keep asking me questions, and I keep telling you I don't want to talk about the past. I'm done with this conversation."

He sat back down, unhooked the clip-on black tie and loosened the top button on his uniform shirt, wrinkled from driving a squad car for hours. The patch on his sleeve had "Liberty Ohio Police Department" encircling the top of the logo, and cornstalks overlaid the embroidered courthouse. At the feet of the cornstalk roots were the words "To Protect and to Serve."

She stared at the patch.

His face had returned to normal Adam. "Not feeling very supportive of my job right now, are you?"

"Protecting and serving is fine in a town where police calls are about lost dogs, an occasional bad check, or drunks who water the sidewalk flowers. I didn't know you when you were in Korea, so your service was commendable, not personal. It's my turn to be protected and served, that was the deal we made."

Adam cleared his throat. "This is not a good time for this, Rebecca. I have my own brochures, and I have to decide pretty quickly." He took out some papers from his jacket that was hanging on the back of the chair.

"I'm signing up to be an advisor to South Vietnamese soldiers. I'd be good at that, don't you think?" The papers were from the local recruiting office. He smiled as though he thought it was an entirely logical decision that she would applaud.

Vietnam? She wanted to slap him. She sat down and folded her arms over her stomach, where the pain sharpened. "So that's what my life will be, no child, and no husband?"

"It would be a year."

"What about our commitment? You promised me, only the Reserves." The salt burned in her eyes. "You already served in Korea. What if you don't come back? You're all I have."

He drew in a large breath, and his fingers drummed on the table, his eyes downward.

"Adam, don't avoid me. Please look at me." She wiped away tears and moved her head to get in line with his eyes. He had earned medals in Korea and handled toughs on the street. Yet he could not look at her when she was angry. "You know how traumatic it was for me to lose my father in a war—to see him lying in that coffin with no arm. I don't want to lose you. It's too much. I need you." Uncomfortable with pleading with him, her heart raced.

That firm square jaw of his lifted toward her. "I have experience they need for advisors. I'm in the Reserves, and with my police background, they let people at my age request orders for active duty. There's a good sign-up bonus, and I won't lose my pay from the police department. It will set us up well for the future." He spread his hands apart to plead his case. "Plus, didn't we both buy into Kennedy's "do for your country" stuff? Hell, we named Clipper after one of Kennedy's dogs, for Pete's sake."

At the mention of his name, the dog looked up and wagged his tail. Adam automatically scratched Clipper's ears, and the dog put his head back down with a satisfied sigh.

Rebecca swiped at a tear that had escaped her eye. She shifted so her feet were firmly on the floor, and she leaned toward Adam with her elbows on the table and her hands clenched together. "You have got to be kidding."

He unfolded her clenched fingers and rubbed his thumbs over her knuckles. "I've been a good provider.

You're always supportive of my police work. This will give us a good retirement."

She pulled back. "But you come home every day, which is not true for a lot of guys who go to Vietnam. And I'm not sure serving in Vietnam is helping our country or those people—what I hear on the news is not all stars and stripes. Newspapers are beginning to say we don't belong there. And that big march in Washington..."

"Don't pay attention to what you hear on the news. And those marches are organized by Commies. The South Vietnamese don't want communism, just like us. We can help them, Becky."

"I think the government is feeding us a bill of goods about Vietnam."

He pointed to the *New York Times* lying on the kitchen counter. "I wish you would stop reading that crap. You take one class on international studies, and you become an expert in Southeast Asia."

"Adam—"

"I have to go. That's all."

She stared past him, digging through thoughts to find something to say that would make him back down. The resolve in his face said that there was no changing. He had made up his mind, without her.

Her mind raced with possible arguments. "Aren't you afraid?" she asked.

His lips tightened, turning downward. "If the pounding in my chest is fear, yes, I have been afraid, but..." He leaned forward. "I'm a survivor. I survived combat in Korea, and now as a police officer I come home each night, to you. And after I serve this one last time, I'll come home to you again forever. I promise. One year. You have your mother here, your friends, your bridge club, and your job at the church. And we can both feel good about my contribution and your contribution for supporting me."

She read the pleading in his eyes. She heard his resolve to convince her he was right and that he would be all right. The urgency of his needs and her needs swirled together in a water and oil mirage. "What about reports of American advisors becoming targets of the Viet Cong?"

"I have to step up to the plate, to do my job, like my father did and my grandfather did." He paused, looked away, then back. "And your job is to support me."

That's when the war became personal. She threw Adam's cup of coffee onto the floor, and it broke into dozens of shards that left slices in the kitchen linoleum. Like spattered blood, coffee pooled on the floor and dripped off the cabinets. They both stared at the mess. Adam stood and pulled her to him. Her tears erupted and soaked through his shirt. He rocked her in his arms until the afternoon light in the kitchen mellowed into dusky grey shadow.

4

They went to bed. Adam slept in manly confidence he was doing the right thing. Rebecca tossed and turned in circles of helplessness in the face of a husband's right to make decisions.

She pretended to be asleep when Adam rose and got ready for the day. She listened to the clink of dishes as he pulled them out of the cupboards, smelled the coffee wafting from the pot to the corners of the house. She heard him softly close the back door.

She sat on the edge of the bed and tried to push back her anger at Adam for re-enlisting. *Why do men need to show honor by going to war?* She thought of a recent news broadcast. Grandfatherly newsman Walter Cronkite pointed out the latest skirmish on a black and white map of Vietnam, a country that most people didn't know until there were newscasts about the "conflict" in Southeast Asia.

Let them fight their own damn war. Her head ached from the back and forth of the argument in her mind. Be supportive. What about supporting her? How dare he go against their agreement. She thought about their early conversations about a childless marriage. *Oh hell.*

She took Clipper out for his walk, avoiding the park and staying on the main street. Maybe there was somewhere else she could read the paper. While he conducted his doggy detective work, Rebecca studied the remaining elm trees shading the street. Their shade had weakened since Dutch Elm disease began its assault. How many wars have these trees been growing through, unaware of the carnage going on in the human world? Maybe the Civil War, or the Spanish American War. World War II? Korea?

The elms had their own modern war to fight with a foreign fungus. Was war inevitable for both plant and animal? The stronger always challenging the weak?

Nearing her house, Rebecca managed to wave to neighbors sitting on their front porches, barely visible from behind the wooden rails. The air was heavy with the scent of juniper pine, growing at the base of most of those porches.

She had almost reached the house when she heard a car's tires squeal as the car came around the corner. Several teenagers hung out the windows of the car and yelled "Commie." They burst into laughter and drove off in a squeal.

Rebecca froze. She felt the heat of embarrassment and shame crawl up her neck. Out of the corner of her eye, she saw Mr. Jackson watching her. He approached the street, looked both ways, and crossed over to her.

He put a hand on her shoulder and said, "Don't you mind those knuckleheads, Missy. You didn't deserve that."

"Why would they say something like that?" she asked. "I'm so embarrassed."

"Well," he said, glancing at the newspaper under her arm. "It's a small town, and people keep track of what side of the political flag pole you stand. If you don't mind me saying, people kind of know where you're standing just because you ask a lot of questions, and your house is noticeably flag free. And you're always walking around with the *New York Times*. Unusual here, if you don't mind me sayin'. People don't abide by others doubting God or the government. Makes 'em nervous."

She tucked the paper farther under her arm. "I probably offend you too. I mean, you're a veteran and all, and you have flags all over the place."

"Look. I don't care what war we have, there will always be those against it, and those for it. You just can't worry about what other people think."

"Please don't tell anyone what happened. I can't stand anyone thinking I'm a Communist. Adam would be horrified. Thank you, for being kind."

"Sure enough." He hesitated and said, "Is kind of strange that you don't even have one flag on your house. Fourth of July and all coming up."

"Long story."

Rebecca went into the house, unleashed Clipper, and sat at the kitchen table to finish reading the *Times*. *I can't be all wrong. I just want to know.*

5

"Do you have to leave Chuckles wrappers all over the house?" Adam stood with his feet apart and holding forth a fistful of candy wrappers. "You're smart enough to read a book like that spy one and yet..."

"The Spy Who Came in From the Cold?"

"Yeah, that one, and eat candy meant for kids?"

Rebecca dropped the towel she had picked up to dry the frying pan. Supporting herself with both hands on the sink's edge, she lowered her head and counted to ten. She loved eating Chuckles, sugar coated jelly candies—her favorite was licorice, which left her with blackened teeth.

"Well, soon you won't have to worry about Chuckles wrappers, will you?"

Without a word, Adam deposited the wrappers in the trash can and left the room.

She swallowed hard. It had been a month since his announcement that he was going to Vietnam. One more week before he went for training at Fort Bragg.

She could have prevented him from going if only she had found the wisest, most convincing words to stop him from re-enlisting. She practiced different versions of her argument, but when spoken aloud her words never changed the outcome and only increased the tension between them. She was like the monkeys she read about in college—when they couldn't control their environment, they began to not care. She wasn't ready to not care. Not yet. There was still time to change his mind. Or, perhaps she should accept his decision and her fate. She would try.

He announced one night that he wanted to see the movie *The Longest Day* at the drive-in.

"I don't want to see a war movie," she told him in a huff. "Are you crazy?"

"Vietnam's different. This movie is about D-Day, a different war, in a different place. It's the US of A against the Nazis." He took her hand. "It was a great book. Come on, we can cheer on the Allied Forces together."

Sitting in a brand new Chevy Impala SS that Adam had bought her as consolation, they munched on popcorn and watched previews of *The Brain That Wouldn't Die,* a film about a maniacal scientist who grabs his girlfriend's decapitated head from a crash scene and plans to attach it to an attractive corpse. Rebecca wished for a different head too. One that didn't love Adam so much.

For the Bugs Bunny film *Dumb Patrol*, Adam turned the volume up on the speaker hanging on the window. In spite of the cartoon's WWI topic, she had to laugh when the "Baron" kept trying to outfight Bugs with bigger and bigger planes.

Adam poked her in the side and pointed to a car beside them "Steamed up windows," he said. "You know what that means."

Rebecca laughed and moved closer.

There was no laughing during the feature movie, and she kept a tight grip on Adam's hand. As the men on the screen fell from fatal shots, they shouted, some grasping their bodies where they had been struck, others dropped to the ground like stones. Some looked surprised as though they couldn't believe they had been mortally hit. She held her breath when Red Buttons dangled in his parachute, caught on the steeple of a church.

"It's a war movie," Adam said when he noticed the vice grip Rebecca had on his hand. He said, "This is war glorified and horrified."

He looked at her more closely and softly said, "I'm sorry." He unhooked the speaker from the window. They left as Red Button's parachute slowly ripped from its moorings and he slipped toward certain death. Adam and Rebecca drove home in silence.

"I still don't understand why you have to volunteer to put yourself in danger," Rebecca said when they were getting ready for bed—the first words either of them had spoken since they left the drive-in. "There are many other ways to serve your country."

Adam buttoned the shirt to his pajamas.

"Did your father drill this "duty to your country" crap in your head?" Rebecca stood with her hands on her hips, facing Adam.

Adam pivoted to look at her. "Leave my father out of this. He died a long time ago, and you know I don't want to talk about my parents. Ten years you've been prying into my past."

Rebecca put a hand on his chest. "Why do you leave such an important part of your life shut off from me?"

Adam glared at her.

"Is there nothing I can say to have you choose me over the Marines? Help me understand."

"Not everything has to be understood, just accepted. We have such a great thing going until you bring up stuff you know I'm not going to talk about. I'm going to bed."

The night before he left, they made love—a last desperate effort to connect before he shipped off. Adam was more urgent, rougher than his usual tenderness. The focus was not on her pleasure but on his. Each thrust seemed to be intent on maximizing his experience as though he were trying to memorize the valleys and folds of her body's intimacy. When he was drained of both energy and passion, he continued to hold her tightly.

Moistness on her shoulder alarmed her.

"Adam, are you crying?"

He didn't answer for a moment. He gave a half-hearted laugh.

"I'm drooling on your lovely neck," he said, stroking her from shoulder to the dip in her spine and back again.

Her own tears were silent, and they fell asleep in each other's arms.

At the airport, Adam and Rebecca stood among other soldiers, Marines, and officers of various ages and anxiety. Rebecca, like most of the other wives, dressed up for the goodbye—shirtwaist dress, pumps, gloves, and a hat. Adam had on his precisely pressed khaki uniform, adorned by several ribbons including the blue and white Korean service bar. Rebecca had an other-worldly sensation in her body—above the scene, observing couples grapple with imminent loneliness and fear, within the scene as an actress, drawing upon inner resources to act as she thought she should act.

A jet waited on the tarmac; the red painted line trailed from the TWA logo on the tail to the gaping door that would swallow the soldiers.

The chain link gate opened, and a line of the men formed.

"Becky," he said, his cheerfulness obviously forced and determined, "I guess this is it."

She raised her face to him, desperation seeping into her voice. "I can't bear for you to go. Please don't," she pleaded.

"Don't do this."

"Can't they give you some leave when you finish training?" The anxiety ballooned in her chest and throat.

"I've explained that before. They need us quickly."

A noose of grief tightened around her throat. She buried her head into his shoulder, hoping his khaki uniform would dam the tears she couldn't control. He gave her a full hug and put his hands on her shoulders to push her away. He glanced at the damp area on his uniform.

"This will be difficult to explain to my commander." He gave her a weak smile.

He looked around and pointed to other damp shoulders. "Seems to be the norm." He smiled. "I'll be back. Be brave, Rebecca." He let her go. "Be ready for the kiss I throw you." His eyes became wet, and he set his jaw.

Adam spun toward the plane, squared his shoulders, and with a warrior's stride, walked toward the gate.

Rebecca grasped the chain link fence that separated them and squeezed until the steel prongs cut into her skin and distracted her from the need to scream. Each step Adam took toward the plane pulled from her whatever sense of sanity she had as though her heart was inside out. Muffled tears from nearby wives joined hers as though they were all attending the same funeral.

When he approached the plane's doorway, she couldn't bear to watch him enter the giant aircraft that would be taking him from her. She didn't want his kiss, she wanted him, home, being the husband she wanted him to be. Wasn't there something she could do? Anger struggled with her grief. She turned away. With guilt and hope she turned back toward the plane. Adam was gone.

What had she done? Within seconds after the door of the plane closed, she wanted to trade her soul to rewind those few minutes from their last hug to his entrance into the plane. "Be brave," she heard echoing in her head. She sent her husband off to war showing her fear, not her support. Her heart broke thinking about Adam's airborne kiss, and his wife not willing to receive it.

She watched his plane moving down the runway positioning for take-off. Oh, Adam, I'm sorry, I'm sorry, she said silently. *What if he doesn't come back??* She prayed that somehow, he had sensed her apology, and her selfish act didn't seal his fate.

She made her way back to the car through the mostly silent crowd of tearful wives and bewildered children. As she walked by a frowning uniformed officer, he looked straight into her eyes. She closed her eyes and saw her father's frown.

6

Rebecca woke to wrens warbling outside the bedroom window, but their songs did not cheer her. Adam had been gone for two months and had shipped to Vietnam. She looked to the empty side of the bed where his ghost lay. She could see him lying on his side, beard shadow on his face, eyes crinkled when he saw her staring at him. But when she blinked her eyes and looked again, the pillow had no dent, the blankets didn't cover any human form. There was no automatic invitation to smooch and cuddle, and there was nothing to keep her hibernating in the warm covers. She threw off the blankets and left her lonely cocoon. "Be brave," Adam's voice said to her.

What does it mean to be brave? she wondered.

She dressed quickly and went to the kitchen, followed by Clipper, whom she briskly walked around the block—the poor dog barely had time to pee.

Rebecca glanced at the clock. 9:05 AM. She had some time before she had to leave for her part-time job as a church secretary. But it was also a job that nagged on her ambivalence about a God who allowed war and forgave people who didn't deserve to be forgiven.

A firm knock on the back door raised Rebecca's hopes that her neighbor Kathleen had come for coffee. She needed some lighthearted banter as an antidote for the empty start to her day. She wanted some regeneration to be strong for Adam, to be strong for herself in spite of the quiet panic inside her.

She pulled aside the curtains on the upper half of the door, and there stood Kathleen—Irish housewife, mother of two children, and the bearer of flaming red hair, made a little fierier with the help of Miss Clairol. She still retained a bit of an Irish lilt, which Rebecca tried to occasionally imitate much to Kathleen's amusement.

Kathleen helped herself to coffee and sat down at the kitchen table. "You look like you're losing weight. That a benefit of being a military wife?" She saluted her friend with the coffee cup she brought, a gas station give-away with a red and black Texaco logo.

"Hoo-rah, I think they say." Rebecca poured her own coffee into a rooster and roses cup and sat down. She turned the cup, so the strutting rooster was in front, his eye following her like the Mona Lisa's. She stared back, wondering if the eye was trying to say something to her. She let go of the cup and burst into tears.

"I'm so feckin' stupid, I'm sorry I brought it up."

"No matter." Rebecca wiped her eyes with a kitchen towel. She pointed to some parfait glasses, obviously rummage-sale candidates, on the counter. "What do you think, keep or pitch?"

"You have t' ask my opinion about parfait glasses with chips and faded bubbles painted on 'em?"

"Pitch." She set them in a box marked "church sale." Rebecca asked, "How's things with your kids?"

"Ooh boy. All they want to do is watch *American Bandstand*. That music drives me nuts. And my husband refuses to take ballroom dancing lessons with me."

"Frustrating. Is there something else you two can do together?"

"He wants me to join the American Legion Auxiliary. More cooking, serving men, at least that's what I've seen them do."

"American Legion. Wow. That reminds me, did you see the news last night?" Rebecca asked. "More Americans are being sent to Vietnam."

"How long has Adam been gone? Two months?"

"Yeah." Rebecca's eyes filled. "I miss him so much. Every day I wonder what he's doing. Is he asleep, is he afraid, is the enemy watching him from the jungle cover ..."

"Of course, ya do." Kathleen patted her friend's hand. "Have ya heard from 'im since he left for 'Nam?"

"No, but I should any day. My day crawls until the mail comes. There's nothing, and I wait for the next day. And the imagining starts all over again." Rebecca took a sip of her coffee. "I still can't believe that we're involved in that awful war, training Vietnamese soldiers to kill other Vietnamese."

Kathleen didn't look up when she said, "Ya sure talk a lot about the whys and whats of something ya can't control." She continued to examine her coffee.

Rebecca put down her cup and looked at Kathleen. "What do you mean by that?"

"You're the only Vietnam wife in town that doesn't fly a flag from your porch, you're always quotin' the news about which reporter says what regardin' our being there, and you don't—"

"Your point is?"

Kathleen took a deep breath. "I guess I would expect ya to be more patriotic, especially t' honor Adam's service. I mean, my parents were so proud to become American citizens, and my brother immediately enlisted when he was old enough."

Rebecca pushed her chair back. "So, to be a good wife I need to be waving American flags and accept everything our country does? Is that what patriotism is?"

Kathleen folded her arms. "Well, what do ya think it means to be patriotic?"

Rebecca pushed some crumbs around the table with her forefinger. "To be honest, I'm not sure."

Kathleen stood up and put a hand on her arm. "As your friend, I think it'd be easier for you t' not spend time, heart and energy trying t' decide if the war your husband is fighting in is right or wrong. Ya' think the universe is waiting to give ya' a medal for making the right decision? Focus on supporting your soldier."

Rebecca stood up and went to the door. "I have to go to work." She gave her friend a weak smile.

"Well," said Kathleen, "I guess that advice didn't go over." She put a hand on Rebecca's arm. "Don't forget about the Police Department's charity auction at the Memorial Building tonight. They are raising money to send supplies to the soldiers in Vietnam. I'm sure you knew about that."

After Kathleen left, Rebecca read the flyer for the auction. If she went, she'd have to endure painful cheerleading about his service. Perhaps Kathleen was right. "Be brave," she heard again.

She put the flyer down, sighed, and said to Clipper, "Well, let's see if I can avoid any patriotic pressures at work."

Rebecca's conversation with Kathleen penetrated her thoughts as she tried to type the Sunday bulletin. Did she have to give up her own opinions to support Adam? Her fingers hovered, frozen above the typewriter, and she stared into space. She shook her head. Rebecca saw the scrawled note detailing something that was to be put in the announcements. "Remembering our veterans and those now serving. Stay after church for a flag cake, baked and decorated by our own Mrs. Gladstone. Wear red, white, and blue to show your patriotism." There was a postscript: "Draw a little flag, Rebecca, on the page. Thnx." Patriotism was as hard to escape as religion.

Underneath the note was a death notice that Rebecca was to put in the newsletter. Always with a black border and cross. "Wonder what old geezer died this time," she muttered to herself. She took a closer look. "We are saddened to learn of the death of PFC Arnold Smith, USMC, killed in action, Hue Province, August 22, 1965..." The words sucked the air out of the room. She put the note under the cake announcement, and typed, typing anything. She rummaged through the pile of notes to find the adult Sunday school schedule.

A door banged somewhere in the building. Startled, Rebecca dropped the pencil she was sharpening, and the point broke. No matter. Sharpening pencils distracted her from worrying about Adam. Rotating the handle, hearing and feeling the whir of the cylinder blades against the wood soothed her. The pristine point on the newly sharpened pencil gave her a needed sense of accomplishment.

She glanced up to see Mrs. Gladstone standing in front of her desk. The woman's mouth was turned down at the corners, and her gray over-permed hair stuck to the edges of her sweaty face.

"May I help you, Mrs. Gladstone?" Rebecca asked.

"I need to see the pastor, please, Mrs. Benson." Her eyes flitted about the room as though she couldn't focus on anything in particular. "I don't have an appointment but it's important." She strained to look into Reverend Kaskell's office, always open when he wasn't meeting someone, but he had cleverly placed his desk so he wasn't visible from the reception area. "I hear useful information when people don't think I'm in," he had once told Rebecca.

Mrs. Gladstone looked at Rebecca and said, "I was driving down your street, and I noticed you don't have a flag on your porch, dear. Did you lose yours? You can get them at the hardware store, you know."

Rebecca squelched a retort and reached for Rev. Kaskell's buzzer on the intercom. He appeared at his office door before her hand reached the button.

"Mrs. Gladstone, so good to see you, and you caught me at the right time." He stood to the side and waved her in.

When he closed the door, Rebecca knew she had some quality work time ahead. She turned on the radio to muffle any sounds that might escape through the heavy door. A local station, WKYZ, was giving the farm report—the right background noise to not pay attention to—and to forget Mrs. Gladstone's critical observation about the missing flag.

She took a moment to look around the office. Various crosses hung on the cinder block walls or were placed on wooden shelves, along with cute wall posters of cherubic Hallmark children being kissed by puppies, heralding love and acceptance through platitudes like "Jesus loves me...even when I'm bad." So many times, Rebecca had been tempted to draw horns on the child who gazed down on the room with such innocence, and she'd planned to pencil in fangs on the puppy. She mentally slapped herself each time for such bad thoughts. She had been raised in the church where she now worked, but the Sunday school lessons had been less interesting than the boys who winked sideways at her.

Her gaze stopped at a carving that had little blocks of wood on it that appeared to be nothing but little blocks of wood. It was the most irritating item in the office. When a person got some distance from it, the blocks merged into the word "Jesus." She kept placing it out of sight so she wouldn't be tortured by the compulsion to see how close she could get before the letters became random rectangles. But Reverend Kaskell would re-position it so visitors would have to decode and be entertained. So where was Jesus when PFC Arnold Smith died?

"Be brave," she heard Adam say.

Oh, Rebecca, stop being such a whiny shrew.

The pastor's door opened, and out walked a calmer Mrs. Gladstone.

"I see you're doing the cake for Sunday's celebration, Mrs. Gladstone," Rebecca said.

"Yes, I am." She beamed. "I'm going to write our servicemen's names on it, and your darling Adam will be right in the middle. We are so lucky that your husband chose our town to settle in. I'll be proud to put his name on the cake."

"Quite patriotic," Rebecca said, trying to rein in her sarcasm. The shrew again.

She wasn't successful. Mrs. Gladstone's smile disappeared more quickly than Rebecca's sarcasm took to say.

"I..." And she said no more but rushed out the door.

Reverend Kaskell appeared and leaned against the door jamb. "That was a little harsh, wasn't it?" He waited for her to answer, but she kept her head down and pretended not to hear as she typed.

"So much anger, so much bitterness. How can I help?" he asked.

"You can't." She stopped typing and looked at the still keyboard.

"It has to be very difficult to have Adam away. Time will go fast, my dear."

"No, it won't." Rebecca chewed her nail, remembering it was a habit she was trying to quit, put her hand in her lap, hiding the offending hangnail.

"Would you like for us to say a prayer together for Adam?"

"Can we also pray for the end of all war?" She made eye contact with the Reverend and mentally dared him to have an answer.

"That's a big order."

She lowered her head. "I'm sorry. I am not in a good mood these days."

Shuffling papers on the desk, Rebecca heard him walk back into his office and quietly close the door. She regretted her adolescent responses. More of the same, she thought. Why didn't Adam's letters from training camp mention anything about the scene at the airport? What if he didn't come back? What would his last thoughts be? She looked up at the Jesus carving and ached with loneliness.

The clock on the wall read twelve-thirty. Thirty minutes to go. She finished the bulletin, complete with death notice and flag drawn on the announcements.

At the clock's chime of 1 o'clock, she grabbed her purse and muttered "See ya," to Reverend Kaskell's door. She heard a partial goodbye as she scooted out. Clipper needed a walk, the carpets at home needed vacuuming, and she needed to brace herself for a patriotic evening of not being herself.

7

She hated being a shrew. Sweeping the carpet was one way to tame unwanted thoughts. The motor of the vacuum drowned out intruding thoughts of Adam, Reverend Kaskell, and Mrs. Gladstone. Rebecca pushed the wand of the canister vacuum back and forth, back and forth, over a piece of lint that would not yield to the suction power of the Hoover. So she picked up the piece of lint, fluffed it, and put it directly in front of vacuum. Gone.

Finished, she dragged the canister to the hall closet and tried to shove it in, but the hose and attachment wand flailed about the door jamb. The harder Rebecca shoved, the more furious was their stubbornness to not fit inside the closet. "Sugarfoot," she said to no one. Her face hot and her jaw set, she gave one final push and closed the door before the wand and hose could escape. She sank to the floor with her back to the door. She punched the door with her elbow, frustrated over the stupid vacuum attachments. She realized she couldn't laugh about it with Adam at dinner that night, and she felt very alone and helpless. *Why does everything happen to me?* She thought about PFC Smith's death notice and felt embarrassed by her conceit.

Back in the living room, Rebecca caught a glimpse of the mailman walking away from the house. The mail! She sprang to her feet and sprinted to the door.

The mailbox had a different aura about it—a cloud of expectation, and Rebecca nervously pulled open the lid.

An envelope of unfamiliar paper stood at attention. It had to be a letter from Adam! It was. She carried the letter into the living room as though it were a diamond tiara. She sat on the sofa and patted the cushion for Clipper to join her. He jumped onto her lap. She held the letter and ran her fingers over the military postmark and Adam's careful handwriting. She slid a finger underneath the flap of the envelope, lifted the gummed paper, and pulled out two pages of thin paper. "Hey Becky" his letter began. He drew funny little hearts and a man and a woman kissing. His drawing was infantile, and it made her laugh.

I love getting your letters. I can't tell you how much that means to me when I hear my name at mail call. The guys who don't get much mail try to hide their disappointment, but you can still see it in their faces. Some guys get no mail, and they disappear when the rest of us are reading ours. If you get my drift, keep those letters coming! Let me know how long it takes for my letters to get to you.

How are things going at the church office? Think you'll pick up any more hours?

I have so much to tell you, but I have very little free time now. There's a whole new language to learn here, Vietnamese and camp talk. The young arrivals are called cherries, new and about to be bruised by reality (ha, ha).

Since I served in Korea and am older than most, I escape that label. "Boo koo" is bastardized French for "beaucoup." Some of the lesser educated guys think it's Vietnamese for "lots." And then there's "boom boom." I'll give you a hint. It's what you and I like to do! The Marines here, for the most part, talk in one syllable, four letter words, mostly beginning with "f." "Sugarfoot," your favorite word, isn't heard here. Ha! And when I get back, you can eat all the licorice Chuckles you want! Many Vietnamese here have stained teeth from chewing betel nuts. But some have black teeth, painted with God knows what. They think it's attractive. At least toothpaste gets rid of licorice!

She put his letter down and closed her eyes to absorb his lightheartedness. She stroked Clipper's fur and remembered Adam's laugh. She picked up the letter again and wished there were a hundred more pages to read.

There will be two of us American advisors embedded with South Vietnamese soldiers (ARVN). My cohort is a guy named Robert Norris, who grew up on a farm only two counties away from us. When we go into the boonies, we'll be living like the ARVN, not like American grunts. We'll have a tight rope to walk, guide yet not offend. We'll be working with Vietnamese officers who will outrank us, so our "suggestions" may not be taken kindly. Should be interesting. I know we can be a big help here, Becky. I hope I can convince you of that.

Well, it's time to "didi" (get out of here). I'll write tomorrow. Sweet dreams, and give Clipper an ear scratch for me.

Love you, Adam

Rebecca put the letter to her face and tried to breathe Adam's scent. Nothing. It was the closest she could get to him. She closed her eyes and traced the channels of the script as though she were reading Braille, but instead of dots, she caressed the indentations made by his pen. She pictured his hand moving across the paper.

She rose from the sofa and sensed Clipper's eyes following her every move. "Let's watch the news," she said.

Walter Cronkite held his notes with confidence and locked eyes with the camera—his presence filled her living room. His authoritative voice narrated the scenes of gunfire between the Viet Cong and U.S. Marines. Rebecca leaned toward the television and focused on the soldiers' faces. They looked like exhausted teenagers who should have been honking their horns at the local drive-in instead of carrying weapons, gear, and ammo. The news story switched to a report on the role of American advisors. She locked onto the screen, her eyes and ears poised to catch any mention of Adam or his unit. No sight of him, no report on casualties. Next was a story about Soviets scoring the world's first spacewalk; a story about President Johnson who said we shouldn't turn our back on a country that needs our help to repel communism; an in-depth analysis of the pacification program in Vietnam "to win the hearts and minds" of the Vietnamese people. *Yeah, right. Let's bomb your rice paddies to win you over.* Westmoreland wanted more troops. She sank lower into the sofa.

Rebecca called her friend Annie for a drink before the torture began in the Memorial Building. Annie was her muse—pragmatic, humorous and a lifetime friend. "Hey Annie," she said on the phone. "Let's meet for a quick drink at Sir Lancelot's. You know, the new bar in town where they have a medieval armor suit greeting you at the door. We can eat and drink like victorious knights and sing bawdy songs like the wenches we are."

Annie waved to Rebecca from a booth in the back. A curl of cigarette smoke rose above her. She had a half-finished Manhattan—the stem of a maraschino cherry resting on the coaster underneath her drink. Rebecca slid in and waved at the waitress.

"No need," said Annie. "I've already ordered you a Daiquiri. Cigarette?"

"Adam doesn't want me to smoke. Have a question, though. What do you think it means to be patriotic?"

Annie sat back. "Whoa, dive right into a heavy topic, will you? What brings that on except your constant need to master every topic you encounter?"

Rebecca said "thank you" to the waitress who brought her drink, and she took a slow drag on the straw and let the morning's church piety disappear. "Can I be patriotic without flying a flag at my house?"

"Well, Professor Benson, I'd have to think about that."

"I'm serious. Patriotism is a big deal in my family. You know that my father was killed in France in World War II. My mother practically wears stars and stripes underwear. It drives me nuts."

"What, that you don't want Lady Liberty panties?" Annie took a drag on her cigarette.

"Funny," said Rebecca.

Annie blew a ring of smoke into the air, tapped a long ash into the ashtray. "Don't worry about patriotism. Accept that you have legitimate doubts about the war."

"I'm getting the distinct impression that the folks in Liberty think I should be more patriotic."

"So?"

With both palms up Rebecca said, "But if the war is wrong, Adam could die for nothing."

Annie sat back from the table. "Don't talk like that." She fanned the air with her hands. "Get those negative words outta here."

Rebecca shook her head. "I can't talk or write any of these feelings to Adam. He's so proud of what he's doing."

"I'm glad you're not bringing him down with your doubts. Be proud of your Marine. You're going to the charity auction tonight at the Memorial Building, right? Enjoy the spotlight. Flaunt Adam's service, try out a little patriotism, make people guess where you stand." She gave a flourished wave of her hand.

"No, I don't think so."

"It'll be good for you to get out. Your friends are missing your irreverence."

"You mean like the pun I told at Uncle Walter's funeral? 'The funeral director had some stiff competition for this gig.' "

Annie hung her head. "As our friend Kathleen would say, 'Sweet Mary and Joseph.' "

"She did invite me to go with them, but I'm pretending to be something I'm not at those affairs. I don't know anyone who feels like I do. It makes me lonelier than I already am."

"From one friend to another, grow up." Annie smiled. "If you don't like the war, you don't like the war."

Rebecca stared back.

"I'm not saying I don't understand your fear over Adam's deployment, but we used to talk about many other, fun stuff."

"I guess I have become a one line song."

"Call Kathleen and tell her you are going," Annie said.

"Why aren't you going?"

"I have a date, dahling. I'll wish you luck if you wish me luck."

"Done."

8

Kathleen, her husband, and Rebecca walked towards Memorial Hall—the venue for most receptions, dancing lessons and bridge tournaments in Liberty. The building loomed as a test for Rebecca on whether she could handle the mantle of being a Marine's wife when she desperately didn't want to be.

The stately Greek revival architecture reflected the colonial obsession of the town and stood on a wide street framed by some remaining elm trees. Twenty-five years ago, she bounced up those same steps for her ballerina recital. She was dressed as a tulip in a pink tutu, as were her other chubby post-toddler friends. Her parents beamed with pride as she twirled in dizzying circles down the long, wooden floor of the ballroom, starting and stopping a couple of times to regain her balance. She kept forgetting to turn her head once a revolution, and the fear of throwing up overcame her delight in being a tulip. Life was maddingly simple then.

For the charity event that night Rebecca wore an apricot sheath dress with a long matching jacket. She added her grandmother's pearls. "Monochrome is in," said the woman at Gilmore's Dress Shop. Rebecca hadn't come very far in three decades—she'd gone from a pastel tutu to a pastel dress. But the possibility of throwing up was again real—from anxiety. She and Kathleen and her husband made their way up the wide stone steps that

ended at a veranda with massive white columns.
American flags hung from the fascia boards at the roof
line.

They were inside the doorway when a high-pitched
voice shouted, "Oh-my-gosh, there's Kathleen!" Kathleen
bolted toward the loud and welcoming voice.

Rebecca turned to Kathleen's husband.

He shrugged. "She loses focus sometimes."

She scanned the room of chatty people, back-lit from
the waning sun coming through the floor-length windows.
The air was loud and thick with "how are you" and "you're
kidding," and "that's so funny" remarks that echoed off
the wooden floors. Smoke danced toward the ceiling,
rising from the cigarettes that dangled from lips and
fingers. The sickening memory of a high school trial with
tobacco still hovered on her tongue, and she signaled "No"
to the black butler who offered her a light.

She heard disjointed snippets of politics, baby care,
and diet tricks. Pirouetting between the conversations
were the ghosts of five-year old ballerinas stumbling
through their pliés. The men were in suits, of course, but
the women were clad in all manner of monochrome and
fruit-colored dresses. Seeing Jackie "pillbox bobs" and
Gidget flips prompted Rebecca to smooth down her hair
that didn't conform to either of those styles.

Before she could find a safe haven, Ruth Middleton
approached, or rather, bounced her way over. Ruth was a
large woman with big feet and pendulous breasts. As she
walked by, Rebecca heard someone say, "Now there's a
fine doorful of a woman."

A successful Realtor, Ruth was famous for a house
selling ritual that usually paid off. Over a newly signed

contract, she would grab the sides of the table at which she sat and swing her fleshy endowment back and forth while chanting "Sell, sell, sell!" But only in the presence of women.

"Rebecca, Rebecca, Rebecca, the person I wanted to see." She grabbed Rebecca's shoulders and planted a wet kiss on both of her cheeks as though she were a French dignitary. "I have the most marvelous idea for you."

"And that might be...?"

"I remembered the other night that your mother is eligible for the DAR, and of course that means you are too!"

Her eyes were bright and animated.

"Huh?"

"You know, the Daughters of the American Revolution. I couldn't convince your mother, she's not big on ceremony since your father died, but being a Marine's wife makes you special. And it would fill some time while Adam's gone."

"I...I don't know. I'll have to think about it." Images of white-gloved women in long chiffon gowns carrying flags paraded through Rebecca's mind.

Ruth patted her shoulder. "We are a good support group, and you could carry on Adam's effort...fighting communism, advancing democracy and all that." She gave an exaggerated wink.

"We shouldn't be there," Rebecca said, and Ruth's smile melted into a frown.

"Oh. Well, you think about it. Adam would be proud of you." She took back her hand. "Oh dear, there's someone I need to talk to over there. You think about it now." And off she went, her breasts leading the way.

The Liberty Police Chief, Rory Walters, sidled up to Rebecca after Ruth's departure. His uniform was polished and pressed, but his breath had remnants of a cigar that many important men in Liberty smoked as a sign of their town rank. "Adam would be glad to know you're here."

"Yes, I think he would."

Captain Walters put his hand on her shoulder. "He always had the ability to respond to a situation the right way, keeping things calm, you know, instead of escalating. And man, he kept his equipment spotless. His Marine training, I suppose," he said, momentarily distracted by a loose thread on his sleeve. He took a deep breath. "How long have you two been married?" He tilted his head to hear a response.

"Almost eight years." She stared off into the depths of the room. Eight years. Their lives had balanced pretty well, except for some major issues like children and war. He could compartmentalize things better than she did. "Love your neighbor but build a fence," he would say. "The enemy becomes a different species," he wrote in one letter, "when we call them gooks. The harsher the name, the easier it is to hate them. We're trained to consider them subhuman, so it's easier to kill. We're not going to die for our country, they're going to die for their country."

"Rebecca?" Captain Walters waved his hand in front of her face. "You left us for a moment."

"Oh, sorry." She met Captain Walters' eyes.

"Let me know if there's anything the department, or I, can do for you."

"Thank you."

Rebecca headed for the bar, and one of the town's widow soothers, Irene Sotheby, approached. She wasn't as lethal as some of the others, she gave more sympathy than advice. Rebecca pushed back the painful thought that Irene might be soothing her someday.

Irene was dressed in a Joan Baez-y way, long straight hair parted in the middle, long multi-colored skirt, and most shocking for Liberty society, very little make-up.

"How y'all doing, Rebecca?" Irene said in her lazy Southern drawl that contrasted with her high energy. Irene hooked her arm through Rebecca's and led her to a corner of the room where few people stood. Rebecca glanced back at the bar with longing.

"Most of the people here don't know whether to look at their asses or scratch their watches."

Rebecca giggled and pictured Captain Walters scratching his watch.

"I hope you don't think I'm being, well, presumptuous," her "I's" being more like "I-uh's, "but I've heard people say you have some doubts about, shall we say, our rescue mission," she lowered her voice, "in Vietnam." Irene took a step back and waited for a response.

"Like what?" Rebecca took a step back also. The space and momentary silence between them stood like a demilitarized zone, where nothing bad is supposed to happen. When Irene didn't answer right away, she decided to cross that social DMZ. "You seem to have some doubts. Am I reading you right?"

"Okay with it? Are you kidding, darlin'?" She came closer. "Do you know how hard it is in this town to question the red, white and blue? I don't care if it's religion or politics. Just hearin' someone like you ask questions is refreshing. And rumor has it that you read the *Times*. What a novel thing to do."

Rebecca ventured a step closer. Someone to talk with about doubts?

"Humans are born to question, but most people let go of their curiosity," Irene said with a wink.

"Thank God, a kindred soul. I lost my father to war, World War II, you know," Rebecca said. "Although I was young, I miss him every day. World War Two had a mission worth dying for, I suppose, but Vietnam?"

"We've both lost fathers to war, and now you have a husband fighting in another war. I can't tell you how hungry I am to have someone I can talk to about this."

"That makes two of us." They turned their heads and scanned the room like cold war spies.

"There are more than seventeen thousand advisors over there now. There's a small group who meets in Columbus to discuss ways to help stop the war from growing." She hesitated. "Sure as shootin' this war's going to get bigger. At least that's how I feel."

"Well, you certainly dress the part." Rebecca laughed.

Irene smiled. "I know. People make assumptions about my politics from how I dress, but believe me, I dressed this way in grade school."

Rebecca asked, "If I go to the meeting, do I have to wear madras?"

"Ha! I like your spirit. I need a Liberty girlfriend with me for the ride and the talk, and you're the ticket. No obligation. I'll understand completely if you don't like what you hear. We all have our own paths to take but do give it a try."

Rebecca played with the pearls at her neck. "TV reports about the constant coups and corrupt officials in South Vietnam make me wonder if it's a country we should be supporting."

Irene's eyes widened. "You're really paying attention to this war, aren't you?"

"I'm confused. We need to defend our country, don't we? But I didn't want Adam to go and didn't handle his departure too well, yet..." Adam's photo in his dress blues came to Rebecca, and she thought of the scene at the airport where she had accused him of caring more about strangers in rice paddies than he did about her.

"Your face took a turn for sadness," Irene said. "What were you thinking of?"

"Nothing worth talking about."

Rebecca pulled Irene closer and bent towards her ear. "Tonight, I was asked to the join the DAR.."

Irene took Rebecca's hands. "They're a good group but be aware of some members' blind allegiance to their country. Adam is a patriot, fer sure, but the government is distorting patriotism, and it's dangerous. That's what we're facing. I understand why some people burn flags. They are trapped by a system that says the flag is a symbol of agreeing with your government." Irene's blue eyes were deep and intense with conviction.

"Am I bad to not support a war my husband is fighting in? What would he think of me going to some anti-war meeting."

"Loving someone doesn't mean you can't have your own thoughts."

Rebecca took a deep breath. "Call me with details." Irene squeezed her hands softly and said goodbye.

Rebecca turned to see if anyone had been watching their clandestine talk. She wondered how flag waving and flag burning could occur in the same evening. She nursed a drink through the evening's silent auction and donated twenty dollars in Adam's name to the police charity." She chalked one up in the "done to honor Adam's service" column.

"I do believe you had a good time tonight," Kathleen said on their way out. "And, it appears you survived encounters with both ends of the political mainstream: Miss DAR and Miss Hippie."

"You were watching me?"

"Just keeping an eye on my friend."

As they left the party, Rebecca spotted Ruth and Irene heading to their cars. Irene swooped into her Volkswagen Beetle and scooped up her skirts into the car. Her car had a bumper sticker that read "Make love, not war." Ruth got into a late model Chevy, a car festooned with a bumper sticker that read "Bomb Hanoi."

Oh Adam, what am I getting myself into?

9

Rebecca sat at the breakfast table the morning after her encounter with Ruth and Irene. She held her head. With her eyes closed, she could see Adam's face, hear Adam's words, sense Adam's unbendable patriotism as he flew away to protect democracy. Patriotic sensibility pulled at her. He was her husband, her protector. *God, why am I so maddeningly stuck? I want so much to do something. Anything to feel I have some control in my life.*

Her mother called that morning, and Rebecca asked about the DAR. "Why didn't you join, Mother?"

"It's such a silly reason. I think it's a great organization."

"And..."

"There was one member who drove me nuts. She thought I was a stuck up military wife and made no bones about it. I couldn't stand to be around her. So, I did the cowardly thing and didn't join."

"Someone told me you weren't much into ceremony and such."

Her mother laughed. "Pretty stupid excuse, eh, to avoid offending someone?" She paused. "Are you thinking of joining? That would be wonderful, dear. Honoring your military roots and your husband's service. Are you softening a little on your stand about the war?" Not giving Rebecca a chance to answer, she continued. "I do hope so. I've tried not to say much, but it was disappointing to hear on the street that you were making friends with anti-war types."

"And just what is an anti-war type?"

"Oh, Rebecca, I don't want to get into this. You know what I mean."

"I don't know, Mother, but let's get back to the DAR. It would make me a better example of a military wife?"

"Adam deserves that, you know."

Rebecca closed her eyes and fought against the words of guilt and anger daring to spill out of her mouth.

She made a mental list of the ways to be the good wife of a deployed Marine. No public whining. Check. Paper American flag on the front door (even she couldn't find the flag she had hidden). Check. Nodding politely when dumb things were said. Check. *I'll give it a try.*

A week later at bridge club, Rebecca hoped the ladies concentrated on their bids rather than on her status as military wife whose husband was at war. A woman to Rebecca's left, who was still trying to decide what card to lead, said "Can you believe those college students protesting the war? They have no idea what it is to be patriotic," she huffed. "They can live somewhere else if they don't want to defend their country. Commie professors are egging them on, I tell you." The woman across the table nodded, the woman to Rebecca's right stayed silent and still, her eyes onto her cards. Someone at an adjacent table said, "Ladies, no politics, please."

The woman's flag-waving comment scraped across Rebecca's heart. What would these women say if they knew she had imagined herself marching alongside those students and carrying her own placard that read, "Bring my husband home?" How could she possibly share her doubts about courage and patriotic duty? What if she revealed the pain in her heart for the Vietnamese children who were dying at the hands of the Americans? "War is sometimes necessary," her mother's voice echoed.

Rebecca took a deep breath. "Do you have to agree with your government to be patriotic?"

The three women at the table froze, their cards held as still as a deer who doesn't want to be noticed, their red lip-sticked mouths slightly open.

Rebecca didn't give them time to answer. "Just wondering. Whose lead is it?"

"Rebecca how are you doing?" asked Susan, the hostess, during a break.

"Fine, I suppose. I miss Adam a lot." Rebecca took a sip of coffee, full-bodied and reminiscent of the coffee Adam would have before he reported to the police station. "The x'd off days are gradually filling up the calendar."

"Oh, I know exactly what you mean. My Jim had to go on business overseas for three weeks, and I thought I would go nuts." She dabbed at crumbs on her lips with a linen napkin. "The house was so empty, and I had to take out the garbage myself. Yuck. At least he wasn't in danger like your Adam is. I don't know how you do it. I would be crazy with worry. All the TV reports of ambushes and such."

Rebecca's heart sank at such insensitivity but managed a weak smile. A check for nodding politely.

The table she went to next had a group of ladies already engrossed in conversation. "I swear that my mother-in-law ruined my husband for marriage. She doted on him, cut the crusts off his sandwiches. To this day, if there's a tiny bit of brown crust, almost indiscernible to my eye, he has a fit."

Another said, "My husband's father was a union man, and so Matthew is so against unions. Won't vote for anything to do with teachers because they are in unions. Just being rebellious, don't you think, ladies? How about you, Rebecca? What were Adam's parents like?"

She fidgeted in her chair. "Oh, I really don't know. Adam never says much about his upbringing."

One of the ladies winked. "Sounds like he's hiding something, don't you think, girls?"

Everyone at the table, except Rebecca, giggled.

At the next rotation her partner was Ruth Middleton. Her breasts came into service before the cards were dealt. She grabbed each side of the table, swung those babies back and forth saying, "Spades, spades, spades."

Rebecca's jaw dropped when she opened the hand— six spades, ace high. Maybe those breasts were magic and deserved more respect. "One spade," Rebecca opened to her partner Ruth.

Pass. Ruth bid, "Six spades."

Rebecca made the contract. "Could you swing those things again and say, 'home Adam, home Adam, home Adam?' "

Ruth did, gladly.

Rebecca was helping Susan put away chairs when Ruth came and pulled her aside.

"Remember when I said you were eligible for DAR? I want to take you to see your Revolutionary War patriot's grave. Your mother had told me once who he was."

"I don't think I have energy for a group like dar."

"Now don't say 'dar', it's D. A. R.," pronouncing each letter, "the Daughters of the American Revolution. How 'bout I pick you up tomorrow?? At least do it for your mother, and Adam. It'll give you something to do to take your mind off things."

What mind? Rebecca wondered.

Standing on the front stoop waiting for Ruth, Rebecca doubted the trip was a good idea. But...what could it hurt? It could hurt... a lot. Why go to a cemetery when Adam could end up in one? Yet she was curious. And she would be doing something. Anything besides think.

"What a blessing to be able to visit the grave of your patriot," Ruth said on the way to the village of Granville.

"I suppose."

So, she was going to see the final resting place of her patriot, her key to the DAR kingdom. Farmland bounded the two-lane road on both sides, tall maples protected the farmhouses with their gold and red awnings. Weeds— Queen Ann's lace, thistles, and errant grasses—nestled against the barbed wire fences that kept the cows in the pastures and out of the road.

"If you give us a chance," Ruth said, "maybe you'll understand the value of lineage societies."

Liberty was the perfect petri dish for an organization like the DAR. Ruth said Rebecca's patriot was a preacher who tended the wounded at the battle of something or other—at least that's what was stated on the historical record for him.

The pressure to join DAR brought out her rebellion against being controlled. She wanted to create her own, maybe the Society of Bitter Spouses—SOBS.

Having finally reached their destination, Ruth parked the car under the shade of an ancient oak. They exited the car, and Rebecca instantly inhaled the fall's perfume—sunburned leaves, gentle decay of plants. She watched squirrels with acorn-filled cheeks scamper up the tree.

"Come on." Ruth stood on the other side of the gate, gesturing for her to come in.

Rebecca stepped through the gate into the world of the dead. She was greeted by a live, and large, squirrel. His rodent face stared at her. The squirrel's front legs, spread and tense on the tree trunk, twitched with anticipation. They eyed one another. Was he, was she, friend or foe? She studied the black glassy eyes taking in the human before him, the small pointy ear lined in red fur, still and exquisite. She saw an acorn hanging from his mouth. Would he drop it to lunge at her, using those sharp little teeth? She risked letting her eyes journey from his snack to his smooth grey back marked by scars of former skirmishes. A veteran fighter. He made the tiniest, almost imperceptible move with his front paws. His movement warned her that his next act might be toward her rather than away from her. She stayed frozen, daring not to cough from the acrid leaf smoke that drifted above. Was this like squaring off with an enemy in the jungle?

The hum of traffic, the rustling of the maple leaves, and the buzzing of insects provided background noise for the world the squirrel and she shared. They were both passersby in this miniscule moment of time at the entrance of the old cemetery.

A passerby coughed. The standoff ended, and the squirrel scampered up the tree to a limb high, high, high. There he stopped on his haunches, held the acorn in his paws, and chewed on the tough shell of the nut. Unlike his human observers, he had no idea death was his inevitable future.

"Rebecca, Rebecca," called Ruth. "What are you staring at?"

"A squirrel." Rebecca turned back to her purpose, visiting her Revolutionary War patriot—whom Ruth hoped would be inspiration for improved patriotism.

The moss-covered bricks of the walk were slippery, and Ruth and Rebecca minced their way along a path that led to a more stable grassy area, the oldest part of the cemetery. Massive oak and maple trees shaded the centuries-old grave stones that leaned in every direction but straight up, like tired old men. The limestone headstones had long given up their fight against wind, rain, and air pollution; the carved tributes to the people underneath were barely visible on the blackened stones. The cool and moist air, the rustling of falling leaves, and the chatter of birds were all part of a lullaby for the sleeping residents of the cemetery.

It was so different from the Arlington Cemetery seen on television—acres of open grass, crisp white monuments, and formal paths. Adam would like the ambience of peace, quiet, and reconciliation in the old Granville cemetery. She shook her head to rid the Universe of the possibility she had put out there.

Ruth's sturdy shoes gave her quick footing, and she seemed to be making determined progress toward her target.

"How do you know where to look?" Rebecca asked as she tried to keep up with her. Catching her breath, she gazed over the headstones, which merged into a sea of grave sites.

"We did grave markings for the patriots here a couple of years ago. The Revolutionary War folks have metal stakes with a star or circle emblem with 1776 on them. We're looking for Elijah Cradlebaugh. His stone is curved on the top with an angel carved on it."

The blur of headstones sharpened into an array of funereal art. Weeping trees, clasped hands, angels, doves, and all types of flowers were etched in various rock. Small lambs sat atop the graves of babies; occasional Stars of David adorned some of the stones. Epitaphs ranged from simple letters showing name and dates to flowery expressions of grief. "Though he's gone, within the hearts of those who cared, his memory lingers on," one read. Focused on an anchor carving, Rebecca bumped into a tree stump, a granite tree stump. Ruth laughed and said, "Watch out for those trees."

"Why would someone have a tree stump for a grave marker?" Rebecca asked.

"It could mean a person's life has been cut short."

"Military cemeteries should be rows and rows of granite tree stumps."

Ruth turned. "Never thought of it that way." She motioned to the last row of the cemetery near the pitted wrought-iron fence that barely provided a barrier between the life outside and the death within.

She stopped in front of a faded marker. "Here we are."

Before them was a brownish gravestone that had a primitive rendering of a crowned angel with wings that formed her hair. Her face was one dimensional, simple, like a ten-year-old might draw. But the decorative swirls that embraced her were skillfully carved, and more swirls (or was it supposed to be ivy?) boxed in the wording below the rounded top.

Ruth stood in silence as Rebecca read the words aloud: "To the Memory of ELIJAH CRADLEBAUGH, who departed this Life April 5, 1798 in the 71st year of his age," she read. "He didn't die in battle."

"No, he didn't. And he never was in a battle. He came here to farm afterward."

"Somehow I thought of patriots as people who fought in a war."

Ruth looked at her with the compassion of a teacher about to kindly correct her student.

"It takes more than soldiers to win a war, dear. The typist in a war office is a necessary cog in the wheel of war, as they say. And someone who tends to the wounded suffers along with their pain. It's all service to their country."

"Interesting. Makes sense." Embarrassed she hadn't thought of the big picture of war, she avoided making eye contact with her tutor.

Rebecca leaned down to read aloud the smaller inscription below the date. "Come blooming youths, as you pass by, and on these lines do cast an eye. As you are now, so once was I; As I am now, so must you be; Prepare for death and follow me."

She stood up. "That's not a happy thought."

"People were more accepting of death." Ruth gazed at the stone. "Imagine the people and events that happened between Elijah Cradlebaugh and Rebecca Benson."

Rebecca studied the lichen on the tombstone. The gray-green scales formed un-interpretable shapes. "I

wonder if Elijah worried about whether or not the war
was worth it."

Ruth gave her a sideways glance. "It wouldn't have
crossed his mind."

"How do you know that?"

"Soldiers don't think, they do what they are ordered to
do."

"Never?" Rebecca asked with wide eyes.

"Discipline wins wars, not lollygagging about what to
do. That's what my husband always told me. I bet your
Adam feels the same way."

Rebecca didn't say anything on the way back to
Liberty, nor did Ruth. Adam and Elijah were in her head,
and she couldn't get rid of them. Ruth had told her Elijah
was a Presbyterian minister who comforted soldiers as
they died. What did he say, what prayers did he use?
When they died, were they content that the cause was
worth their lives? Rebecca put her fingers on her temples
and tried to rub out the voices of past battles.

The gentle breeze grew into a wind. The leaves of the
maple trees along the highway turned over as though the
souls from the cemetery were following Rebecca and were
trying to answer her questions.

Ruth stopped in front of Rebecca's house

"Are you all right, dear?" Ruth lightly touched
Rebecca's arm before she got out of the car. "You looked so
sad a minute ago."

"The Revolutionary War makes sense, I suppose, but
Vietnam? I don't know."

Ruth withdrew her hand. "We're helping people in
another land fight off a Godless regime. Don't you think
that's important?" She put both hands on the steering

wheel and looked out the front windshield. "You don't want to dishonor Adam by not believing in the war that he's fighting in, do you?" She broke her stare at nothingness and focused on Rebecca with a maternal smile that Rebecca understood as "You know better, don't you, dear?"

"So many young men gone. Doesn't that make you angry?"

Ruth's maternal smile turned into a maternal sigh. "Freedom isn't free, you know. You're not becoming one of those anti-war people, are you?" She looked at Rebecca. "I thought you had more patriotism than that. We are in Vietnam to protect Asia and our democracy against the Communists."

"But Ruth..."

"You know those war protesters put our young men at greater risk."

"Why would you bring that up?"

"I've seen you with Irene. She'll drag you into that anti-war stuff. Mind my word."

"Can't I wonder?"

"Not with your husband fighting for our freedoms."

Rebecca felt the tightening in her jaw, the tightening that happens when she is offended but lacks courage to speak up.

"You think you're too good for us, don't you?" Ruth scowled. "I've heard your comments about flag waving and all that. I've seen the look on your face when we talk about our ancestors and get excited about finding a new patriot. We aren't war mongers, you know. But we are about honoring the folks who have served and who are serving. Is that so bad?"

Ruth's words stung and embarrassed her. "I –"

"Frankly, I'm sorry I took you to the cemetery. You're probably going to make fun of me and the DAR to all your anti-war friends. We know that men don't gleefully go off to war." Her voice caught. "But those left behind can at least help them believe they are doing the right thing. And if they die, they know they'll be remembered for answering their country's call."

Ruth hung her head, her eyes glistening with unfallen tears.

Rebecca had no words. Like the thousand thoughts in her head, the wind blew harder, and the sky looked dark in the east. She got out of the car. Ruth leaned across the passenger seat before Rebecca closed the door.

"I'm sorry if I came on too strong. I really think you'd understand Adam better if you give us a chance."

Rebecca hesitated, not yet closing the car door.

"You better get inside before the storm comes," Ruth said, looking straight ahead.

She left, and Rebecca stood in the driveway, letting the coming storm whip her hair. She tried to drink in the sweet pungent air of the approaching storm, but Ruth's words still stung. "You're right," she spoke to Ruth's departing car. "I need to be more supportive. I do want to be a good wife."

A bolt of thunder in the distance sounded like a Revolutionary War cannon. She turned and went into the house.

10

It would make a lot of people happy if I joined the DAR.
Rebecca stood at the bay window in the living room and watched the storm approach. The wind increased its ferocity and forced the rain to an almost horizontal assault on the window. Each thunderous boom made her jump and Clipper whine. She and Adam used to make love on stormy days, their passion stirred by the pounding of rain on the windows, their afterglow mellowed at the storm's end as they listened, lazily wrapped into each other, to the slow dripping of water off the roof and trees onto the grass below.

She took a deep breath and stepped back from the window. The storm was brief and had left leaves and small twigs scattered about the street and lawns. The sun emerged between the lightening clouds, and she readied Clipper for a walk. She walked him to the town square, a hub of activity, serving as the conduit for north, south, east and west foot traffic. Each person shuffled or sprinted by. No one spoke, but she kept hearing herself read the tombstone, "As you are now, so once was I."

She plunked onto a bench and watched the humanity parade in front of her. Clipper lay at her feet. So many people walked by. So many different people. Was there a good wife among them? Were the bad wives discernible? Did patriotism ooze from people's pores so their politics became an identifying scent?

Rebecca studied them all. Bent backs and cast-down eyes, straight backs and forward gazes, skin drooped by gravity and years of heartache, wrinkled skin that still glowed, perfume wafting from women of means, stink emanating from ragged clothes. Arms swinging, hands stuffed in pockets, confident strides on black leather Oxfords, tentative steps from broad heeled walkers. Arthritic couples holding on to each other for support. Some couples had barely any space between them, others walked as though they were afraid to touch. She saw young people, whose swagger communicated that all things were possible. They hurried by, carried along by their polished saddle shoes and monkey chatter. Where would she and Adam have fit in that parade?

She wondered whether the spirits of fallen soldiers welcomed the newly dead to the other side. Who would have greeted her father? Did her father miss his arm? Where did that arm, and the magic tattoo, go? Rebecca's thoughts stayed inside her head, and neither freed nor shared, they were unable to stretch their words and fly, testing their truths on drafts of wind.

Maybe she was self-centered and close-minded about ways to be a military wife. And Ruth was right. She had been judgmental about the DAR ladies. She rose from the bench. "Come on, Clipper." He sprang up from the ground, shaking lawn clippings and leaves off his coat.

Home again and hungry, Rebecca looked through the pantry, and spotted a can of Spaghetti O's—the sugary sweet tomato sauce and limp pasta could be had via a can opener and a single pot. Sitting on the sofa, she watched the evening news and slurped the runny noodles. Probably a treat for battle worn guys in the jungles of

Vietnam. A battle scene from The Longest Day played through her head as well as her father's cotton batten arm, and Reverend Cradlebaugh's tombstone. Her sacrifice, she admitted, included lonely days with Spaghetti O's for dinner. The sacrifice of soldiers and Marines included paralyzing fear in the face of an enemy, possible death, and watching comrades die.

She was tired of the patriotism seesaw. She wanted to be a supportive wife and citizen. She'd give the DAR a try.

On a cold early December day, Rebecca and Ruth approached the doors of the Liberty Community Library. They had patched up their disagreements over coffee one day—Rebecca apologizing for being so judgmental and Ruth apologizing for being so sensitive. Ladies were dressed in Sunday-go-to-meeting clothes, dotted with red, white, and blue accents: scarves, hats, bracelets, earrings, and rings. Once the ladies hung their coats in the closet, she noticed the pins. There were gold pins of all shapes, pinned onto blue and white vertical ribbons that hung from the left shoulders of the women. The blinding gleam of the pins across their breasts filled Rebecca with an old desire, badge envy from her Girl Scouts days. Susie, her 7th grade nemesis, had numerous merit badges that covered the front and back of her green sash. Rebecca's badges barely covered the front, all sewn wide apart to take up more room.

"What's with all the pins?" she asked Ruth.

Ruth pointed to the collection of gold on her chest. "These are the patriots I was able to prove." She straightened a large pin with "Virginia" inscribed on the top and a medallion hanging below. "They are all from

Virginia. And this one," she caressed with her forefinger, "is a chapter officer pin. This here," pointing to the bottom of the ribbon, "is the DAR insignia. That's a spinning wheel, to honor the role of women, and the blue and white represent the colors of Washington's army. And—"

"Everyone is wearing white gloves," Rebecca interrupted. She felt the shame of the ungloved. She slipped her hands crosswise into her sleeves, her purse hanging on her forearms.

"Don't worry. Let's go meet some of the ladies," Ruth said. She motioned to a woman who was the exception in the room; she was pin poor. "Diane Hadley, this is Rebecca Benson."

Diane took Rebecca's bare hand with both of hers, gloved. Her hair was gray, and her eyes were warm and direct. "Welcome, Rebecca. I love your mother! She is so much fun. Did she ever tell you how well she could do the Lindy?"

"The Lindy?" She pictured her prim mother abandoning social composure long enough to swing and hop her way through a four-minute dance. "I didn't know."

"I'm not surprised," Diane answered. "We parents have secret lives, you know." She paused. "Actually, I don't think we hide our lives, I think our kids aren't looking."

"Good point," Rebecca said.

Diane released her hand and patted Rebecca's arm. "If you have any questions about this crazy group, don't hesitate to ask. They're good hearted and support a lot of genealogy work, if you're into that kind of thing. A lot of flag waving though."

"What's wrong with flag-waving?" Ruth asked. "It's a sign of loyalty."

"Oh, you know me, Ruth," Diane replied. "Always the skeptic."

Diane turned to Rebecca. "See? The DAR has room for many philosophies." She winked. "If you decide to join, I will be helping you with your papers, you know, proof of your lineage to a patriot. I'm the Registrar."

"Oh, ok."

Ruth introduced her to several other women, all of whom were gracious and welcoming. She felt watched and turned to see an older woman in a walker staring at her. The woman smiled and rolled over.

"Rebecca Benson? I knew about some Bensons in my hometown years ago. But it can't be your family, not your kind of people."

"Why's that?"

"They were not, shall we say—"

Someone rapped a gavel softly on the front podium, and the woman said to Rebecca, "No matter. And we're being summoned." She turned and joined the other ladies moving to chairs, lined up in neat rows. She sat next to Ruth.

What town? What Benson family? Could she dare ask Adam in her next letter? Remembering how he reacted whenever she brought up his past, she knew she couldn't. For Adam's sake. When he gets back, she'll ask him.

Another rap and everyone stood and put their hands over their hearts while Ruth led the group in the Pledge of Allegiance. They sang, they prayed, they recited the American Creed.

Rebecca needed a tissue, and when she opened her purse a Chuckles wrapper fluttered to the floor as loudly as newspaper driven by the wind across a sidewalk. Not wanting to make more cellophane noise, she took the wrapper by the fingertips. Ruth gave her a quizzical look but quickly refocused on the opening ceremonies. Rebecca's purse slid off her lap and landed with a thump, spilling its contents, including a Tampon that rolled under her chair. She felt the heat in her face as she gathered everything. Everyone else stood to sing *America*.

The program was about sending packages of gum, chocolate, and magazines to the troops in Vietnam. "I bet they aren't Playboy Magazines," Rebecca, with a giggle, whispered to Ruth.

Her response was a glance that said, "Not funny."

At the end of the program, the leader announced there was a special guest.

"We have with us today the wife of Gunnery Sergeant Adam Benson, United States Marine Corps, who is risking his life so that we may live in a democracy without the threat of Communism," she read from a script.

There was that word "Communism" again. It sounded more and more paranoid with each utterance, and it evoked images of Senator McCarthy's twisted face decrying the Communist threat to freedom. *Oh, come on, Rebecca, let's be a little more respectful.*

"Rebecca, would you stand and accept these flowers in honor of your husband and in gratitude for your support?"

All the ladies stood and turned toward her; their applause was muffled by cotton clad palms. Their sincerity evoked guilt in her, and she smiled back with an aching jaw.

The leader added, "I would like to add that Rebecca took the trouble to visit the gravesite of her Revolutionary patriot, something we should all do when we add our patriot's pin to our ribbons." Another round of muffled applause.

By the end of refreshments and the goodbyes, the maternal group of women had adopted her. Her shoulders and arms received numerous pats of friendship. She was sure Adam would be proud if she were to be in such an organization. Anything to erase her guilt about that scene at the airport. She looked around for the woman in the walker. She was nowhere to be seen.

A kindly-looking woman approached her. Her name badge said "Betsy Thomas."

"What do you think of our little group?" she asked.

"Everyone was friendly. I appreciated that."

"Patriotic collection of people, aren't we?"

Rebecca laughed and surveyed Betsy's array of pins. She was small-chested, and the pin-laden ribbons trailed down her torso. "I guess that's what it's all about."

"For many it is." She smiled. "I wouldn't trust a flag-waving patriot as far as I can throw a VW bus." Betsy tapped her pin-laden chest. "I know, but I'm into the genealogy. I put up with all the flag waving because of the bigger picture, which is to honor our ancestors who served."

Remembering Ruth's question, Rebecca asked, "Would you call this a flag waving group?"

"Doesn't matter. I've decided a country needs to deserve our patriotism."

Rebecca studied the woman's grandmotherly smile, maternal soft blue eyes, and sisterly caring. Betsy's comments made her think of the protestors—the government didn't deserve their patriotism.

"Oh dear, you're frowning. I hope I haven't offended you."

"No, not at all. I've been wondering about the same things."

"I kind of guessed that about you. You looked quizzical during much of the opening ceremony. Oh well, there are so many ways of thinking and such a short time of living."

Rebecca smiled.

Betsy gave a little wave and continued out the door.

"What were you talking to Betsy about?" Ruth asked a few minutes later.

Rebecca answered, "Something about flag waving."

Ruth dug for keys in her gigantic purse. "She doesn't like stuff like that."

On the way home, they saw police cars and flashing lights up ahead. Rebecca recognized Dan, Adam's friend from the police department. "What's happening?" Rebecca asked across the seat through the window Ruth had rolled down.

He leaned into the car. "A little car chase. Big event for Liberty." He had the glow of a Christmas morning. Adam had once told her that cops lived for excitement to break the monotony of small-town law enforcement. "Hey, nice flowers," Dan said, nodding toward the bouquet on Rebecca's lap, now leaking onto her dress.

"What did the person do?" Ruth asked.

"Robbery. Imagine in our own Tidy Mount Idy. He crashed during the chase," he said with his eyes twinkling. "We got up to ninety-five miles per hour." Dan shook his head. "We don't think he's going to make it. Guess he paid for his crime. You be careful now when you pass by. Don't drive through the glass." He gave a couple of "God speed" slaps to the car and walked back to the scene.

Ruth and Rebecca proceeded slowly around the wreck where tow trucks stood ready to pull the car from the ditch. They turned to watch. One truck was already pulling the mangled auto out. On the bumper was a sticker that read "Make love not war."

"That's one less hippie we have to deal with," said Ruth.

Oh, Ruth, don't give me a reason to check the do-not join column.

"Oh, I'm sorry. We agreed to not let our politics interfere with our friendship."

Rebecca smiled. "We'll keep working on it."

"It used to be so easy," she told Kathleen later. "There were good guys and bad guys. The good guys were Eisenhower, the Lone Ranger, and John Wayne. The bad guys were cowboys in black, the Germans in Nazi uniforms, the Kamikaze pilots who dove into American ships."

"Makes sense. What's the problem?"

"In Liberty it has become whether or not one opposes the Vietnam war or supports the war. It all depends on which side of an idea one stands. On the other side from you, stands the bad guy."

"Your Adam is one of the good guys, don't you think?"

"I know he thinks he is. I'm sure some Vietnamese peasants don't think so."

11

December 1965.

After working at the church, Rebecca relaxed by playing solitaire at the table near the front window. The whir of shuffling the cards made the only noise in the house, the outside sounds muffled by new snow that covered the brown and grey hues of the winter day. Mr. Jackson opened his garage door and dragged two plastic reindeer to his front lawn. Liberty was beautiful during the holidays, and Mr. Jackson was adding to it. He looked toward her, and she waved through the window. Smiling big, he waved back.

It was the first Christmas without Adam, and she wasn't sure how she was going to make it through the holidays.

Not a time for a pity party. It had to be a lot worse for Adam. Strange country, no department store Santa, no wreaths on neighbors' doors. "It's not all about you, Rebecca," she heard her mother say from time to time.

A couple of weeks ago, she sent Adam a tiny artificial tree. She used cotton balls for snow and made ornaments out of soda lids. One had Clipper's picture, hand-drawn and looking more like a cow than a dog. She glued hearts on some of the lids, not Christmassy, but the season was about love, wasn't it? A last-minute artistic decision was to write "Boom" on about six of the lids, hoping he would connect the "Boom booms" and get a laugh out of it. She had also made a string of popcorn garland, and she had put so much tinsel on the little tree she thought it could be used as an antenna. She wondered if reminders of home were helpful or sad. She landed on helpful.

Watching Mr. Jackson working to add Christmas cheer to the neighborhood made her determined to get in a holiday mood. She turned on the radio and dialed stations until she heard Bing Crosby crooning Mele Kalikimaka. She foxtrotted across the living room, arms up to hold on to an invisible Adam, keeping the beat to the 4/4 lyrics about spending Christmas in Hawaii. She sang along to the music, and Clipper's tail wagged to the beat. The twirling fed oxygen to her brain, and she had a lightness in her step for the first time since Adam left.

Out of breath she motioned to Clipper, "Come on, let's go to the basement."

In the kitchen she passed by the wall calendar on which she marked off the days until Adam would be home, or as he said, back in "The World." It was close to dusk, so she marked off another day and smiled.

She descended the stairs, narrow and dark, in spite of the hanging bulb overhead. Clipper surpassed her and waited at the bottom as though he knew he had won the race. At the last step was a light switch that turned on the rest of the basement lighting. The sputtering of the fluorescents over Adam's workbench reminded Rebecca of the hours he would spend down there tinkering with things.

A musty smell reached her nostrils.

She pushed aside Adam's old childhood bike, a Disney affair with Donald Duck's head protruding from the handlebars. Some of Adam's police uniforms were hanging on the clothesline, waiting to be ironed, which she hated doing. She brushed her hand over the blue twill of his trousers as a promise to get them done before he came home.

The floor looked shiny near the corner where the Christmas decorations were. A millipede scurried away from the boxes that looked like they had collapsed a little. She picked up one container only to have the bottom drop out and all the glass ornaments dropped, splashed, and broke onto the cement floor. Sugarfoot, she said to the Universe.

An hour later she had pulled all the boxes from the corner and found the dripping water coming from the seam of the first cement block up. "Pulled" was not the correct term—more like drag, scoop and tear cardboard pieces from their moisture laden hell. Everything was mildewed and water stained. Anything cloth was a swirl of colors run together like Indian batik.

So many memories ruined. The Christmas stocking her mother knitted for her. The nutcrackers she and Adam had collected. The kissing ball her grandmother made from little pill cups they used in the nursing home where she lived. Plastic candle lamps fell through the bottom of a damp bag and crashed to the floor, breaking all the red lights. The sequins and felt elves that her grandmother Barnes had carefully glued onto a felt tree skirt fell off as she carefully unfolded it. She saw a mildewed baby doll from her childhood that she had kept for a daughter. More loss.

One box was still intact, slightly damp but holding together enough to protect the contents. She could only hope it was something memorable worth saving, not leftover wrapping and gift boxes. She opened the flaps, and her heart jumped. It was the wreath that she and Adam had made their first Christmas. It was ugly, but it was THEIR wreath. They had bought a large one with fake white pine branches and decorated it with fake poinsettias and those tiny pseudo velvet bows that had probably been stapled together in some prison workshop. And it was in perfect shape.

"Look Clipper! Our wreath!"

He growled when she pulled it out of the box.

"It's okay, boy, it won't hurt you."

She took the wreath, handling it carefully by the hook on the back. Looking at the mess on the basement floor, she said to Clipper, "I'll worry about that tomorrow."

She proudly carried her find up the stairs into the living room where the radio was playing Benny Goodman's *Jingle Bells*.

She took a no-name landscape painting from above the fireplace mantle and placed the wreath on the nail.

She lit a fire, turned off all the lights, and pulled Clipper onto the sofa. She hugged his warm body and nestled her hands into his long fur. A wave of violin strings introduced a Crosby song that oozed across the airwaves like the water in the basement, spoiling everything in its path. *I'll Be Home for Christmas* crooned with the sadness of a soldier who would be home "if only in my dreams."

Rebecca looked up at the wreath, and her mood switched like a bulb from "On" to "Off," replaced by poisonous resentment of a war she didn't understand. She opened a drawer from the sofa table next to her and found the brochures from the adoption agency. She ripped them in half and threw them into the fire. When they had turned to ash, she scattered the logs so the fire would die out.

The warm front came as the weatherman had promised. The silence of the snow turned into the pounding of rain. Rebecca sat with Clipper and wondered how she was to survive the holidays. Not only did she want Adam to comfort her, she wanted to comfort Adam. *At least I'm not being shot at.*

Early the next morning, Rebecca met with Diane, the DAR registrar, at the library. Diane had a folder of old, official looking documents. "We have to document your lineage back to the Reverend Cradlebaugh for the DAR application. Your mother's mother had documented her ancestry for her membership, so a lot of the work is done."

Rebecca shuffled through the papers, keeping their order intact. "Is that my marriage license? How did you get that?"

"At the court house. I had to get Adam's birth certificate as well."

She started. "His parents would be on there?"

"Of course."

She grabbed the birth certificate and studied the information typed on the document. "What if I wanted to know more about his parents?"

"You'd go to the library or the courthouse. Maybe something in the in the newspapers. Or you could get his parents death certificates and find out who their parents were."

"Do you some paper I can write on? And a pencil? I want to copy down some of the details."

"Well, you'll get a copy of all this when we submit your application."

Rebecca's look of impatience had to be obvious. Diane handed her pencil and paper.

Rebecca wrote down the information most important to her.

Date of birth: May 23, 1925

Place of birth: Zanesville, Muskingum County, Ohio

Mother: Caroline Stevens Benson

Father: Charles Benson

What a Christmas present.

12

By nine in the morning, Rebecca was on the road. Mr. Jackson was going to watch Clipper, she called in sick to the church, and she collected a couple of legal pads, pencils, and of course, a folder with the notes from Adam's birth certificate. And she cancelled playing Bridge that day, which really was a no-no. *They'll survive. I know I'm being selfish, but this is so important.*

She pulled up to the courthouse in Zanesville about ten-thirty. Looking at the three stories of ornate limestone, and the clock tower, she wondered what secrets about Adam's parents sat on the courthouse shelves. It was like Christmas, she thought. She couldn't wait to see what's inside this present.

Rebecca approached the clerk, a young and dour looking woman who was sorting papers on the wooden counter.

"May I help you?"

Rebecca nervously stepped forward and said, "I'd like to see some birth and death certificates of family members."

"Their names?"

Rebecca looked into her folder with the single piece of paper. "Adam Benson, born May 23, 1925, and death certificates of his parents Caroline Stevens Benson and Charles Benson.

The woman looked up. "Date of deaths?"

"I don't know." She held her breath.

"That information would be helpful, but as long as there aren't too many Bensons, that shouldn't be difficult. Do you have an approximate idea when they might have died?"

Rebecca thought through any remarks Adam may have made during their arguments about his past. "I've been on my own since I was eighteen," she remembered him saying. "Maybe around the time he would have graduated from high school, about 1943?"

"That helps."

Rebecca was glad to see the woman's dour expression change to a warm smile. "I've never done this before."

"I can tell. It's fine. I'll be right back."

Rebecca sat on a wooden bench, more like a church pew than a bench to relax on. She looked at the stark circle clock on the wall and watched the second hand go tick tock in excruciatingly slow movements. Everything in the room was brown. Wood floors, wooden counters, oak doors, beige walls. She smiled to herself to think she was also dressed in brown...and brown shoes. Aside from the flag in the corner, she didn't see any more red, white, and blue.

She had heard at one of the DAR meetings that many courthouses had burned down, taking decades of records with them. She was glad this courthouse hadn't succumbed to fire.

I'm going to find out about Adam's parents, she thought. Feeling a little guilty, she wondered if she were betraying Adam's wishes to not reveal anything about his family. Yet, knowing about his past could help explain his secrecy, his motivations about...well, a great deal. And she could understand him better. "Do what's good for the marriage," the Reverend Kaskell said to her once. "Secrets aren't helpful."

The clerk came back into the room with a small ledger type book and a large bound book about the size of a dinner tray. "We're in luck. I found what you're looking for."

Rebecca appreciated the attribution "we." She felt like the clerk had joined the search as a team member.

"Let's see." The clerk opened the smaller ledger to 1925, then to May. "There it is."

Rebecca looked down on the page at Adam's birth certificate, just like the one Betsy showed her. "May I have a copy?"

"Of course," and she put a sliver of paper between the pages. "Now about death certificates. You'll see something very interesting." The clerk opened the massive book to a marked page and pointed. "Look at the dates of their deaths."

Rebecca leaned closer and saw the death date of Charles Benson – June 29, 1943. The clerk's finger slipped down a line. Caroline Stevens Benson – June 29, 1943. Rebecca looked up at the excited clerk's face. "Oh my gosh. They died on the same day?"

"Look at the cause of death."

She looked back at the page and saw that the cause of death for both of them was "massive bleeding in the brain due to gunshot wounds."

"That's horrible. How do I find out more? Was there a robbery or something?"

"That happened long before I came to Zanesville. I suggest you go to the library and look at newspaper archives on or after that date. And look for their obituaries. I'll make you copies of these death certificates also."

Rebecca sat in her car studying the documents. *What could possibly have happened? Was Adam there, maybe? Could he have...no, that couldn't possibly be.*

The librarian in the newspaper archives was much older than the clerk in the courthouse. Maybe she knew of the Bensons, she thought.

"What dates of newspaper reels would you like to see?"

"Around June 23, 1943."

"Alright. That date sounds familiar for some reason. I'm older than dirt and I've seen, and heard, much that's happened in this town."

"Oh? Did you know the Benson family?"

The librarian's eyes widened. "The Benson's? Oh yeah, why are you researching the Bensons?"

"My husband is Adam Benson, born here, and his parents died on the same day. I was wondering if there might be something in the papers about how they died."

Her face turned somber. "I'm afraid you may not like what you find out, but go ahead. You can ask me questions later." She helped Rebecca position the roll of celluloid tape into the reader and scan ahead to June 24, 1943. "Let's look at the day after their deaths. Read and let me know what you think." She gave Rebecca a concerned look and walked back to her desk

She didn't have to scan very far. There on the front page was the headline "Tragic Murder/Suicide." Before she could read any further, she reread the headline several times. *Poor Adam, no wonder he doesn't want to talk about it.* The news article read "Police were called to 408 Martins Road in Zanesville by a neighbor who reported loud arguing and two gunshots. When police arrived, they discovered two bodies in the living room and a handgun lying nearby. The deceased, a middle-aged man and a middle-aged woman, were identified, but more information won't be released until next of kin are identified. Police will continue their investigation."

Looked toward the librarian's desk and realized she had been watching her. Her face registered sympathy for Rebecca.

"Murder/suicide? How can that be?"

The librarian came to her side and sat down. "I'm so sorry. Your husband must not have told you about the horrific conditions in that home. How much do you want to know?"

"Everything."

"It was known all over town Charles Benson was a thug who beat on his wife, and his son. The wife was a sweetie and doted on Adam. That was his name, right? There was some talk Charles was schizophrenic but that was never confirmed. All that's left of the family is Caroline's sister, Debra Stevens. She never married." She squeezed Rebecca's hand. "Have I told you too much?"

"I needed to know. Thank you."

"You're awfully pale. Are you going to be alright."

"Yes, I think so."

Back in the car and with Debra Stevens' address written on her research folder, Rebecca drove away from the library and toward the Benson residence. She had thought

she was going to be sleuthing into Adam's past today, not
digging into the bowels of a sadly dysfunctional family.

13

Rebecca stood on the front stoop of Debra Stevens's immaculate home, a white clapboard cottage surrounded by carefully tended flower beds. With a prayer for strength to a God she wasn't sure about, Rebecca knocked firmly on the door.

"Yes?" a firm voice answered. "I'll be right there."

Rebecca liked the voice, which came through the door as welcoming, inviting, lyrical.

An older lady with white hair, blue eyes, and a dish towel in her hands stood before Rebecca. "What can I do for you?"

"I'm Rebecca Benson, Adam Benson's wife. I hope you are Debra Stevens."

Why is she staring at me? What is she thinking?

Debra reached for Rebecca and said, "Please forgive my rudeness. I don't mean to stare, I just...just never thought I hear anything of Adam after all these years. Please come in."

Debra signaled Rebecca to sit in an oversized, quilted armchair, covered in bright flowered fabric. Debra took a seat on the sofa.

"I'm just overwhelmed. How? Why did you find me?" She put a hand to her heart. "Adam pretty much disappeared after his parents died. Is he OK? Where is he? What's he doing?"

"I know this must be strange coming out of the blue, but Adam was always secretive about his past. Paranoid, actually. And when I came across his birth certificate, I discovered who his parents were. That led me to track down their death certificates, and..."

"Oh yes. You read about their tragic ending. My poor sister..." Debra struggled to continue. "I imagine you want to hear the whole story."

"I do. I want to understand why my husband hides his past. He doesn't want children and I do. He's such a wonderful person, but this one part of him..."

"Please tell me a little about him first. Caroline so loved him. I've imagined her guiding him through life, giving him direction that he so deserved."

Rebecca willed herself to talk first about Adam. She wanted so much to learn what she could about the Benson family. She told Debra the story of Adam's military service, their marriage, his generosity and gentleness, his reenlistment in the Marines. She left out his betrayal of his promise to not soldier again.

"I can tell you are a thoughtful, smart, and loving person, Rebecca. I'm so glad he has you in his life. I imagine it was very difficult to accept his reenlistment."

"More than you realize."

"He was such a good looking young man. Is he still handsome?"

Rebecca smiled. "Very."

Debra sighed. "My sister would be so proud."

"Please, please tell me what Adam's childhood was like. And what happened to his parents."

Debra looked away and then back at her. "I suppose you've seen the scars on his back?"

"Y-yes."

"His father was a very cruel man. He was mostly unemployed, and during those times he took out his frustration on my sister and Adam. I tried to get her to leave and come live with me, but she was afraid that he would hurt me too. I didn't understand why she stayed with him. I told her he was dangerous." She looked off into nothing. "Why would a woman choose to live so horribly?"

Rebecca put her hand to her mouth. "I had no idea. What a horrific situation."

"I'm not surprised Adam doesn't want children. He told me once that he was afraid he would have a temper like his father. And the scar on his back is from a time that he tried to protect his mother. They both ended up in the hospital."

Rebecca stood up and paced a few steps back and forth. She looked intently at Debra. "Was there some mental illness, like schizophrenia or something?"

"Nothing was ever said." Debra cleared her throat. "I'm embarrassed I'm telling you all this. It seems, cheap, somehow. But I have never had the courage, or the gossip monger in me, to do otherwise."

"Can you tell me what happened that day they both died?"

Debra's eyes were wet. "Charles had just been fired, again. Caroline didn't know that, and expecting the next week's paycheck she had splurged on a new dress to please Charles." Her voice caught. "Oh this is so hard."

"Please, if you can, go on. I want to understand Adam's struggles."

"He erupted when he saw the dress on her, accusing her of being a spendthrift, using all his money for her frivolities. He slapped her. Then I heard her yell that she'd had enough and was going to leave."

"How did you know what was being said?"

"I was standing on the doorstep. Ready to knock on the door. Oh, I wished I had, maybe I could have interrupted the whole thing, but I was frozen by the violence I heard."

Rebecca couldn't move. She wondered where Adam was that moment. "The death certificate said they both died of massive bleeding in the brain due to gunshot wounds."

"When Caroline said she was leaving, I heard a drawer open, then a gunshot. I opened the door, and that man looked me in the eye and put the gun to his head. In an instant he was gone."

"Oh my God." Rebecca moved to the sofa and held Debra in her arms. "I'm so sorry. I'm so sorry." She rocked Debra like Adam had rocked her when she had first told him about her father. When Debra stopped sobbing and wiped her eyes with tissues from her pocket, Rebecca asked, "I...I have one more question. Where was Adam?"

Debra sat back, more composed, and said, "He walked in from school just after the second shot. He blamed me for not stopping his father."

On the drive back to Liberty, Rebecca felt the exhaustion in both mind and body. She and Debra had said their goodbye with hugs of shared truth. Rebecca had promised to stay in touch and keep her informed about Adam. And they had talked about ways to tell him that Aunt Caroline was alive and well, and anxious to connect. Rebecca's Christmas present had become a conundrum—how was Adam going to react to her snooping into his family?

14

The revelation about Adam's parents overshadowed the holidays. Every letter she wrote omitted her newfound knowledge and her developing relationship with his aunt Debra. The few decorations she had displayed made her wonder what Christmases Adam had experienced. Her guilt doubled over the selfish way she said goodbye.

She had been a good wife and had played the patriotic life the last month or so. Adam deserved no less. A new flag flew at the front door although each breeze made the flag flutter and whisper to her an uncomfortable reminder—Americans were dying in Asia as were the Vietnamese who defended or wanted the land. At least the ladies didn't avoid her at the grocery store, and conversations at bridge were more lighthearted and not so carefully crafted. Her mother fawned upon her and repeatedly told her how proud she was of her "return to sanity."

Rebecca was bursting with Adam's past. She was not the town pariah as she once was, but she knew she was on probation.

She joined the kind ladies at the DAR meetings and learned more about the courage of the men and women who bravely fought independence from British rule. She wondered if she would have been so determined. The woman with the walker never returned to the DAR meetings, and it seemed the woman's unfinished sentence about the Benson family would remain unfinished. Rebecca wasn't sure she wanted to know more anyway.

It was another cold day in January, and Rebecca picked up a pen to put an "x" on the calendar. She had twelve x's on the new calendar—carefully drawn every morning. "So many empty boxes, Clipper. And so many days until I can let Adam know I understand."

A day without a letter from Adam was many times longer than other days. The mailbox had become a Pandora's box. Anything could be let loose by opening the mailbox lid. His letters were changing. They began as lying letters—funny, loving, and void of the chaos she saw on TV. The letters had evolved into telling her more truth. But with truth came reality, and the reality frightened her. Adam's lying letters were comfortable, the truthful ones were not. More and more she pictured him in danger rather than in the monotonous life he initially portrayed.

I can't hit him with what I know. Would he be angry or relieved? Best to wait.

She removed the dried-up wreath on the front door, needles falling with the slightest touch. The oranges and other once decorative fruit were mummified, and the wires holding the pine cones were visible. By the time she got it to the trash can, it was a skeletal reminder of a past season.

She spotted the postman coming up the street, and she pretended to be busy as he approached. She fiddled with the trash can lid, making sure it fit tightly. From the corner of her eye she watched the postman's progress, like a school girl waiting for her latest crush to ride by on his bicycle.

The postman placed a letter in her mailbox and took the letter she had written to Adam. Rebecca's heart pounded.

"Howdy, Miz Benson." He tipped his hat as he departed for the house next door.

Rebecca grabbed the letter and went into the house for her letter reading ritual—a cup of tea, sitting on the sofa, a signal to Clipper to jump up with her. The letter sat on the coffee table, propped on its edge so she could study what stationary he used and what that might mean. She savored each detail. She took note of the postmark, January 3. In the right most corner Adam had written "FREE," a perk of being in a battle zone, she guessed.

She slid her finger under the flap, and a piece of typewritten paper slipped to the floor. It looked like a poem. Weird. Adam didn't write poetry. She focused on the letter.

January 2, 1966

Hello Beautiful!

During the day, we go about our business on the base. It's like Main Street in Liberty. Guys are going back and forth to the mess hall, there's the PX where we can buy candy or cigarettes, radios are playing all the latest songs, there's constant traffic of jeeps and trucks (not Buicks and Chevys!), horns honking and people waving.

I haven't had any incidents, but I will admit that when night comes, there's a whole different feel to the camp. At night, we can't see a thing, and our ears are open to the slightest sound. But don't worry about me. I'm in a huge base camp with lots of Marines, soldiers and artillery all around the perimeter, and they are always vigilant!

Starting next month, I'm going to be going on patrol with the ARVN. My charges tend to shoot blindly and poke their rifles out of a bunker and fire. No aiming like we're trying to teach them. And they don't always appreciate our attempts to instill discipline. But they love to smile for American reporters! It'll be a lot different going out with guys who aren't the Marine buddies I've been used to. You can always count on your buddies to watch your back. This group, I don't know.

She stopped reading once she realized that Adam had slipped into truth telling. Be brave, she told herself. He trusts me to know. She focused again on the letter in her hands.

My letters will be more sporadic since we may be gone several weeks at a time. I've wanted to lose a little weight, and I think eating in the field like the Vietnamese do, I'll get my wish.

I hear horror stories about elephant grass. It's taller than us and as sharp as knives. The guys get pretty sliced up going through it. Plus, you can't see anything. I may come home striped!

I have to tell you how the VC get through the wire. An NVA who came to our side (we call him a Kit Carson) showed us how permeable that razor edged wire could be. To maneuver through it, he retrieved cutters from his jaws and made a silent and precise cut to allow the next forward movement. I swear he had a rubber torso. It was like watching a cobra crawling over and through rocks and debris, all without disturbing the earth. The whole point was, of course, to teach us not to assume the wire keeps the VC out. "Always vigilant" our commanding officer says.

I'm including a poem that my buddy Robert "Longfellow" had written. (All the guys get nicknames related to some personality trait that is an easy tease. Robert pretends his nickname refers to his manliness, not his poetry.) You'd be surprised at the number of poet soldiers we have. I was really taken by Robert's "sensitive side." Don't want to make you worry with this poem. It's so good, I wanted to share it with you. But I am very safe.

A new year, eh, Sweets? That means I will be back this year. Scratch Clipper's ears for me. Love you bunches. You numba one!

Hugs and Kisses,
Adam

After reading the letter several times, Rebecca looked for the sheet of paper that had fluttered to the floor. Poetry?

Songs of the Concertina Wire
Da Nang
by Robert Norris

Concertina wire
coiled
    protecting
    vigilant.
Trust me
    Sings the razor edge
    as the wind sweeps past.
Danger muted by melodies

a lullaby of wire.

Soldier,
jungle tired.
Eyes
Closed,
Muzzle
Down,
Finger
nestles in trigger guard.

Clip, twist
clip twist
wire cutters in expert hands,
a plasticine Viet Cong,
a sapper in black,
flowing under and through.

Knife meets flesh,
soldier blood
drowns soldier song,
Black clad ghoul
slips back into jungle darkness
to songs of the concertina wire.

Rebecca placed the poem on the coffee table and watched the living room grow dimmer with the waning light of the late afternoon. The graying room sank into her as deeply as the poem's rendering of danger and murder. She refolded it and returned it to the envelope that had carried its menacing message. Adam must be around so much carnage that he doesn't even realize that the poem was powerfully _ominous.

The images in the poem overwhelmed Rebecca. She forced herself to swallow the worry, the whole lumpy gelatinous ball of anxiety that was trying to make its home in her throat. She pushed the images into that do not disturb portion of her brain that was already crowded with unreckoned realities. Desperate for distraction, she looked wildly around the room. Heart pumping, breath shallow, Rebecca looked to the phone.

"Hey...if hubby is at another dinner meeting, wanna come over and have a four course Swanson dinner with me? We can watch the news," she asked Kathleen.

"What a great way t' celebrate removal of a ratty wreath from your door," she said.

"You saw that, huh?"

"Small town, big eyes. I do live next door t' ya." She added, "What are the courses?"

"Let's see, there's an entrée, of course, vegetables, fruit, and...dessert, probably with a maraschino cherry no less. Haven't picked our poison yet."

"Yum. Do you have any Chianti?"

"Yep."

"The kids are at a basketball game. I'll be over in about twenty minutes."

Rebecca turned on the oven and went to look over the TV dinners in the freezer. Meat loaf, green beans, Tater Tots, and brownie. Turkey and dressing, cranberry sauce, and mashed potatoes. Franks and beans, ugh, that one was a gagger. Spaghetti and meatballs. Yes. That would go with Chianti. She took out two of them, rolled the aluminum back from the cherry crisp and slipped them into the oven.

Of course, the TV dinner was small, but the Chianti bottle was big, so they didn't care if there were only a couple of tablespoons of spaghetti and a few questionable meatballs. They finished before the second half of the news.

"Want t' hear a good one?" asked Kathleen during a commercial.

"Sure."

"An Irish priest is driving down t' New York and gets stopped for speeding in Connecticut—"

"Not another one about a priest." Rebecca mockingly slapped her forehead.

"You're so—"

"Wait." Rebecca turned up the volume on the TV.

"U.S. Advisors helping South Vietnam Army. More than twenty-three thousand Americans serve as advisors." The camera cut away from the news desk to a video of smiling Vietnamese soldiers talking with a US serviceman, whose back was to the camera. "American advisors have extensive training on the Vietnamese language, culture, and military goals," intoned the voice-over. "The rapport they build with their Vietnamese counterparts has immensely helped the war effort against the spread of Communism in the peace-loving hamlets of South Vietnam." More shots of happy Vietnamese farmers talking to US Marines.

"Are y' glad Adam is part of that, doing some good and all?" asked Kathleen.

Rebecca turned off the television and retrieved the poem Adam sent. "There's another side to all that. Take a look at what I received in the mail from Adam. Some friend's poem."

Kathleen read the poem and frowned. She handed it back. "Geez."

"Adam says the advisors are getting pretty discouraged. Not enough training, overestimating our ability to develop rapport. The more he tells me, the more I worry. And this poem…"

"Ya want him t' lie t' ya so ya feel better?"

"Yes, actually. I think I do."

"That's putting a big burden on 'im, you know. Smart woman like you would want to know as much as ya could. When he's telling you how things actually are—it means he trusts you t' be able t' handle the truth."

Rebecca inhaled Kathleen's advice, and by the time she exhaled she agreed. "You're right. I tend toward playing ostrich. Let's watch some more." She turned the TV back on. "If I hear bad news, you're toast," she teased.

"Developing story. Two American advisors have been killed while on patrol with ARVN soldiers. Details to follow after the break."

Rebecca jumped up and Kathleen came to her side as they waited a million years for the commercials to end and the newscast to resume.

"Two Army advisors were killed in Cam Thien three days ago…"

"Oh Rebecca, they're Army not Marines."

Rebecca put her hand over her mouth to hold back the bilious acid rising in her throat. Truth is so hard.

15

"Mother." Rebecca wedged the phone between her neck and her chin while she folded her laundry. "Only a few more months until he is home."

"Let's plan a big party for Adam. Before you know it, he'll be back. He certainly deserves a hero's welcome. I only wish I had been able to do that for your father."

"Oh, Mother..."

"Back to the party. Where? Whom will we invite?"

"I'll start making a list, and I'll have to get a new dress, a must for a big occasion like this."

"And I have plenty of decorations we can use."

"This will be so much fun," said Rebecca. "We always do enjoy planning parties together, don't we?"

She went to the living room and re-read one of his letters. He was fine, didn't get to shower as often as he would like, the C-Rations made Spam seem like a gourmet meal, and please send him some more hot sauce to cover the real taste of whatever they ate. And Kool-Aid to flavor the musky water they drank. He also described a scruffy but friendly mutt that followed their unit from village to village. *Reminds me of Clipper, he said. He sits and stares at me when he wants something. Of course, I have to guess what that is. We have to keep him hidden though. They eat dogs here.*

Rebecca smiled, picturing Adam trying to interpret the dog's steady gaze.

Only four more months in country (Nam), Sweets. I told you I'd come back. What a reunion we will have!

Awkwardly drawn hearts, that she called man-art, decorated his prose. Adam always said he was lucky and would come back safe.

Movement on the street caught her eye. A black car pulled out front. At first curious, then terrified, Rebecca put a hand over her cotton-dry mouth. *Not here, please, not here.*

Two spit polished Marines exited the car, pulled on their jackets to line up with the crisp creases in their pants, put on their hats and adjusted them with both hands. Their movements were in slow motion, and sunbeams like warning lights bounced off the sheen of their spotless black shoes. They turned onto the sidewalk up to her house. *Not Adam, please not Adam.* The doorbell rang a death knell.

Rebecca jumped off the couch but couldn't answer the door. The doorbell continued its ominous toll. She finally made the thousand-mile journey to the door.

Her sweaty hand slipped off the knob. She tried again and opened the door.

"Mrs. Adam Benson?" The older one wore a silver cross on his uniform. She stared at the silver symbol—how did he hang it so straight? Its shiny surface had a tiny scratch at the bottom. She studied the curved groove of the scratch, its depth, its path. Her brain would not let her accept the message of the man at the door.

"Ma'am?"

With great effort she raised her eyes to look at the man's face. He had a set jaw and eyes that were a hundred tragedies deep. He was accompanied by a younger Marine who held a briefcase and kept clearing his throat.

Rebecca nodded but she wanted to shake her head and make them go away.

"I have an important message from the Secretary of the Navy, may I come in?"

She opened the door wider and pointed to the living room. Her legs trembled, and her heart was on the edge of exploding. The Marines took off their hats.

"Would ... you like to sit down?"

Almost in harmony, the two men shook their heads. "No, thank you, Ma'am."

The three of them stood facing one another, forming a triad of somber and hesitant participants. Rebecca's mind was outside her body, looking down at the scene, powerless to direct the action.

"Something to drink? Lemonade? Water? How about some cookies I made yesterday?" She pushed back the hair hanging near her eyes, and she gestured toward the kitchen. "Oh my, I'm being an awful hostess... Adam would be embarrassed for me to treat fellow Marines like this. Please let me do something for you. A...a drink, maybe? A beer, would you like a beer? Maybe a—"

The older Marine with the cross took a small step closer. "No thank you, Ma'am.

Rebecca put her hands to her chest. "Please tell me he's alive. Wounded? He's only wounded, isn't he? Which hospital?" She looked back and forth at the two somber men.

"The Secretary has asked me to express his deepest regret," she heard from the younger Marine.

The Marine doing the speaking was nervous, his voice breaking during his script. Rebecca's heart pounded against her ribcage. *Shut up! Shut the fuck up!*

The rest of his words sounded like they came through a long, dark tunnel, mixed and tumbled by the invisible wind that blew through. She heard something about "killed in battle" and "casualty assistance officer."

Rebecca fell to the floor, rocking back and forth on her knees, arms wrapped around her exploding chest. She wanted God to strike her dead, right then.

The chaplain gently helped her up. Once she was on the sofa he asked, "Is there someone we can call to assist you?"

Rebecca stared at him.

"Mrs. Benson, we will stay with you until we are sure you are with someone. Are you certain there isn't someone we can call?"

"I'll do it." She walked stoically to the phone beside the TV chair, Adam's chair. The receiver was lead in her hands. With trembling fingers that wouldn't fit into the circles on the dial, she managed to call her mother.

"Hello?"

Rebecca opened her mouth, but no words came. She handed the phone to the older Marine and sank onto a chair. At that moment, Rebecca could not face tomorrow let alone the next minute.

PART TWO

Do the best you can until you know better. Then when
you know better, do better.

Maya Angelou

16

June 1966.

Adam came home as promised, only not alive and breathing. Rebecca stood at the small gathering at Arlington National Cemetery where Adam wished to be buried. Dan was there, and sweet Aunt Debra made the long trip to say goodbye to the nephew who was the last connection to her sister Caroline.

"Mother, I'd like you to meet Debra Stevens, Adam's Aunt, his mother's sister."

"Oh, I didn't know Adam had any family left," she said to Rebecca. Turning to Debra, she said, "I'm so glad to meet you. How did Rebecca find you?"

"I read about Adam's death in the Muskingum newspaper," she lied. "That's his birthplace. I suspect the military put notices in hometown papers."

Her mother looked at Rebecca with an expression of "Is there more to tell?"

So many questions and lies in Rebecca's head. She glanced at Dan and saw he was looking at her. *I wonder what he knows.* Each of us has our own history with Adam, to be mourned in our individual ways.

The pills she had taken to numb her emotions suppressed her ability to cry. She wanted to get through the funeral as a standing, coherent widow. She felt other worldly, like her tears were out there somewhere, abated, waiting to return.

"I know you're disappointed that Adam won't be in the family plot," her mother said to her.

Rebecca held her mother's hand as tightly as she had at the funeral of her father. Her mother was so stoic, perhaps some of that strength would pass into her. She looked at row upon row of white gravestones glistening in the sun, each whispering "don't forget me."

"Yes, Rebecca said. "Here, though, Adam has the whole country mourning and honoring him."

"Now that I've seen this, I wish your father were buried here."

"How can such a beautiful place hold so much tragedy and grief?" Rebecca asked her mother.

"It also holds a lot of love, Rebecca. Your love is as deep as your grief."

The Marines lifted Adam's flag-draped casket off the caisson and solemnly sidestepped to begin the long journey to his grave. The young Marines holding onto the casket were immaculate in their dress uniforms of blue jackets and white pants. Every shiny buckle, every exact pleat, every perfectly pinned medal were reminders of the respect the men had for their fallen comrades. Did they think Adam's sacrifice worth it? Rebecca let go of her mother's hand to cover her eyes with one of Adam's cotton handkerchiefs.

The chaplain's words floated about her but she heard little. The twenty-one gun salute made her jump and brought her out of her wandering thoughts about times she and Adam shared. At the mournful tones of Taps from the trumpet, she froze. Was this real? Was Adam really in that casket?

The Marine detail removed the flag from the casket and ceremoniously folded it. The chaplain came forward with flag and knelt in front of her.

Her mother put her arms around Rebecca and said in choking words, "I'm so sorry you have to go through what I did. This isn't something a mother wants to have in common with her daughter. But he died for his country. There is no greater honor than that for a family."

Back home in Liberty, memories slammed into her dreams and created twisted versions of the somber ceremony. Sometimes she ran in front of the Marines conducting a twenty-one-gun salute, and she steeled herself for the impact of bullets. With each round of gunfire, she heard the rifle explosions and the bullets whizzing by her ears. The dreams always ended with her dropping the precisely folded flag handed to her, and the fabric became a puddle of red, white, and blue paint at her feet.

Adam's sense of duty also left her a footlocker with a return label: "Camp Pendleton Personal Effects and Baggage Center." She hadn't been able to conduct an important rite of passage for Vietnam War widows—the careful opening and examination of the contents of a husband's personal effects. She had briefly opened the canvas bag of his washed uniforms, and she was disappointed it was void of Adam's scent. But the locker of personal effects was more ominous. She assumed his watch and wallet were in there, proof that it was he the

Marines had sent back in the aluminum coffin. If she didn't look at his things, he's not really gone.

"I can help them," she recalled Adam saying. *Yeah, semper fi.*

Images of the disciplined Marines at Adam's funeral halted her sarcasm. Had they been thinking "As you are now, I might be?"

It had been three months since Adam died. Three long months. During the weeks between the notification and the funeral, she had cried until all the wastebaskets in the house filled with tissues. Her freezer filled with casseroles and desserts her friends brought, but she had little appetite. Unread condolence cards piled up on the hallway table.

Gradually the wastebaskets didn't fill as quickly with used tissues, and she enjoyed a rare moment when she actually smiled one day at a little girl who was skating on the sidewalk.

By the second month some appetite returned. A licorice Chuckles was one day's pleasure. Her teeth still black from the sugary treat, she erupted into sobs that seemed to have no end. Wastebasket nearly full again. She walked in a fog most days and hoped it was all a dream. Mornings she found mascara stains on her pillow.

By the fourth month, she actually slept several nights without crying herself to sleep, and some mornings there were no mascara stains. One day Rebecca noticed how the roses in Jackson's yard perfumed the street. When she inhaled their sweet aroma, she allowed herself to enjoy the flowery scent.

What she missed most was the touching and intimacies that she and Adam shared. She missed the warmth of his body next to her in the bed, on the couch, on the floor wrestling with the dog. She still wore Adam's shirts to bed. And every night, she lit a candle that stood beside a photo of Adam in his dress blues.

Rebecca asked her friend Annie to meet at Bobby Jo's Restaurant to mark the end of the "Period of Constant Crying," as she liked to call it. It was a good place for a celebration of any type. Cheap wine, good food, and walls decorated with things that many people had thrown out as trash years ago but now served as amusing wall art— clocks that explode in star shapes, prohibition signs (the largest one hanging behind the bar), black and white Mickey Mouse drawings, Charlie Chaplin movie posters, photos of modestly dressed bathing beauties with hats and parasols, rusted saxophones. The noise of the bustle and juke box would protect her from eavesdroppers.

At the restaurant Annie ordered her usual, a gin and tonic, and Rebecca ordered a daiquiri.

"You know, Annie, when Adam pulled me over for failing to signal a turn, I got a ticket and a husband, a husband who promised to take care of me, protect me."

Her friend swirled her drink, pinched the lime with the red plastic swizzle stick. "Still fighting against independence, are you? Marriage for protection is the cave days." She looked at Rebecca.

"We did have a 'A Groovy Kind of Love', like the song." Her eyes teared, and she fought to gain control.

Annie put down her drink. "Reality is that four months ago your world did shatter, and you survived, albeit mostly in your house and at work. Time to break free, my friend, move on." She lifted her glass.

"Move on? Sounds like I would be leaving Adam behind."

"Maybe 'go forward.'"

"That sounds better." Rebecca shook her head. "I want to stamp my feet and punish Adam for dying. I want to shake my fist at the VFW and make the President and those generals pay for sacrificing my husband." She gulped the rest of her drink and signaled the waitress for another. "And the widow of a local war hero? Life without Adam, in a small town where my grief is so visible and my patriotism so scrutinized? And the scene at the airport will not stop turning in my head."

What Rebecca didn't tell her friend was that the child issue was no longer an anger point. But the war? She could never talk to him about her new understanding.

She was glad her back was to the room so her tears wouldn't be visible to anyone but Annie. "I'll never know if he turned and blew me a kiss. I've tried to throw that image in the trash, but my guilt ignites it, and its smoke of shame drifts over me."

"Very dramatic, Rebecca." Annie took her hand. "You're a very reluctant widow, aren't you? The problem is you have no choice, so reluctance is only going to drag out your recovery. And it seems to me that you are looking for a magic wand to make all this go away."

"Ya think so? It's so much easier to hide. The Marines gave me one of those white flags with a gold star in the center that I'm supposed to put in my front window. I'm a Gold Star widow, can you believe that?"

"Have you opened the footlocker yet?"

"No." She studied her drink.

"Rebecca, are you nuts? Don't you want to know what's in there?"

She shook her head, unable to look at her friend.

"There's something else about being a widow that is difficult to talk about," Rebecca said to her drink, not to Annie.

"What, my friend, would that be?"

"I miss the...the intimacy." Rebecca felt the heat in her cheeks. "If Adam were alive, he'd be coming home next week, and..."

"Look at me," Annie said. "There is nothing wrong with that, except it's frustrating."

"I suppose," she answered.

Annie shifted in her seat. "Did I see a For Sale sign in your yard? Don't you think it's a little early for that?" Annie picked at the salad.

"Too many ghosts in the house. A change would be good, don't you think?"

"Whose ghosts are they? Yours or Adam's? And, would moving be moving on or running away?"

"Both, and I have a realtor, Ruth Middleton."

"Ruth Middleton of the swinging breasts? How funny. I hear she sells though."

"That's what I'm counting on, but you know I'm not sure about anything, or anybody anymore."

"All the more reason to not make any sudden changes." Annie shifted in her chair. "You've got to let go of your resentment."

"How would you react if someone betrayed you?" Rebecca's eyes burned. She studied the salad and pulled out a suspiciously wilted piece of lettuce.

"Remember...I was betrayed, by a cheating husband," Annie said. "Now there's a broken promise. At least Adam had a cause he believed in that was bigger than the two of you."

"The war, you mean. Great cause. Why did Adam think he had to save the world anyway?"

"In the end, I'm sure his training efforts saved some lives. And who knows why he had to die, that's unanswerable. We humans aren't meant to know."

"Annie, what would I do without you? You keep me sane."

Annie didn't answer. Odd. Annie always has something to say.

They ate in silence for a few minutes. Annie leaned forward and took both of Rebecca's hands.

"I have something to tell you," she said.

Rebecca looked at her, puzzled, having no idea what she might be saying. Annie's hands felt moist and a little shaky. Was she stalling about something? Her concern grew. Was she ill? Cancer?

"I understand Adam's need to serve." Annie took a deep breath. "I've enlisted in the U.S. Army Nurse Corps to be a surgical nurse in Vietnam. It's what I need to do. I leave in a few weeks for Fort Sam Houston."

The room grew cold. Annie, her life raft, was leaving for the war that killed her husband. "Not you too!" Rebecca pulled back. Her voice was no longer discrete but loud and shrieking. "How long have you been planning this? You couldn't tell me, your best friend?"

"Lower your voice. People are looking at us."

"I don't care." She looked at her friend in shocked puzzlement.

"I tried to tell you, but you were in such pain over Adam, and it seemed selfish somehow. . . "

"You're abandoning me too?"

"It's not abandonment. It's a choice I'm making for myself. I...I'm so sorry, Rebecca. I really am, I guess I was too chicken to face you, you've been struggling with Adam's death, the war itself and such."

"I didn't take you for a flag waving patriot."

"It has nothing to do with flag waving. Those boys over there need our help regardless of the good or bad of the war, and I'll be Lieutenant Henderson." She gave Rebecca a salute, smiling.

Shock waves traveled down Rebecca's spine. She couldn't, wouldn't, see Annie's pride.

"I'll be back before you know it. I promise." The look on Rebecca's face told Annie her words were hurtful.

"That's what Adam said and look what happened to him." Rebecca could no longer control her tears. She buried her head in her hands, tears trailing down her wrists.

"That was thoughtless of me to say," Annie said.

"Please don't go."

"It's got to be a shock for you, but right now I need you to be strong for me. I'm scared too. I need to know that my best friend understands my need to help and will be there for me with letters, and cookies, and Kool-Aid."

"And I need you to hold me up while I move forward. Couldn't you have waited? I don't think I can do this without you."

"Yes, you can. I'll be a letter away. You have other friends like Kathleen, your mother, and of course, yourself." Annie took a deep breath. "Friends take turns supporting each other."

The boulder in Rebecca's stomach sat heavy. She stared at the remainder of her salad and wondered if she would ever be able to eat again. *How dare she abandon me?* Fear and helplessness emptied whatever reservoir of strength she had.

"Rebecca?"

"Yes?" *What could be worse?*

"You know my parents are gone, and I'm not close to my cousins. I gave your name for notification purposes."

17

Rebecca slammed the door shut after she walked Clipper in the morning. He hid under the table.

Guilt gnawed at her as she replayed the last evening's conversation. What was it Annie said? "Friends take turns supporting each other." *Maybe Annie was right. I am a crazy, reluctant widow. And self-absorbed.* A whisper of strength nudged her. Damn helplessness and damn Annie. How dare she leave me for Vietnam?, and I ain't afraid of no damn locker, either.

Rebecca went upstairs to change out of her public clothes into clothes for getting chores done. She chose an oversized Ohio State sweatshirt with torn off sleeves, jeans with paint stains and holes in the knees. Ugly and comfortable, perfect for doing an ugly task. Once downstairs in the guest bedroom, she directed her gaze toward the unopened locker of Adam's personal effects, sitting on the floor of the open closet. The dented corner and black scuff marks told a story of rough handling on its trip from Camp Pendleton to Liberty, Ohio. The postmark was stamped on Rebecca's brain as well as on the package—March 20, 1965—their ninth anniversary.

She stared at the box, and the box sat without comment. "Oh, Adam. Did your dying have any purpose other than to make me a widow?" she said aloud. At the sound of his master's name, Clipper whined, his nose upward and twitching toward the smells the box held. His black ears were at attention, and his spotted tail wagged. He was panting, yet Rebecca was hardly breathing. She took a deep breath, grabbed the wooden handle on one end, and pulled. The footlocker stayed put. Another pull. One inch toward her. "Come on, you bleepin' piece of wooden shit." Rebecca bent her knees, grabbed the handle with both hands and pulled. The plywood box yielded to her determination and let go of the carpet that held its splintered feet. She dragged it to the center of the room.

Clipper sniffed and walked around it, taking in every bit of information a dog's nose could gather. He sat, looked up at her, and whined.

"I suppose you want me to open it, don't you?"

Clipper whined again and wagged his tail.

An aura of doom emanated from the locker. What more disappointments lay inside? What difference would it make anyway? Adam is dead. Nothing in there is going to bring him back.

She slipped some cardboard under the rough areas and dragged the locker to the living room. She pushed it back among other boxes waiting to be examined and sorted for things worth keeping and things to pitch. She had been weak rather than strong. What was strength anyway? And who decides? Rebecca rubbed her forehead with both hands.

Clipper walked over and scratched at the quarantined footlocker. He lay beside it, so close it looked like the footlocker itself was dressed as a springer spaniel. He let out a sigh and closed his eyes with a final soft whine. The dog had such drama.

At least it was out of the closet.

She went into the kitchen to pour herself a cup of coffee from the only modern appliance in the kitchen, her own PolyPerk. Her mother scoffed at plastic coffeemakers, although she seemed to approve of the orange, brown and yellows daisies that adorned the off-white plastic. "So colorful," she had said. That was mother talk for "I see you got one of those (fill-in-the-blank), and the color is the only nice thing I can say about it."

Kathleen appeared at the kitchen door. Her orange and yellow pedal pushers and matching blouse reflected the June day, though it was still cool with the morning dew.

"Little early to be throwin' stuff out, isn't it?" she asked as she stepped in and surveyed some boxes in the kitchen. With her came the perfume of lilacs from somewhere in the neighborhood. Holding a steaming coffee mug, she sat down at the kitchen table. Its metal edges were worn from years of neighbors absentmindedly rubbing while they kibitzed and snacking. The smell of coffee mixed with the summer floral odors she let in.

"What have you been up to?" asked Rebecca.

"It's time for the Liberty Garden Club to start arranging programs for the coming year. Have any ideas?"

"Afraid not. I'm a black thumb."

"Whoa...what is that look on your face?" she asked.

"Did you hear about Annie?"

"Yeah. She made me promise not tell you until she had a chance to let you know. Happened kinda fast."

"So, she told you first?"

"She was worried about how t' tell you. She's a good friend, ya know."

Rebecca sat, unsure how to react.

Kathleen scanned the living room, visible through the arched doorway. She looked at the cartons that would be hauled onto a moving truck someday. "Looks like you haven't gone through Adam's locker yet."

Rebecca studied a hangnail on her thumb.

"Three months and ya still haven't opened it, eh?" She blew on the hot coffee.

"I can't." Rebecca sat down with her coffee. "There're probably snakes in there or poisonous spiders that hitched a ride from the jungle. Mosquitos waiting to bite."

"They'd be dead by now." Kathleen looked up. "What other excuses have ya been using lately? Your fear of a malarial mosquito is your lamest effort."

"Go ahead and make fun of me. What if there are things in there that Adam didn't want me to see, like girly magazines? I hear Marines take advantage of not having wives around to indulge in some good reading."

"Good try. I read a while back that the military removes sensitive materials like girly magazines from personal effects. And there's usually an inventory list." She studied her friend. "You did read the inventory, didn't you? Wasn't that sent to you separately?"

Ignoring her, Rebecca adjusted the dotted scarf over her hair and re-tied the ends underneath.

"By the way, I hear you signed up with Boobie Shake Ruth to sell your house."

"Well, she has an interested buyer already."

Kathleen looked again at the boxes around the living room. "Seems a little soon. Are you moving or running away?"

"Moving, of course," Rebecca answered quickly.

"I'll miss ya, ya know." She patted Rebecca's arm. "Where do ya think you'll go?"

"My cousin Robin found a couple of apartments in Cincinnati for me to investigate. I'll rent first. You know, maybe having a new start will help. I won't have Adam's ghost in every room. Reality is a little hard for me."

Should I tell her about Debra? That moving to Muskingum was another option? Not yet.

"At least you're smart enough t' realize ya tend to dodge reality. What does your mother think about you selling the family home she gave you when she moved into an apartment?"

"She doesn't care about the house, but she doesn't want me to move. Did you notice the flag out front?"

"What made ya do that?"

"I'm pretending to be patriotic. Until I decide for real."

They exchanged smiles.

When she left, Rebecca scratched behind Clipper's ears. *I can't wait to get away from the reminders of a life I used to have.*

Did she really want to get rid of the good memories too? Adam didn't mind the twenty pounds she had gained over the nine years they were married. "More to pinch and kiss," he'd said. And if she failed at something, Adam was the net to catch her so she could spring up and climb again.

Adam's death had cut a hole in that net, and she wasn't sure how to mend it. She was miserable in her suffering, yet to not suffer was to let go of Adam. A proverbial conundrum. And now a best friend is also going to war and probably won't come back, like so many others.

Be brave, she heard Adam say. *Yes, I need the courage to go through that damn locker.*

A few hours later Rebecca showered and perfumed herself for nobody. She put on her pajamas so if anyone called about going somewhere, she could say she was all ready for bed. She went into the kitchen and poured lime juice, rum, and sugar syrup into the blender, and with ear splitting crunching, the daiquiri was ready. The clock read 4:45. Close enough. Jackie Kennedy liked daiquiris too. Poor Kennedys. Rebecca remembered the night she and Adam cried during the evening news on November 22, 1963. The terrible news invaded their small town through the TV antennae into living rooms, and people began the vigil aided by black and white televisions.

Clipper had unwrapped himself from the footlocker to come and check what she was doing in the kitchen. He wagged his tail. He looked like he was smiling. "You're such a good boy." Clipper shoved his wet nose into her hand to accept the compliment. Hanging from his mouth was a piece of soggy newspaper, and she looked into the living room to see the local and world events torn, chewed and scattered in front of the television. In a magical snippet of time that's too fast for human understanding, he had managed to destroy the daily paper. Headless politicians, soggy grocery ads, farm bureau prices, and wedding announcements with wadded up brides were the remains of Clipper's play. He ran back to his newspaper play yard. Oblivious to the damage, he gamboled in the paper bits, and his joy displaced her displeasure. He was a good dog, except for his penchant for paper, especially newspaper. "Clipper, you bad dog."

After cleaning up the mess, she retrieved her drink and sat on the living room sofa that she and Adam had bought together nine years ago, a style they called "Danish pandemonium."

From the lamp table beside her, Rebecca picked up a photo Adam had sent from Vietnam. He stood on the splintered steps of some shot up hooch, grinning and waving at the camera. He had a cloth bandolier of ammunition draped around his torso like Miss America's sash, and he casually held his rifle at a downward angle. The family that used to live in that hut was nowhere in sight. *Who were they, and where did they go?*

"Whaddya think, Clipper? Are we doing the right thing by moving?" He sat up and put a paw on her knee. That was "yes" in Clipper talk. A signal pat to her lap, and up he jumped.

Maybe Adam saved all my letters, the way I saved his, wrapped in a ribbon. He had such purpose. What is my purpose? It had become an unanswered question that she revisited over and over.

The front doorbell rang, and Rebecca could see an unsmiling Ruth through the peephole, which gave her a fish face. She opened the door, threw up her hands to excuse herself for the bedtime attire, and led the realtor into the kitchen. Ruth sat heavily in a chair.

"Things have changed," she said.

18

Rebecca sat down. "The buyers want to close sooner?" The reality of leaving Liberty sunk in.

"I wish." Ruth handed her some papers. "The buyers backed out."

Rebecca's mouth hung open. "Backed out?" She looked at Ruth's ample breasts. "What about the boobie shake?"

The realtor sighed. "There's a first time for everything, I suppose. Turns out they heard a rumor this property sits over an Indian grave. Did your parents ever say anything about that when you were growing up here?" She put out her hands as a question.

Rebecca jumped out of her chair. "An Indian grave? Holy Toledo." Ruth's news popped the thin skin of her courage. "How...how did they find out something like that?" she asked, seated again and arms folded. "Seems contrived to me."

"The buyers are good friends with a hippie type in Columbus, and when they told him about the house they were buying, he rang the alarm." Ruth attempted to smile. "He said there is a rumor that some Shawnee chief lies right under this table, about twenty feet down, under the fill they used to raise the lot. If this house had been built with a deep basement, he'd probably have been found. Hard to prove, hard to disprove." She folded her hands on the table. She leaned toward a stunned Rebecca and said, "I'm so sorry. Unfortunately, it makes this house difficult to sell if the buyers backed out because of an alleged burial ground. And the reason for the buyers backing out has to be disclosed to potential buyers."

"Jesus, Mary, and Joseph."

"And the wee donkey," Ruth added.

They stared at each other. "I guess I'm not getting my fresh start," Rebecca said, surveying the carefully packed boxes. She had been so proud for getting rid of things— mismatched glasses, the earrings with no partners, the worn blankets she had snuggled in as a child.

"This sounds like something out of a bad novel."

"What do you want to do?" asked Ruth.

"Maybe it's a sign to not move."

"Does that mean you want to take the house off the market?"

"I don't know."

Ruth left, and Clipper re-emerged, pacing and whining at the back door.

"Let me get dressed," she told the dog.

Dressed, she took him outside where he baptized Mrs. Walker's prize rhododendron, sniffed and turned down a chance to water the evergreens in the Smith yard, put his head up for an ear scratch from an unnamed neighbor, lunged fruitlessly at a squirrel who taunted him with chirps, and circled and peed on a fire hydrant that had most likely witnessed hundreds of dogs marking their territory. Each time Clipper peed, Rebecca thought how fate had pissed on her.

They walked around the block twice before Clipper completed his "daily constitutional" as her grandfather used to call it. Back home, he plopped on the floor beside his food bowl, too tired to eat. But Rebecca was too wired to settle down.

Indian burial ground? Well, it was Ohio. She went to the front window and looked at the For Sale sign. How many realtor signs signaled running away? How many foretold new beginnings? She imagined the town talking about how difficult the house would be to sell. The longer the house was on the market, the louder the talk would become.

Rebecca went outside, pulled the sign out of the ground, and stashed it behind the garbage can. She was nearly to the door when she turned back, retrieved the sign, and stuck it back in the ground.

Once inside, she imagined Adam holding her as he did when she needed to cry about something. What was it that the minister said at the funeral? "Get up every day and make the bed...have a routine," and for the first few months, she struggled to follow his advice until she was no longer tempted to stay under the covers, willing her pain to go away. Just that morning she had wakened early, energized to do more packing, buoyed by taking action. An Indian battle, a hundred or so years ago, disrupted her plans.

She looked around. Maybe cleaning the kitchen was in the same league as getting out of bed. Do something. The boomerang patterned Formica table with chrome legs cried out "skuzz-eee" as she wiped it down. It was so fashionable a decade ago. She had planned to get a new kitchen set for Cincinnati, not early American, not Mediterranean and especially not Danish Modern. Rebecca glanced at the clock on the wall. The hands emanated from a black and orange rooster on a wood grain background. Going from the kitchen to the living room was like going through an American barnyard into a Copenhagen hotel lobby.

She called the hospital and left a message for Annie to call her the next morning. *Oh, Annie, how am I going to survive my drama without your counsel? Adam, what am I supposed to do? Mr. Shawnee chief, anything you want to add?*

19

Rebecca went to the church office even though it was not her day to work. Reverend Kaskell always encouraged her to work extra if she need to. Annie called to say she would come to the house after her shift.

When Annie arrived, she breezed in like the East wind, ready to dispel any falsities in life. She was still wearing her white starched uniform, white hose and sensible white shoes. Her immaculate nurse's cap, striped with a black band, sat at attention on the table where she placed it.

Annie shook out a mane of long blond hair, held hostage for the day under her cap. She slouched, letting her head lean on the back of the chair. "Holy shit, what a day," she said. "Pun intended. I gave five enemas today."

"Yuck." Rebecca sat opposite and compared her own hair, pulled back into a put-off-the-shampoo ponytail, to Annie's clean and full tresses.

"So, I see the For Sale sign is gone. Tell me about this grave, it was the talk of the hospital—between enemas. You've been sleeping on top of Indian bones? What kind of nut job made that up?" She sat up, holding in both hands the cup of coffee Rebecca had offered her.

"It's not funny," she said to her smirking friend. "First, tell me how your plans are going for your journey to the jungle. I think I'm ready to talk about it."

"Thank you, friend. I was afraid to bring it up. You know how you hate shots? I have to get lots of them."

"Will they give you a lollipop for each one?"

"Uh, I don't think the Army gives out lollipops, helmets maybe. Back to the Indian bones. This could only happen to you."

"Seriously, Annie, I can't believe it." Rebecca put her head in her hands. "And what am I going to do without you? I need a drink," she said to the Formica.

"Me too," Annie said. "It's only four, but what the hell."

Rebecca busied herself fixing both of them a daiquiri and hoped that the blender would spin some answers. She watched the ice get crushed like she felt life was crushing her.

Annie glanced at Clipper who came into the kitchen and sat beside Rebecca, looking up. "He senses your moods, doesn't he?"

"Last night he slept next to Adam's locker, I think he can smell him." Rebecca tussled his ears. "You miss your dad, don'cha, boy?"

"I'm sure he does," said Annie. "You know, Adam was the reason you stayed in Liberty instead of spreading your wings somewhere. Now you're trying to leave, and this damn Indian thing comes up. Doesn't it make you wonder if you're not supposed to leave yet?"

Rebecca looked at her friend.

"I have a crazy thought," Annie continued. "Maybe your life can't go on until you face what's in that locker. Maybe some mystical force is making you finish one of life's tasks before you can reap the benefits of another. You know," she paused, "taking that unopened locker to

Cincinnati would be like towing this house and all its memories right behind your car. And every morning, it would all still be in your damn driveway, begging to be faced."

The heaviness of Annie's truth fell on Rebecca. She looked off into the distance. *Could Annie be the one I could trust with Adam's past?*

"Tell you what," said Annie.

Rebecca turned her attention back to her friend.

"Let's go to dinner tomorrow night and when we come back, I'll sit with you while you open the locker. Or, I'll open it and describe to you what's in it. You don't even have to be in the room. I'll shout to you what I find."

Annie, said, "You can do this."

"You see me through all my crises and know all my secrets, don't you? Accidents, lost loves, pretend loves, public humiliation."

"It goes both ways, Rebecca. You've seen me through my divorce, and you're very entertaining, too, especially when you say "sugarfoot" in public instead of "shit" or "damn.""

"Perfect lives are perfectly boring, aren't they?"

"Yes, they are." Annie sipped her coffee. "And bruised lives are really more interesting to talk about. Just don't bruise yourself."

"You mean the locker, don't you?"

"Yes."

"Do you think less of me because I avoid it?"

"Yes."

"I thought you were my friend."

"I am. And friends tell friends the truth."

20

When Rebecca woke the next morning, she emerged from a dream that lingered in the half awareness of early dawn. She was riding in the cab of a little blue train engine, and Adam's locker was in one of the cargo cars. His locker was surrounded by happy dolls, giggling monkeys, and tall giraffes whose heads stuck out through the roof of the train cars. Adam's smiling face was on the front of the engine, and he was singing, "I know you can, I know you can, I know you can." Rebecca lay there in the warm sheets and pondered the meaning of the dream. Was the message from Adam or was the message from her own mind? Unsure, she rose from bed and began her day.

A loud knock on the kitchen door startled her. Clipper barked, and she signaled Clipper to go to his bed.

Rebecca pulled the café curtains aside to see a young man in a Marine uniform standing on the stoop. He wore summer khakis, the uniform she thought made Adam so handsome, but the man on the other side of the door was not handsome. Before her was a Marine with a dingy belt buckle and wrinkled creases on his pants. And a nasty mole on his chin. When he took off his hat, his hair curled behind his ears, not a jar head razor cut. She quietly put the safety hook into the eye bolt, a security feature that Adam had installed, but never used—not necessary in a town like Liberty—except when people like the one before her appeared at one's door.

"Hello," she said through the window.

"Uh, ma'am, are you Rebecca Benson?" His eyes flitted from her to the street.

She followed the direction his eyes took and saw an old red Chevy, not a black car. It was as unkempt as the Marine—faded paint, scrapes on the fenders, mismatched tires.

"What can I do for you?" She glanced at her watch, mindful of the time she needed to be at the church office that morning.

"I'm Corporal Benjamin Friend, and I served under your husband in Vietnam."

Her heart skipped a beat. She removed the safety hook, and her hand trembled on the door handle. "Come in, please." Her eyes locked onto the young Marine, and she pleaded with the heavens that she was going to hear that it had all been a mistake. Adam was a POW, now rescued, he was at Camp Pendleton being debriefed. What poor soul was mistakenly put in Adam's coffin? Why is this man not in dress blues?

"Is he...?"

He didn't move but said, "Ma'am, certainly you know he is deceased." He shifted on his feet and looked away.

"Oh, of course...I was hoping, maybe. Never mind, please come in." She stood aside to let him in. Church office be damned, the mysterious visit was more important. Yet, as he passed by her, his wrinkled appearance made her nervous. *Maybe this is not such a good idea.*

They proceeded to the living room, and Rebecca motioned toward the sofa. Corporal Friend sat and leaned back. He crossed a leg over the knee of the other. His shoes were scuffed, not like Adam's police or Marine dress shoes. She had to force herself to not look at a very black, hairy mole on his chin.

He looked at the piles of boxes on the floor. His gaze fixed on the locker from Camp Pendleton.

"Can I get you something to drink?"

"No, thank you. I'm here to talk, you know, make connection to a buddy I miss."

She leaned forward. "You were friends with Adam?"

"We were both in the operation near Khue Linh. There were a few of us Marines in a training patrol with the Vietnamese army."

"Where Adam died," she whispered.

"Yes, ma'am, but I wasn't with him. I was, um...across the way."

Her throat thickened, and she coughed to talk. "The letter I received from the commanding officer said that Adam was a fine soldier and a good ARVN advisor. He respected the South Vietnamese."

The Marine cleared his throat. "The operation didn't have the greatest outcome." He sat up and looked at the pile of boxes in the room. "Did he write to you much? Maybe send you some gifts?" He turned his gaze back to her.

She forced herself to move her gaze from the mole to his eyes. "Why do you ask?"

"Making small talk." He shifted in the chair. "I wrote my girlfriend a lot, I kinda of used to tell her..." he cleared his throat again and said, "...well, vent about how things were over there. Did your husband?"

"No, he didn't want to upset me. In one of the last letters, he joked about needing General "Chesty" Puller."

She waited for Corporal Friend to laugh, but instead he gave a puzzled frown.

"Is he on the Gomer Pyle TV show or something?" he asked.

Was this guy a fake or extremely dumb? Everybody in the Corps knew about Chesty Puller, the most decorated man in Marine history.

He looked at his watch and said, "I should go."

"But you only got here; can you tell me more about Adam? You're the first connection I've had to him for so long." She leaned toward him. "Did he talk about home? Did he mention me? Was he a good leader, of course he was a good leader, did...did he suffer when he died? He—"

"It's difficult for me to talk about all this, ma'am, I thought meeting Gunny's wife might help me close a chapter, you know." The young Marine stood to leave.

His hand was limp when they shook, and he made a fast retreat out the door. A "Watch it, Rebecca" flag popped up in her mind, and a chill floated over her. The corporal's misidentification of Chesty Puller as a character on Gomer Pyle alarmed her. Yet something he said about closing a chapter sounded legitimate. She wondered how many slaps to the side of the head she needed to close one of her own chapters. She clenched her teeth and went straight for the locker. She pulled it to the kitchen and positioned it in front of a chair. The locker sat. She stared. The locker said, "I dare you."

21

All the voices in her head said she couldn't continue to put off reading what the Marines had sent in the footlocker. The voices were real and imagined: her mother, Annie, Kathleen, Reverend Kaskell. Adam's chant in the dream joined in. "I know you can, I know you can."

She shuffled through the desk drawer, the one containing correspondence easy to ignore—March of Dimes solicitations, thin and thick rubber bands, paper clips, hard candy. The drawer was a pack rat's collection of papers and unrelated objects. Where was that thing? She had seen it recently. Frustrated, she jerked the drawer from the grip of the desk. She flew backward and landed on her back. The drawer slammed into her chin and came to a rest on her chest. Her face was covered with office supplies. Clipper nosed under the paper and junk to lick her face. His rough tongue stung the wound on her chin.

Rebecca pushed aside the mess and gingerly stood up, went over to a mirror and saw the beginnings of a dent in her chin, reddened and showing some purple. She winced.

The sounds of ripping paper and gnawing drew her attention. She turned and saw Clipper pulling and shredding some paper as though it were a rawhide bone. In the gummy, shredded mess was a corner of an envelope, and she strained to read the words "...Pendleton Personal Ef..."

"Clipper!"

He slunk away, leaving the soggy remains of the letter on the floor. He had not eaten the footlocker key.

She moaned with each wet and tattered piece of paper she picked up.

"Annie," Rebecca said over the phone, "the night of courage and truth is here. I'm ready, if you're still interested in doing this with me. I also had a strange experience today I want to tell you about."

"You read the inventory?"

"Long story. The inventory letter is in Clippers stomach."

"I'm so glad you've come to your senses," Annie said as they walked downtown to the Main Street Restaurant. She took Rebecca's arm and steered her past an uneven place in the sidewalk.

Rebecca felt a familiar weight in her gut. "Maybe we will only have dinner."

Annie stopped. "What about the night of courage and truth?"

"The truth is," Rebecca whined, "that I don't think I can handle seeing Adam's things. Don't you get it? The thought of it makes my hands clammy, I'm afraid I'll burst into tears, and the whole damn dam will burst."

Annie walked again, dragging Rebecca. "Did you read the inventory in the locker?"

"No. I want to see and touch things first. A typed list seems cold."

Annie turned to her but kept in step. "You're postponing the inevitable, and I think this dinner is extending your avoidance."

Rebecca could think of nothing to say in her defense.

They entered the restaurant where the white table cloths and the maroon carpet softened Rebecca's anxiety. Waiting for a table, she watched the waitresses with white uniforms and flowered hankies tucked into their bosom pockets. They wrote orders on little pads with carbon paper. A short waitress approached. She had gin on her breath and a hairnet on her salt and pepper hair.

"Here comes Gin-Breath. I wonder if we'll see her duck into the kitchen closet tonight. Though she always exits more relaxed than when she went in."

"She's a good waitress, though," Annie said. "We're getting a little gossipy, don't you think?"

"True. It makes me wonder, though, what she avoids in her life?"

"Yeah, we all have closets, or footlockers, don't we?" Annie added.

"Touché."

The waitress, hairnet a little lopsided, came to take their drink orders—daiquiri for Rebecca, and a gin and tonic for Annie.

Rebecca held her drink aloft. "I want to celebrate brave women. To Jackie Kennedy and her indomitable spirit!"

"To Hell with Jackie...to brave friends," Annie said. "Tonight's the night for discovery and truth."

"To scared friends who need courage," Rebecca offered.

Annie cocked her head. Drink still raised above, she said, "Aren't they the same? You're not brave unless you're scared."

"My wise friend Annie. Too bad your husband didn't know what a great woman he had."

"Well, I should have wised up sooner. People assume marrying a doctor was the answer to a happy life. At least one's mother thinks so. There are so many women for the doctor to "practice" on, shall we say." Annie set down her drink and directed her attention to Rebecca. "Before we get into this heavy subject," she leaned forward, "don't look, but there's a man staring at you. He's sitting to your right, across the room."

"Great, how am I going to see him without him seeing me see him?"

"Drop your napkin on the floor."

Rebecca did. When she peeked, she had no idea who he was, but he was good looking—dark thick hair, trim, darker skinned. Greek descent maybe? Napkin back in her lap, she smiled at Annie. "Don't know him. Two strange men in one day. Anyway, back to my question."

"If you don't want him, I'll take him."

"Not interested," Rebecca said.

"Of course. Sorry. So, tell me more about this Marine who stopped by."

Rebecca retold the events that unfolded with the mysterious Marine's visit. Annie looked at her friend with incredulous eyes.

"I don't think you should have let him in the house."

"But I did. I thought he might know something about Adam." She fingered her drink, making streaks through the condensation that coated the glass. "Have you ever tried to not look at a person's pimple or mole, and the more you try the harder it is to not look?"

"Oh my gosh, yes. Why? Did this guy have one?"

"A really nasty, hairy mole on his chin."

"Ugh." Annie flagged the waitress and showed her the empty glass. "Speaking of strange, what pushed you into making the decision to open the footlocker?"

"Adam would have said. 'Go for it, dammit.' I don't want to disappoint you either. I think I'll have another drink to bolster my resolve" Rebecca caught the eye of their waitress and showed her empty glass too. "Even the scruffy Marine said to get on with things."

"Makes sense."

"But the way he focused on Adam's locker was kind of creepy. It actually made me more curious than fearful about what's in it."

"Good. So that means we're going back to open the locker, right?"

They had an indulgent dinner of prime rib and a dessert of vanilla ice cream rolled in pecans and topped with hot fudge—a signature dish of the restaurant.

They walked back to the house where the porch lights welcomed them. Rebecca stepped ahead of Annie to unlock the door but heard the crunch of glass underfoot. "What the sugarfoot is that?"

"Stop," Annie said. She took Rebecca's arm. "Look at the door."

She looked up to see the curtains framing jagged glass, the door was ajar. Her hands turned clammy. "Oh my God."

"Don't go in. Someone may still be there."

They ran next-door and asked the neighbor to call the police.

"I can't wait here," Rebecca told the neighbors. She grabbed Annie's hand and pulled her to the door.

Back at the house, she grabbed a broom that was on the porch, and used the handle to push the door all the way open. She cocked her head to listen for any sound, and she leaned forward to look into the kitchen. She leaned forward a little more. "Hello?"

"Holy crap, Rebecca, do you expect an intruder to answer?" Annie whispered. "I don't think we should be doing this."

"The door is open."

They crept in, holding hands, making small steps. Nothing seemed out of place, except for more glass on the floor.

Rebecca used the broom to sweep a path for them. The living room was as tidy as when she left it. They stopped in the middle of the living room, holding each other and tilting their heads in several directions. All was quiet.

Whining came from under the couch, and a shaking Clipper crawled from his hiding place.

"Great watch dog," Annie observed.

Rebecca patted Clipper to calm him.

She looked about the living room. The row of moving boxes had a hole, as though a front tooth were missing. "The footlocker is gone."

"What?" Annie took a step forward.

Rebecca felt as empty as the spot where the footlocker once sat. A thief had taken the locker and robbed her of her reunion with Adam. She had been ready to touch the things Adam had held, to connect with him through the minutiae he used so many thousands of miles away. How many times did she have to lose him?

"Why now?" she cried to Annie.

Rebecca sat. Weariness, that's what she felt. Exhausted from both avoiding responsibility and trying to do the right thing. Drained by the assault of things over which she has no control. Void of knowing a next step.

Annie took Rebecca's hand again. "Do you think it was the scruffy Marine? You said he was staring at the footlocker."

"I can feel evil in the room. Someone came into my home, walked through my rooms, eyed my books, and boxes, and furniture." She lifted her face to Annie. "Now what do I do?"

"Let's see what the police say."

The detective, Adam's friend Dan, told her he had no idea why someone would take only the personal effects from a deceased Marine. Rebecca had given him the name of the visitor, Corporal Friend, but Dan doubted that was a real name. She could see anger and sadness in his eyes as he surveyed the scene.

"It's awful, Rebecca, I'm sorry." He took up his pen and notes. "Can you give me any details of the man and what he was wearing?"

"Well, he had khaki pants and shirt with a tie. He wasn't groomed like you would expect a Marine to be. There were stripes on his shirt. Three, I think."

Dan stopped writing. "Three stripes? Didn't you say he introduced himself as a corporal?"

"Oh, that's right. I could have been mistaken, maybe."

"Hmmm. And what was in the locker? The military would have sent you an inventory."

She picked at her cuticles. "I don't know. I hadn't opened it. And now I don't have it." She avoided his eyes.

He pulled his pen away from the notebook, and she chanced a glimpse of him as he studied her for what seemed a long time, but it was probably only a second or two. "And where might it be, Rebecca?"

"Clipper ate it."

Dan looked at Clipper who wagged his tail at the sound of his name.

"I see."

"I'm sorry," she said, "I'm embarrassed I avoided seeing Adam's things. I planned to open it tonight."

"That's understandable. I might have done the same thing." He smiled at her. "Was it locked. Was there a key?"

"Yes, I put it on top of the footlocker."

"I see." He put his pen away. "I'm sorry this happened, Rebecca. We sure do miss Adam. I miss him too." He ripped the blue-inked copy from the notebook and lay the report on the kitchen table. His eyes were glossy. He turned and left before Rebecca could respond.

After a restless night, Rebecca dragged herself from bed and peeked into a gloomy kitchen. The police had taped cardboard over the broken window, blocking the sun from the kitchen's eastern exposure. The room was gray rather than gleaming with the morning sunshine. She went to the door and checked the bolt. Tight.

The mirror by the door reflected how she felt—hair frizzy, dark circles under her eyes, no make-up, no lipstick.

On the table sat the copy of the police report from last night's robbery. The purple impressions made on the carbon-less paper detailed her loss. Incident type: Aggravated Burglary. Check. Method of Entry: Forcible Entry. Check. Property: Marine footlocker, addressed to the Complainant, contents unknown. Check. "Entry was gained by breaking a glass pane, unlocking the door. Scuff marks were observed on the exterior siding below the window, broken glass was found on the interior floor indicating the point of entry."

Now that the locker was gone, she wanted more than ever to see what was inside. She wanted to see, touch, and mourn over the last things Adam touched.

Adam wasn't coming back. She let a small amount of truth sink in. Adam is dead. *Now I have to figure out how I'm going to live.*

22

Loud knocking on the kitchen door reminded Rebecca of her appointment with Ruth. She came into the kitchen, a clipboard tucked under her arm. "I saw the lights late last night." She gave Rebecca a once over, eyes taking in the bathrobe and disheveled hair. "Lord, you look awful. And the cardboard on the door window? What happened?"

They sat in the kitchen over cups of coffee as Rebecca told Ruth the story of Corporal Friend and the missing box.

"Oh, dear, dear. I'm so sorry. What can I do?" She clasped her hands.

"There's nothing to do but wait and see what the police dig up." Rebecca paused to listen to the leaves of the maple trees rustling outside. Trees that Adam would never see or hear again. And that damn footlocker she will never see again. Her heart actually hurt; she had heard about breaking hearts, and hers felt as though it were being squeezed flat.

"You still there?" Ruth waved her hand in front of Rebecca's face.

She refocused. "So, what did you find out about my Indian problem? Bad news comes in threes, you know, the second being the theft."

"Now, think positively. Your property lies between a creek and a rocky outcrop that was the scene of an alleged skirmish. And," she paused, "that's not a friendly chief that's supposedly buried beneath us, he was a Shawnee, rumor goes. I also found out that some idiot at a local rest home loves to entertain school kids with the story. He even shows a photo of your house."

Rebecca put her head in her hands. "Yep, number three."

"The skirmish is fact. But I saved the best news for last. I have a buyer who thinks the history is quite fascinating and not a barrier. He wants to buy."

Rebecca sat straighter. "Really?"

"Really. Here's the offer." She put the papers in front of Rebecca. She surveyed the boxes lined up around the room.

Rebecca looked up from the sales agreement. "I guess the boobie shake worked."

"Of course." She smiled.

"So, what do you think of the offer? Just a couple thousand off the asking price. Buyers don't need a loan."

Rebecca looked at the boxes in the living room. She pictured a moving van pulling away from the house with memories in the driveway waving goodbye. The van she saw in her head drove towards darkness, not light. *Be brave.*

"I can't."

"What do you mean?" Ruth leaned toward Rebecca.

Rebecca was relieved she saw concern in Ruth's face, not anger. "So many people warned me, including you, that I might be running away rather than starting a new life. The robbery of Adam's things reminded me I'm not ready to give up his presence either. I'm sorry."

Ruth was silent for a moment. Rebecca wondered what awful things she was thinking about her decision, and her.

"I hate to lose a sale, but I have to agree you are doing the right thing. I admit feeling a little guilty, as though I were taking advantage of your vulnerability. If it doesn't feel right, don't do it." She took Rebecca's hand. "No hard feelings."

Rebecca let out a sigh of relief.

They walked to the door. Ruth bestowed a maternal smile on Rebecca and gave her a hug. Enveloped in the realtor's ample bosom, she had the sensation of falling into a mattress of goose down, an oddly comfortable sensation.

She extracted herself from the soft refuge of Ruth's breasts and stood while she fiddled with her necklace, a gold cross—a wedding present from Adam. "Yes, Ruth, take the house off the market."

When Rebecca closed the door, Clipper's nails tapped on the linoleum floor as he trotted in.

She sat and petted Clipper. She felt less burdened than she had in months. The tightness in her chest had lessened, the urgency to sort and pack things had abated She hadn't realized the tension she had been holding until the tension disappeared. The house seemed to wrap its walls around her instead of trying to evict her. She realized she had been forcing change when she needed to be pondering change.

Rebecca watched Ruth as she pulled the sign from the front lawn. The sign gave no resistance as though it had some sense to not fight its fate.

I wish I could live in the present moment like Clipper. He romps, pees, and eats. He doesn't know about wars and death.

She looked at the broken window, the police report, the fingerprint powder that revealed the pattern of the robber's prints. The line-up of boxes in the living room exposed the empty space where Adam's box had been.

Rebecca heard, or imagined, her mother's tsk-tsk when she called to tearfully describe the robbery.

"I'm sorry, but I told you, didn't I, to go through the footlocker? That was the first thing I did when I received your father's things."

Rebecca knew complaining to her mother usually brought forth some life lesson regardless of the circumstance. *Why did I call?*

"You cried over losing your baby teeth," she said once, "but they were replaced by new, better teeth. Same with life. A loss usually results in something better gained."

Rebecca stayed silent. A heavy blanket of guilt lay over her as she thought about her refusal to face the contents of the footlocker. She yearned to apologize to Adam for her lack of courage at the airport, for not honoring his sacrifice, for not facing what had come home in the locker. And Debra, the phantom aunt? She didn't know if her mother had told anyone yet, or even thought about it.

Later she sat on the sofa, engulfed in one of Adam's sweaters, saved for those times when she yearned for him. The white cable knit draped over her like the mourning dress of a Spanish queen. His scent had disappeared from the sweater months ago, so she had spritzed some of his cologne along the neck line. His presence flowed upwards into her face. The odor was soft and comforting. She wrapped herself in her own arms and listened to her breathing. It was the only energy she had.

Clipper lay in the corner, facing the wall, occasionally sighing. Whatever dog guilt was possible, he was displaying it. Regret smothered both of them.

Rebecca wondered why she waited to open the letter. A list of bad decisions floated through her mind, caused by reluctance to face what had to be faced. She told herself the loss of the locker and the inventory letter happened because she had been unwilling to face reality. "See what's really there, not what you want to see," she had heard Adam say.

She called to Clipper. He jumped on her lap, and she threaded her fingers into his silky fur. His heart beat strongly and rhythmically, and she let its energy flow to her hands, veins, throughout her body. Clipper yelped from the tight clutch she had on him, and he jumped to the floor.

She listened for Adam's advice. None came. She was on her own.

Maybe I am dishonoring Adam by questioning the war. He believed in what he was doing. Perhaps that was enough. Dammit. All my anger has been focused on my loss rather than Adam's contribution. She went to the phone.

"Ruth?" She asked into the receiver. "I'm calling about DAR. Betsy had told me my papers were ready to send, but I haven't given her my dues yet. Adam would want me to join. Let's get on with it."

"But do you want to join? I know we've been saying that Adam would be pleased. But most of all, it's what you want."

"It's what I want."

"Great." Ruth's voice sang over the phone. "Shall I pick you up for the meeting next Thursday? Bring your checkbook."

A police car pulled into the driveway.

"Gotta go, Ruth. Something's come up."

Rebecca opened the door before the police officer had a chance to knock. It was Dan.

"We found the locker. Could you come to the station first thing in the morning?"

23

To the right of Dan's desk, on a side table, sat Adam's locker. The locker was only a few feet away, and Rebecca imagined her arm stretching, pulling the box toward her. Or maybe pushing it away. There the locker sat, a symbol of her cowardice to face Adam's death and a symbol of her loss.

Annie sat beside her.

Dan's office was not much different than any detective arena seen on television or during the occasions she had accompanied Adam to the station for an off-duty errand. It had an atmosphere of bureaucracy and testosterone. Piles of papers and folders surrounded the battle-scarred desk, and dark gray metal filing cabinets lined the wall behind him.

"We've recovered Adam's locker from the vehicle driven by the deceased suspect," Dan said.

Rebecca grabbed Annie's hand. "Deceased?"

"He died in a car accident. Driving at a high rate of speed. He lost control of the vehicle, crashed into a utility pole."

Dan pushed a photo toward Rebecca.

"Here's a picture of the suspect, it's gruesome—the crash was severe. But I'm sure you've seen photos like this before from Adam's work. Is this the man who came to your house?"

Rebecca leaned over from the chair and pulled the photo toward her. A sheet covered the body up to its neck, and she saw a bruised face, eyes closed as though he were sleeping. His hair was matted with blood. And there was that nasty mole. There was no doubt who it was. She felt a little nauseous.

"Are you alright? You look a little graey," Annie said.

"I'm okay, I think."

Rebecca put the gruesome photo back on the desk.

"That's definitely Corporal Benjamin Friend, who came to my house asking about Adam."

"Are you sure?"

"Yes. I'll remember that mole a hundred years from now."

Looking inside the folder, he said, "According to his driver's license his name was Frederick Smith. We found a Marine Corps uniform in the car, but the Marine Corps has no record of him."

Annie picked up the photo and carefully studied it.

"Put it down, please." Rebecca grabbed the photo from Annie's hand and placed it on the desk.

"What about fingerprints?" Annie asked.

"We dusted for prints, and of course the package had been handled by many people. You'll see powder on some of the things, including the exterior. I expect they will match those of our Frederick Smith."

Rebecca looked at Annie. "This is the break-in, all over again."

"We believe he is part of an organized group of smugglers who place contraband in personal effects parcels of deceased military." Dan stopped and looked at both ladies. "These packages are sent to the member's

Home of Record in the U.S. Once the parcels are in the Postal System, they are stolen by insiders and the contraband removed."

"What kind of contraband?"

"It can be anything from gold, to jewelry, to drugs."

Rebecca got up from her chair, walked to the door, hesitated, and returned to her seat. "Go on."

"I'm sorry, but it seems you have been a victim of these people, but we didn't find any contraband so either it's already been taken, or there never was any."

"Do you think Adam was dealing drugs?" she asked, alarmed.

"No, no, no. Most of the time contraband is placed in the lockers by a third party. You'll be glad to know there was an official inventory from the Marine Corps Office of Personal Effects inside the locker, and it all seemed to be there. We're done with the contents, and you can take it with you. If you notice anything that might be important, will you call me?"

"Of course."

"I'll have a couple of officers take the locker out to your car. Give us about ten minutes. What does your car look like?"

"Chevy Impala SS."

"Adam treated you well." He grinned.

When they got to the car, Rebecca pointed to the trunk. "It should fit in there," she told the officers.

Annie volunteered to drive, which Rebecca appreciated. Once home, they both wheezed and panted to get the locker out of the trunk, up the steps, and into the kitchen. Rebecca patted Clipper and turned on the coffee maker.

"Whoops," Annie said. "I left my purse in the car."

Over the sounds of percolating coffee, Rebecca heard Annie re-enter, her steps sure and quick.

Annie took hold of Rebecca's shoulders and spun her around. "Damn it, Rebecca, enough hiding. We're going to go through Adam's things together. You owe it to him to check this out."

Rebecca threw herself into her friend's arms. "I can't do this. I want Adam back, not his stuff."

"Adam is here with you, honey." She patted Rebecca's back in loving, healing strokes. "He would want you to face this." She pushed her back a little. "By the way," she said, her voice softening, "I hope you made strong, strong coffee. Sit down and I'll pour." She led her friend to the table and sat her down. She poured a cup of coffee for them both. "I'll pull out one thing at a time and we'll look at it."

With cup of coffee in hand followed by a slurp of the hot stimulant down her throat, Rebecca was ready.

24

Annie pulled the inventory sheet out. "Do you want to look at this first?"

"No."

Annie put the inventory aside, stuck her hand in the footlocker, and extracted an opened but unused plastic bag of socks, which Rebecca recognized as ones she had sent.

Annie handed them over. "See, that's not so bad."

Rebecca shrugged and put the bag on the table.

Next, she pulled out an envelope that jingled. "I'm surprised the robber didn't take this. Let's count it." Annie counted the money—twenty-two dollars in bills and fifty-seven cents in change. She retrieved a Gideon bible, cracking with newness when she opened its pages. She pulled out two other books, *Armageddon* by Leon Uris and *The Good Soldier Švejk*. "Good grief. I don't know how to pronounce this one let alone know what it's about." She held up *The Good Soldier* for Rebecca to see.

She took it and wondered why in the world Adam would be reading such a thing. Thumbing across the edges, she noticed some dog-eared pages. She read one aloud to Annie, "Potting at an Imperial Highness is no easy job, you know. It's not like a poacher potting at a gamekeeper. The question is how you get at him. You can't come near a fine gentleman like that if you're dressed in rags. You've got to wear a topper, so the cops don't nab you beforehand."

"Weird," said Annie. "Sounds like someone was thinking of offing an officer. I've heard that if an officer is incompetent, they get rid of him but make it look like enemy fire."

Rebecca flinched. "You think—"

"No, absolutely not." She reached inside again. "Here's another surprise. Marlboro cigarettes," which she held in the air. "I didn't know Adam smoked."

"A long time ago. Maybe the stress of it all."

"And here's a Zippo lighter. Something's etched onto it."

"Let me see." Rebecca took the lighter and flipped it over. Someone had scratched the letters "UUUU" on it. "I have no idea what that means."

Annie leaned into the locker to pull out more, but she backed off and said, "Let's take a break."

"No, let's keep going." Rebecca took another sip of coffee, the cup rattling when she set it back on the saucer.

Annie shrugged her shoulders. "Okay." She pulled out a stuffed manila envelope with black powder smeared on it. Fingerprint powder.

Rebecca grabbed it and ripped it open, not taking the time to pry the metal tabs upward and slip the flap out. She shook the contents onto the table, and all the letters she had written him tumbled out. She caressed them, knowing Adam's hands had opened the envelopes, his eyes had read the words, and his brain had translated her verbiage into feeling. There were postcards and a Valentine she had sent him, a drawing of a worn sock with the inscription "Darn It, You Have to Be My

Valentine." Rebecca smiled. "I remember buying this at the drugstore knowing Adam would think it funny. I sent it to him early." There was also a postcard that read "Admit it, life would be boring without me," and a Christmas card with "Peace" on a peace symbol.

Rebecca gathered up the pile of letters and held them to her chest. She closed her eyes and tried to inhale the image of Adam reading them.

"Don't quit now," Annie encouraged.

Rebeca reluctantly put the letters down.

Annie dug in again and pulled out two more bags, one which held Adam's wallet. In it was his driver's license, a AAA card, and some medical cards. The other bag had something covered in tissue, and when Annie unwrapped it, there was Adam's watch, with a dark spot—blood. Rebecca lightly touched the stain. "This was my wedding present to Adam."

"You okay?" Annie asked. "They should have cleaned it better."

She set the watch down close to the edge of the table, and Clipper came over. He sniffed. He cocked his ears, sniffed again, and whined.

Annie and Rebecca looked at each other, knowing Clipper had smelled Adam.

"My turn." Rebecca inhaled a breath of courage and pulled out a smaller manila envelope. When she opened it upside down, Adam's dog tag tumbled out. She gently picked up the smooth-edged metal tag, its ball chain hanging from the grommet. She held it softly in her palm as though she were cradling an expired sparrow. Annie placed her hand on Rebecca's shoulder.

With her forefinger, Rebecca traced the stamped name "Adam J. Benson," and placed the tag against her heart and closed her eyes.

"This may have been the last thing that felt Adam's heart beat," she whispered.

She opened her eyes to see tears in Annie's own. Rebecca bit the insides of her cheeks and showed the tag to Annie. "Look," she said. "I wonder what the "M" stands for?" She fingered the letters that read "USMC M."

Annie took a closer look, frowning. "I have no idea. "Male" perhaps?"

Rebecca pulled out a small wooden box, and when she opened the hinged lid, she saw Adam's wedding ring. She picked it up and held it. She recalled the day she slipped it on Adam's hand, the gold shiny and promising, now scratched and worn. Inside the ring was etched "3-20-1957." She traced the tiny inscription with a finger. "I remember the day I went to the jewelry store to pick out his ring," she said to Annie. "The jeweler asked, 'Simple gold band?' I looked at the case of men's rings and spotted a two-tone gold ring encircled with Celtic knots. 'I'll take that one,' I told him."

"What was special to you about a Celtic knot?"

"Adam was part Irish, and he wanted to go to Ireland someday."

Rebecca remembered images of the travel magazines Adam had collected about Ireland—the sheep blocking the narrow stone-lined lanes, the emerald green countryside, the three-hundred-year-old inns where one could get the rawest jokes and the freshest stout.

"Yoo-hoo. Are you still there?" Annie asked.

"Thinking about the plans we had." Rebecca unhooked her gold necklace, the one with the cross Adam gave her on their wedding day, and slipped his ring onto the chain—a kind of alpha and omega symbol of their marriage.

"Do you want help with that?"

"Yes, please." She yielded to Annie's gentle hooking of the necklace.

"Do you want to go on?"

She nodded.

"Let's see what else is in here."

She re-examined the small wooden box. Inside were some Vietnamese postage stamps. Colorful, but useless. The little box went into the pile of the other looked-at items.

She grabbed a larger envelope and dumped its contents on the table. Looking up at her were photos of Adam and other Marines with and without shirts, posing with basketballs and sweat on their chests and faces, or standing by tanks and other armaments.

"Pretty hunky guys," Annie said. "I hope I get to see some of that!"

But Rebecca saw only Adam's bare chest and remembered what it was like to have it against her skin.

"Wait a minute," Annie said. She handed Rebecca a group shot and pointed to one of the men who stood right next to Adam. "Isn't he the guy we saw at the restaurant?"

Peering closely, Rebecca realized Annie was right. "So, he was a friend of Adam's." She turned, excited. "We need to go back and see if we can find him."

"Okay, but don't get distracted. We have more to look at."

Rebecca set the picture aside and reluctantly returned to the other photos. There were several she had sent to Adam, some loose, a couple in frames. One was her engagement photo. In their early years whenever they had a fight, he would tap on the glass and say, "Now where's the sweet Rebecca who's in this picture?" Rebecca noticed a crack in the glass that went from the bottom of the frame to the top.

"Take the photo out before you cut yourself," said Annie. "I don't want to be wiping up your blood."

The clasps on the back of the frame were stubborn, and Rebecca broke a nail trying to pry one loose, but she eventually succeeded. She expected to see her handwriting, "All my love, all my life" on the back of the photo. Instead she saw unfamiliar handwriting, on the back of a second photo. The writing was stylized differently than anything she had ever seen. The inscription read, "Love always, Lan." In Adam's handwriting was "Lan Nyguen, Saigon, January, 1966."

"What the hell?" Rebecca looked up at Annie.

"Take it out," she said.

"I'm not sure I want to."

Annie wagged her finger. "There's a perfectly good explanation."

Annie and Rebecca leaned in, their hair blending as they hunched over the frame. Rebecca pulled away the photo hiding behind hers. Adam and the woman who must be Lan stood in front of a hotel that lacked paint and had many other signs of poor maintenance. Adam had his arm around her tiny shoulders. Lan looked up at him with adoration.

Rebecca dropped the photo and its frame. The cracked glass became broken glass, scattered onto the kitchen floor.

Lan Nyguen stared out from the photo and mocked Rebecca with her adoring smile. She looked at Annie, expecting to see disbelief and pity in her face. But Annie's eyebrows were drawn together in a quizzical pose.

"Certainly, this can't be what I think it is," Rebecca said. "He was having an affair."

"Don't jump to conclusions."

"What else could it be?" She cried. "Maybe I deserve this."

Annie put her arms around her.

"What? No words of wisdom? Anything else you want me to face?" She scowled at Annie.

"I am so sorry. I—"

"I've read about soldiers having Vietnamese lovers, who end up pregnant. I once heard Mother and Daddy arguing about a woman in France. It never made sense until now."

"You're jumping to conclusions because you expect the worse. Have some faith in Adam. You don't have any proof of anything."

"Isn't this proof? Look how she adores him. Why would he be hiding her photo behind mine? If she were a friend, he would have told me."

"Maybe, maybe not."

"Oh my God. What if he had a child with her?"

"Slow down. I think you're being pretty quick to judge."

"I want to be alone." Rebecca turned her back, Lan's photo in her hand.

"Don't close me out, not at a moment like this, Rebecca. Let me be with you."

Rebecca stayed silent, her back like a concrete wall between her and Annie.

"Please?"

"It's too much. Please go."

The kitchen door closed softly behind her.

25

Rebecca threw everything back into the footlocker. She didn't care what else was in there.

She got a broom and dust pan from the kitchen pantry. Each tinkling sound of the glass against the metal dust pan scraped across her heart. But the truth, she was sure, lay in the shards that covered the linoleum.

Former loves crossed her mind. Jim, a good looking cheat. Ron, a liar with a gambling problem. Was there no one she could trust? A random swipe of the broom revealed the gash she had made when Adam said he was going to Vietnam and she threw the coffee cup on the floor. The linoleum had become a story book of Adam's betrayals.

Alone. The word had a moanful quality like a wolf's howl. At least a wolf had strength, cunning, and intelligence. Unlike me, she thought. She slammed the contents of the dustpan into a wastebasket. Adam had abandoned her for some swashbuckling military mission, and if she were to interpret the photo correctly, he had been giving his strength to someone else. Annie said it could have been a friend. Fat chance. The war had taken away her husband in body and soul.

"Mother?" she said in the phone through sobs.

"Rebecca, what's wrong?"

"I hate this war."

"Nobody likes war, dear, it's one of those necessary evils. You know that. Why are you crying?"

"You won't believe what I found out."

Rebecca heard her mother inhale and exhale quite loudly.

"What's wrong now?"

"It's Adam. I found a photo."

Her mother laughed. "That doesn't sound like a reason to be crying."

"But he's with a Vietnamese woman, his arm around her, and she wrote 'Love always' on it. He was... having an affair."

Silence. "You're imagining things. Adam wouldn't do that."

"I'm not imagining the 'Love always' written on it, Mother."

"Maybe it's someone who had a crush on him, or a local he helped."

"Why would he have kept it?"

"Men like flattery, dear. You know that."

"But Mother—"

"You're always looking for the worst."

"What about the woman in France I heard you and Daddy argue about?"

There was a heavy silence on the other end of the phone.

"That, that was a long time ago, and I...I was jealous about a friend your father made. It, it was nothing."

Rebecca hung up. Feeling more hollow than before she called her mother, she went to her bedroom and pulled out a decorated box of Adam's letters. She had glued heart and flower wrapping paper around a shoe box like she did for Valentine boxes in grade school. The box was full with his letters.

She sat on the bed and dumped the letters. Surrounded by correspondence with an APO return address, once read with longing and affection, she reread each letter and looked for any words hinting at unhappiness, a crack in their trust. All along she had assumed the lying letters were untruthful about the dangers he experienced, not about his love for her.

Each letter had a miss you, Baby; you're the greatest; the only one for me; look at your photo several times a day; can feel your hair in my hands; no other woman for me; some guys go on leave for boom boom, but not me, I can't imagine anyone else but you.. Each loving phrase should have strengthened her faith in Adam, but Lan's admiring smile upon him bore into her. She had known betrayal before. She swept the letters onto the floor.

Clipper whimpered and watched from a safe place in the hall. Rubbing her stiff legs, she rose from the bed, staggered like a Zombie to the kitchen. She poured more coffee into her cup. More human like, she walked to the bedroom and put the scattered letters back on the bed. She signaled Clipper to join her, and his eager leap to her side comforted her.

Clipper had his paw on one of the letters—maybe a sign of importance—so Rebecca picked it up. It was written on paper with reddish water stains and a muddy thumbprint. Adam must have written the letter while he was in the field. She reread the letter.

Hi Sweets,

Taking a few minutes to write to the love of my life, my wife! We're in the "boonies" as they call it, and let me tell you about a Purple Heart we all should have from walking through the elephant grass. It is taller than Ohio corn, its leaves are razor sharp, and they leave slices in your skin like paper cuts. And the mosquitoes. I counted thirty-five bites on one arm!

Thanks for sending me the article about the Liberty Police Dept. Big crime in Liberty, eh? I miss the guys (but not as much as I miss you!). If you see any of them, say hello for me.

I'll write more later.

In the envelope was a slip of paper she hadn't seen before. It was a poem titled "Hiding." Curious, Rebecca read it aloud.

Hiding
Da Nang January 10, 1965
By Robert Norris

Another poem by his friend. Hiding is a good title for me to be reading tonight, she thought.

Hiding in the wood,
Hiding under the floor,
Search for me.
Finding me brings golden life.
Search for me.

Rebecca sighed. It was a strange poem, and it was strange Adam had sent it. Too impotent to understand what she needed to think, to feel, or do, she put the letters back in the box. The voice inside her was strong and filling her with fear she hadn't been enough for Adam—that she was indeed a failure as a wife. Why else do men stray?

She spent the next two weeks on auto—going to her job at the church, taking care of Clipper, and watching TV in the evening. Interactions with Annie were bittersweet. She wanted to retreat so she wouldn't miss her, but she wanted Annie's wise words and companionship. Annie called several times and tried to get together. Two nights before Annie was to leave, Rebecca relented.

Sitting across from each other at the bar where they had seen the mystery man, they nursed their drinks.

"Do you think we'll see the guy from the photo?" Annie asked.

Rebecca swished her drink. "I don't want to talk about photos."

Annie looked at her with pleading eyes. "Please, Rebecca, don't shut me out. I need you now. In fact, we need each other, each for our own struggles. Friendships go both ways, you know. It's not only about your pain. What about my pain? My fear?" Annie paused. "You can't turn your back on people because they live their lives differently than what you need them to do."

Annie's words stung. Was this what she did to Adam? Freeze him out because of her own pain?

Annie's face reddened. "You turned your back on Adam and now you are turning your back on me." Annie's face changed from anger to instant regret. "Oh, I'm sorry...I shouldn't have said that." Annie paled and her eyes searched Rebecca's for forgiveness.

"You're right. I am a coward. I felt so abandoned, so...unvalued. Is that how Adam felt?" She grabbed some tissues out of her purse and wiped her eyes.

"Unvalued?" Annie took Rebecca's hands. "If you were unvalued, I wouldn't have kept calling you. If you were unvalued, Adam wouldn't have kept writing to you. And he never mentioned the scene at the airport. I think he understood your pain and didn't want to hurt you by bringing it up. That's love."

Rebecca looked at her friend with new respect. Yes, Annie was the one to tell.

"There's something I want to share with you. Something I found out about Adam."

Annie nodded.

Rebecca told Annie the whole story about Adam's parents, the murder-suicide, and Aunt Debra. Annie focused on every word Rebecca said.

"There that's it," Rebecca said. "You've been awfully quiet. What do you think?"

"Wow. Just wow. That explains everything about his reluctance to have children. He was wrong, of course. The child doesn't have to repeat the sins of the father."

"I want so much to tell Adam I understand."

"I have to admit your anger about his not wanting children hasn't been at the forefront of your despair recently. It's all been focused on his re-enlistment."

"Do you think he knows I understand?" Rebecca looked hopefully at her friend. "Do the dead forgive us?"

"I would hope so. What's important is that you know. And you have a new family connection, his Aunt Debra. She must be pretty special to travel all the way to D.C. for his funeral. Have you told anyone about her?"

"I introduced her to my mother at the funeral. We haven't talked about it since. I don't know why. My mother hasn't asked, and I haven't wanted to give her the grisly details."

"Hang on to this Aunt Debra. I think she's going to be very helpful to you."

She went to the airport with Annie to see her off to her new adventure. She watched her board the plane. Rebecca waved and blew her a kiss. So opposite of how she sent Adam off to war. She went home and cried.

She put the offensive photo of Lan in a hall closet. At least once a day she retrieved the photo and stared at it. Who was she? Why did she look at Adam with such trust and affection? Adam wasn't looking at her but at the camera. Her mind filled with see-saw thoughts. And she didn't have confidence in any of them.

One evening, she looked around the bedroom that was decorated with teenager taste. Her mother gave her and Adam the house and had moved into an apartment. The bedroom had the same faux French Provincial furniture her father bought when she was in high school. Adam tolerated the floral ensemble with ruffled curtains and matching bed spread and bed skirt. The crystal lamps and ruffled lamp shades added to the ambiance of a Gidget boudoir. He said the room made him into Moondoggie, Gidget's surfing boyfriend. Rebecca smiled. On passionate nights, Adam became Kahuna, the older man who fell under Gidget's spell. As a Gidget wanna-be, Rebecca would play coquette one moment and seducer the next. "Best friend, best lover," she used to tell him.

Enough of Gidget and Moondoggie. Rebecca surveyed the room and saw an ugly, dated bedroom and ghosts of painful memories. Echoes of Adam's soothing whispers in her ears filled her with sadness, wafts of his aftershave floated around the room and settled on Rebecca with memories that had become full of doubt. Time to redecorate. Afterall, she was staying.

26

Shopping for happiness, that's what her mother called it. The next day Rebecca found herself at JC Penney's in the domestic goods department—wooden planked floors, wooden display tables, and a pneumatic tube system rushing change back and forth from customers' hands to the store office.

A display of modern bedding contrasted with the old-fashioned architecture of the store. Rubbing her hands over some Wamsutta sheets, the urge to break free of Moondoggie and frills overwhelmed her. *I can't do anything about that woman, but I can change something.* Another voice within her countered. *Would Adam think I was abandoning our history? How would he know anyway? Would the world think I was leaving Adam behind?*

She spent the next week painting the walls a soft white with n tint of yellow, each downward stroke of the brush covered up the relentless photo of Lan lingering in her brain. Occasionally an unreleased sob caught in her throat as she erased the ambience she and Adam had shared.

Rebecca hung border wallpaper of green lattice. She ironed and hung the lime green and white Williamsburg design draperies of the same lattice as the border. She slept in the guest bedroom, away from the reminders of change in the other room.

"What in Heaven's name are ya' doing?" Kathleen asked one day from the screen door in front.

"I'm painting," Rebecca shouted through the bedroom window where she could see Kathleen on the front stoop. "Wait 'til you see what I'm doing."

"Where have you been?" Ruth asked over the phone one evening.

"I'm redecorating the bedroom. I've already painted. Goodwill is coming tomorrow for the old furniture."

"When can I see it?"

"I'll let you know."

"How's the redecorating going?" Rebecca's mother said on the phone.

"Would you like to help me pick out some furniture and bedding?

"That would be wonderful!"

At the furniture store Rebecca and her mother browsed the furniture department. They stood in front of a display of Queen Ann night stands and a dresser, painted in a darker lime green.

"What do you think, dear. It would contrast nicely with the wall color."

"Sold. I'm thinking of keeping the white carpet. It's still in good shape?"

"Agreed. Oh, Rebecca, thank you for having me along. I've missed you. You've been sort of AWOL, to use a military term, since Adam died."

"No military terms, please. But yes, I need to take action, of some sort."

They agreed on a quilted bedspread that perfectly matched the walls and some decorative pillows in soft lime and yellow colors, like she had seen in a Good Housekeeping magazine.

She hung some Williamsburg prints on the wall, put a floral Hadley vase of her grandmother's on the dresser, placed new brass lamps with white shades on the nightstands, and bought a new yellow princess phone. She had plenty of insurance money from Adam, and she spent it quite well. During the whole process Clipper watched patiently from the hallway, yawning through much of the redecoration.

Before she transferred her clothes back from the guest room to the new dresser and freshly painted closets, Rebecca stood in the room to admire her work. The Gidget boudoir was gone. So was Adam, she realized. She softly closed the door.

The next morning, which happened to be Veteran's Day, Rebecca emptied the guest bedroom wastebasket—filled with tissues from a night of hating Adam, missing Adam, hating herself, and hating the new bedroom. She felt she had erased him.

Reading about bitchy, pathetic women might distract me from my failures. Some trashy fiction perhaps.

Visine for her bloodshot eyes, a little extra foundation, rouge to brighten pallid skin, and a spritz of Avon's Unforgettable. Ready to go to the library.

Rebecca planned how she could avoid the Veteran's Day activities. Ruth had invited her to attend and watch the DAR regent lay a wreath at the Civil War statue, but the possibility of being in the war widow spotlight compelled Rebecca to ignore the invitation.

Determined not to be cowed by patriotic fervor, she walked south on Main Street and quickly encountered the puzzled glances of people who passed by. Not only was Rebecca going the opposite direction, she was patriotically naked—unadorned with an American flag in her hand and wearing green and orange instead of red, white, and blue.

Many people were walking up Main Street to the town "square," which was a circular traffic round-about to guide cars from the center of town to the east, west, north and south roads. The Square was a bane to older drivers who couldn't remember the rules for the right of way, many of whom Adam would pull over and give a warning instead of a ticket. For the duck tailed teenagers, the Square offered the perfect setting for Friday night gatherings— teen drivers revving and honking, onlookers smoking at the feet of the Civil War soldier forever frozen in his bronze stance looking South. Rebecca imagined his stare on her back as she walked in the opposite direction.

A familiar hand waved in her direction, and when the face came into view, Rebecca saw it was one of the DAR women she had met.

"Are you alright? I saw in the paper your house was broken into." Her voice softened. "Did you lose anything valuable?"

Anything valuable? Everything in a house has some kind of value because of their memories: souvenirs, gifts, family heirlooms, and a dead husband's inventory of his warrior home away from home.

"All recovered," Rebecca said. She moved on before the woman had an opportunity to ask why she wasn't going to the Veteran's Day ceremonies.

She stopped in front of Candyland's plate glass window whose displays sang a siren-song about the soda bar and array of confectionery promises. Most of the time she was able to tune-out the call for chocolate, but the gnawing in her stomach had not been soothed by a quick dive that morning into the Chuckles drawer. The thought of a butter-cream chocolate pulled her toward the candy store door.

Thinking about the crisp chocolate shell and the celestial creamy vanilla center set her salivary glands into full drooling mode. She anticipated the sugar and cream flowing over her tongue, the sweetness firing all the pleasure neurons in her brain. Seduction by chocolate would leave no room in her head about wars and sacrifice and duty. She opened the door, which gave a welcoming tinkle of the overhead bell.

Focused on the glass case of chocolate, arrayed by flavors and fillings, Rebecca jostled a woman beside her. It was Irene Sotheby, the Southern anti-war woman from the police charity.

"Irene, I'm so sorry, I didn't see you standing there."

"Seeking chocolate comfort, I see. Bless your pea picking' heart. Y'all have the look of a woman on a mission." She grinned. "Which ones are your favorites?" She pointed to the display of butter creams. "I'm partial to the maple creams. I'm so hungry my belly thinks my throat was cut."

Rebecca laughed. "Maple cream is blasphemy. Pure, unadulterated vanilla cream for me."

They looked at each other and giggled.

They each chose a chocolate treat, plus a cup of coffee and sat down at a bistro table for two. Their sugar induced moans further bonded them as women sharing a sinful treat. They didn't need words, eye contact, or touch. The chocolate formed a sensual, if temporary, bridge between them.

"I'm sad for you, having lost your husband in Vietnam," Irene said while stirring her coffee. "And a father in World War II."

Rebecca waited for the rest of the widow-soothing talk about his sacrifice, courage, blah, blah, blah. Don't people realize the pain is too tender? And no one except Annie had been witness to Rebecca's new pain.

Irene gave a soft smile. "Have y'all thought any more about going to Columbus with me, to an anti-war meeting?"

"I, uh, I don't know." Rebecca stirred her coffee and stirred some more. *What would Adam think if I went to an anti-war meeting, a war that he died in? And today, do I care?* Rebecca looked to see if the store clerk, busy behind the white marble counter washing parfait glasses, could hear them. She leaned in toward Irene. "I'm confused. Isn't the war supposed to save the Vietnamese from Communism? Make the world safe and all that?"

They were the only customers in the shop. The only sounds heard were the rhythmic clinks and scrapes of their spoons against the glass cups as well as water running and the splashing from the clerk's washing duties.

Head down and concentrating on the swirling coffee whose steam had disappeared, Irene said, "That's what the government wants us to believe. Let's go up the Square."

"I was heading to the Library."

"It's Veteran's Day. The Library is closed."

"Oh." Rebecca felt silly she hadn't thought of that.

"I bet we'll both see something worth remembering."

Startled, Rebecca stopped stirring and looked up at Irene. "What do you mean?"

She pulled her chair closer. "Well...there will be patriotic speeches for sure, but I heard there were going to be some injured Vietnam vets there too, who plan to speak out against the war, uninvited, of course. Do you think the good folks of a small Ohio town can handle hearing two sides of a story?"

"Vietnam veterans?" Rebecca sat back and tapped her forefingers on the edge of the table. "I don't want to be pointed out."

"If they haven't contacted you to be part of the program, I wouldn't worry."

A dim memory came to Rebecca. "I wonder if that was the call I got a couple of weeks ago from a VFW guy. I thought he was going to ask for a donation, and I hung up."

"We'll sit in the back."

Rebecca crossed her arms. "Why are you so determined to get me involved?"

"I detect a kindred spirit, honey chil'. Plus, when my father died in Korea—career Army—I found it helpful to distract myself with 'Why the hell is there war?' "

"Do you think you're a little disloyal because he was, after all, a soldier?"

"Father used to say to me 'Babydoll, war is hell, but a soldier doing his job well is a peek at heaven.' It took me a long time to figure out what he was saying, but I decided he said soldiering was a job, a noble job most times, one of which is to help keep your buddies alive. And if you do that, you're mighty proud." She took a sip of her coffee. "Then this light came on. What if we are lied to about the purpose of the job?"

"Huh?"

"World War II was obvious, especially after evidence of Hitler's plan for annihilating Jews as well as the attack on Pearl Harbor. But Vietnam? Why are we getting involved in countries' civil wars? Still, soldiers carry on, doing their job with pride, believing in the mission they're fed."

"You think President Johnson is lying to us?"

"Like a no-legged dog."

Rebecca laughed at the image, but Irene's charge was sobering. "My God, what if Adam died for nothing?" The candy turned sour in her stomach. The mixture of love and anger for Adam roiled in her. *Damn you, Adam.*

"Adam did what he wanted to do. I'm sure he was a fine Marine. Now what do you want to do with your life?"

Rebecca looked up. "You've got me curious, you know, about the speeches and all." She resumed tapping her fingers on the metal rim of the table and looked, unseeing, at the glass cases in the shop. "I'm not sure I'm doing the right thing, but I'll go, and I'm counting on you to not get me into something I wish I hadn't."

"Darlin', I'm the lead dog, with legs."

The pulsing drums of the Fife and Drum Corps prompted Irene and Rebecca to a regular and rhythmic walk up to the Square. The cadence drove Rebecca forward into a battle of unknown outcomes. She was invincible, the drums beating in sync with her pulsing blood. When she heard the high pitch of the fifes along with the low beat of the drums, her pace quickened. The musical cadence of the instruments left no room for doubt or fear. She was going to face her patriotic demons. She would prove to herself she could stand among soldiers and flags.

The music stopped, and they stood at the edge of the crowd. Rebecca's feet took root in the grass, and she stood motionless among all sorts of flag-waving men, women, and children. She pulled her coat closer around her to fend off the chill of an early November cold front. Old men in loosely fitting uniforms of World War I and middle-aged men in tightly fitting uniforms of World War II lent a visage of graying hair to the crowd. On the outskirts of the gathering was a small group of protestors carrying signs disparaging the Vietnam War. Some teenagers pushed one of the protestors holding a "Hell no, I won't go" sign. "Commie," they yelled at him.

She chilled with the memory of being called the same thing.

She looked back at the men in their uniforms, wondering how many had been face to face with their enemies, not with music to infuse them with courage, but with only the deafening explosions, yelling, and screams. Adam's face floated in front of her.

Irene jabbed Rebecca with her elbow. "You have a 'deer in the headlights' look. What on earth are you thinking about?"

"Too much," she answered.

Irene pulled Rebecca toward a back row of chairs, and they sat down among the other women, children and patriots of various wars. To their extreme left was a man in a wheelchair. He wore Marine dress blues, shoes shined like black diamonds. Polished medals hung from his thin chest. Below his crisp white hat hung a ponytail. On his lap was a sign Rebecca couldn't read. Toward the podium, Ruth Middleton, hatted and gloved, held a flag draped wreath. Rebecca caught her eye and waved. Ruth signaled back, but her smile turned to a frown when she saw Irene. Near Ruth stood Kathleen. Rebecca waved to her, who nodded towards Irene and held up two fingers as a peace sign.

The men of the Fife and Drum Corps stood up and walked toward the podium. A flag bearer held the American flag. As they marched forward in silence, men of large and small girth in their woolen reproduction uniforms, were visibly limping on arthritic knees. Sweat dotted their puffy and wrinkled faces. Everyone stood. After they placed the flag and spun to face the crowd, the leader gave a signal and the corps moved forward, playing their rhythmic call to battle.

Irene leaned over. "The British liked to announce their arrival. In the Revolutionary War that music was the last sounds heard by many, you know.

Rebecca turned to her in surprise.

"Yeah, war marches were common during the Civil War, too. I would gladly have taken up arms if rifles were being handed out against the inspiring rhythms of a fife and drum corps."

Rebecca watched the men retreating from the podium. Under the influence of the music, the men became younger, smoother, and more agile. She didn't see sweaty old men anymore, she looked upon brave and determined soldiers, marching with discipline and bravado. The faces of the audience were smiling and full of admiration.

People waved small American flags, and children sat on their fathers' shoulders and fluttered their own flags in little hands.

Once the band was fully withdrawn, everyone sat down to the shouts of the corps leader, "Ready, sit." The mayor of the town came to the podium and made the usual niceties about the big crowd, the patriotism of the city, and the freedoms they all shared. The muscles of his face hardened, and he began his introduction of "Marine Major Stephen Langley, having distinguished himself on the battlegrounds of a nation three thousand miles away, fulfilling his duty to his country who asked that he help a beleaguered nation push back the claws of communism." He gestured to his right, and a model U.S. Marine came to the podium, straight as the wood in the podium he stood behind.

All the bravura the drums had beaten into Rebecca drained as she looked at him. It was Adam who stood before the crowd, who took off his hat, and who tucked it under his arm. His dark hair framed a squared and angular face. He looked at the crowd with the confidence of a man who knew what he wanted to say was something the people wanted to hear. He scanned the crowd looking for friends, and he waved a few times with the certainty of men who had been trained to lead and save lives. Rebecca wanted to jump in his arms, inhale his aftershave, savor his strength, and hear his words, "It's all a mistake, Becky." The beating in her chest took away her breath and strength. She blinked twice. It wasn't Adam at all, it was Major Langley who came into focus. And he was blond, shorter than most men, and his eyes darted about the crowd.

Irene took her hand. "What's wrong," she asked. "You're pale as paper."

Standing up, Rebecca steadied herself on the back of the chair. "I saw a ghost. I have to go."

Irene's puzzled face glanced toward the podium, and when she looked back at Rebecca her face had softened. She understood.

Rebecca stumbled through the row of people saying, "Sorry, sorry" each time she banged into knees or stepped on toes. When she got to the end of the row, the Marine in the wheelchair pushed back so she could pass. His eyes were deep pools of past ghosts and a determination for the future. Rebecca touched his shoulder for balance and the jolt of pain and lonely days reverberated through her hand. The placard on his lap read, "I asked my country what I should do, but all I got were lies." She gasped. Rivulets of scars ran down his neck.

"What are you starin' at, lady?" His voice was gravely and terse with defensiveness. "Haven't you seen a man in a wheelchair before?"

"I'm...I'm sorry, your—"

"Yeh, the scars. I left some flesh in 'Nam somewhere." He looked away.

Rebecca could taste the bile in her throat, and she reeled away from the man with the horrible scars. Stumbling toward the sidewalk, she wiped sweat off her forehead, and she thought she might faint. Behind the trunk of a large maple tree, she hid from the injured man, but the ghost of her father followed her. She shut her eyes so tightly that her face hurt, and the pain chased away the Marine and her father. Her breathing gradually slowed so she was able to resume her return home.

Ahead of her was a monument listing Liberty's lost sons. She stopped. In the first column, his name was a beacon, and it burned into her heart: Gunnery Sgt. Adam Benson, March 15, 1966, Vietnam.

27

Back home on the sofa, Rebecca burrowed her hands into Clipper's fur. Adam's apparition had opened a protected cave where she had been storing sensations too painful to replay: Adam's morning sandpaper beard, the lingering aroma of Old Spice in the bathroom, the way he slurped the milk out of his cereal bowl, so annoying but now so missed. But it wasn't Adam on that dais, the apparition at the Square was only from some embedded synapses firing in her brain.

The wounded Marine. Seeing the results of war's carnage was unsettling, repulsive. Yet, she felt badly for him that he survived a battle only to endure the stares of strangers.

She cried for her father. She shivered a little as she remembered the sensation of the cotton arm in her hands. He was lucky he didn't have to live his life maimed like the man she saw.

Clipper snuggled deeper into her lap and lay his head on her thigh. What if Adam had come home in a wheelchair instead of in a casket? Gentle, proud Adam. What a couple they would have made in a world of prosthetics and altered lives. She hadn't known Adam when he served in Korea; she was spared that year of suspended living, as most wives of men serving overseas described the experience. She had had only five months between the time he was deployed and when he was killed. She fingered Adam's ring on her necklace, which she still wore, to prove Adam was hers, not Lan's. With the explosion of a bullet, her life as she had planned, went from suspended to canceled.

The phone rang.

"Rebecca?" a tentative Irene asked. "I wanted to see if you are alright. I, uh, shouldn't have dragged you to the Veteran's Day thing."

"I'm not that strong, I guess."

"You are as strong as you need to be. Each emotional whack peels another layer of bandages away."

Rebecca's face tightened. "I must have a very thick bandage."

Silence. "I guess I should be more careful with what I say. Sometimes I feel like I ain't got the sense God gave a goose. I'm sorry."

"The Marine in the wheel chair. I wondered what he meant by 'my country lied.' "

"That's Rory Walters' son, Billy. Rory's very upset with him and kicked him out of the house because of his anti-war activities and drugs. He comes to the meetings I was telling you about. His reaction was ruder than I've witnessed before."

Rebecca studied the spots on Clipper's fur, which swirled into a pattern like a map of Asia.

"Not a real pleasant guy."

"Wait 'til you hear his story, and the others' too. There's a meeting at the Columbus YMCA next week. I'll call you a few days ahead to see if you want to go. It might answer some questions for you." Irene cleared her throat. "I don't mean to push you."

"No need to call. I'll go, I have a lot of questions."

Rebecca squirmed on the hard folding chairs of the Columbus YMCA. She was surrounded by strangers, many wearing t-shirts with anti-war slogans like "make love, not war" and "draft beer not students." In spite of her discomfort, Rebecca reminded herself why she was there. *I want to understand, I have to understand, why we are at war and why so many people are against it.* Her heart spun in the opposite directions. *I want to be against it, dammit. I lost my husband's heart and life. Or maybe I wanted to be for it. Then maybe Adam would have died for a goodly cause. Or maybe his death was punishment for abandoning me.* She hung her head.

She could barely breathe in the stuffy room. The whir of a movie projector distracted her, and she noticed the stream of fanned light reflect off the silvery screen. It was a newsreel of a women's march against the war.

The marchers in the film were in Berkeley but they wore pearls and pumps, pencil skirts and saddle shoes, slacks and sweater sets. They looked like anyone's next door neighbor. Young mothers and grandmotherly looking women walked in a crowd that streamed down one lane of the highway. Wheelchairs were the chariots of some of the protesters. "Bring our boys home" read one sign, "refuse to kill or die in Vietnam" read another. Their destination was the Oakland Induction Center. What Rebecca saw were mothers who didn't want their boys dying thousands of miles away.

After the lights came back on, Rebecca raised her hand. "We helped people in Europe in World War II. What if we had turned our back on England, and France?" Irene, sitting beside her, inhaled deeply.

An ominous murmur rose with a timbre of accusation in the unheard words, and the antagonism in the room crawled over Rebecca like fog. Why did she come to this stupid meeting just to make a fool of herself?

The leader in front of the room spread his hands toward the crowd and yelled, "Come on, folks, it's a legitimate question. Not everyone's been enlightened." Light laughter ensued. "Who wants to help, uh, what's your name, please?" he asked as he looked toward her.

"Rebecca."

"I will," said a voice from the side of the room. The room turned in unison towards the voice, but the owner wasn't visible until people moved aside to reveal Billy Walters, the wounded veteran Rebecca saw at the Veteran's Day ceremony. He pushed the wheels of his chair with gloved hands. With less repulsion and more interest, she watched his deft maneuver of the wheel.

He headed to the front while the audience applauded. Wearing no uniform this time, his hair was loose and framing his bearded face. He looked like a Sunday School Jesus, but he wasn't sitting on a rock, and he had no children sitting on his lap. He did have an angry, sad expression that begged an audience. Polished medals and pins decorated his green vest; his muscular arms emerged from the shirt embroidered with "Vietnam Vets Against the War."

He rolled to the microphone. The room was quiet, the kind of quiet that makes a person lean forward in anticipation of words worth hearing. Billy scanned the crowd. Expertly pausing for dramatic effect, he took the microphone, handed to him by another vet who stood behind the podium.

"Washington lied to me." Hoots and applause met his statement. "I enlisted to fight for our freedom and the freedom of the Vietnamese people. 'They are being invaded by outside conquerors,' the generals would have us believe. Let me tell you, it didn't take much time in the rice paddies and villages of South Vietnam to realize that they saw us as the invaders." He paused, scanned the room, and made eye contact with anyone who dared to meet his challenging gaze. "They've been fighting a civil war for hundreds of years. Who are these Americans, they asked? Why were they burning down our houses and bombing our rice paddies? Guess what, folks, we're not saving them from anything," he pumped his fist, "we're destroying everything our planes fly over. Our boys are dying for the American war machine."

Billy's words slammed into Rebecca's conscience and she thought of Adam's flag-draped coffin. The room grew hotter, and she struggled to breathe in the increasingly thickened air.

"I'm proud that I enlisted." Billy put a hand over his heart. "Freedom isn't free, I know that. But don't be fooled by slick Washington salvos like "Domino Theory." Give me a battle that means something, give me a war that sets people free, not one that supports a corrupt government. Give me a people who want the freedom that our guys are dying for. Give me a purpose other than taking a hill, counting bodies, and climbing back down that corpse strewn trail. There are no Iwo Jimas in Vietnam. We didn't plant the American flag on any hills because our job was to count the enemy dead and leave. Never mind the body bags of our own men."

People were applauding Billy, some standing to show their approval, and a chant rose over the cacophony, "One, two, three, four, we don't want their fucking war. One, two, three, four, we don't want their fucking war..."

Rebecca picked up her purse and coat, made her way down the row and up the aisle, stepping on feet, and pushing empty chairs aside.

Once outside, she stopped and sat on the steps. The chant inside the auditorium was muffled by the steel doors that closed behind her. She held her hands against her pounding heart and felt it begin to slow. The sound grew louder again as Irene emerged, holding a handful of Chuckles candy in her hand. Puzzled, Rebecca looked down at her purse and saw it was open, the brass ball clasps un-linked.

Irene held out her hand and smiled weakly. "Y'all left a trail of these as you left. Were you worried that I wouldn't be able to find you?"

Rebecca clasped her head. "I don't know who I hate most—the people who killed my husband, my husband for being killed, or the woman my husband kept secret. Oh, and there's the Marine Corps and the President and the military machine."

Irene sat down. "That's a lot of space being taken up by anger. Do you have any room left for living?"

Startled, Rebecca looked at Irene. "It would be so much easier if I were a devoted patriotic wife who believed Adam died for a purpose, and our country has our best interests in hand." She wiped tears from her face with the back of her hand and slumped over to rest her head in her hands.

"I'm saying," Irene said, putting her arm around her friend's shoulders, "that you'd save yourself a lot of energy by accepting you're in a conundrum. It's not about Adam, it's about you. You're the one living. You get to decide what to do with your grief and Adam's memory." They sat in silence for a little while, watching the traffic on the busy street in front of the YMCA.

The door opened behind them, and they both sat up. There was clunking against the door frame, a couple of spoken "fuckin' doors" and wheels rolling. It was Billy.

"Hi, ladies." Billy sat in his wheelchair, and he cocked his head to the side as though his greeting was more of a question. He sat looking at them. "You're Adam Benson's wife, aren't you?"

She glared at him. "What if I am? And how do you know?"

"Some folks inside told me who you were. I saw you leave. Sorry if I upset you, today and on Veteran's Day." He seemed to be scanning Rebecca's face, and she wondered what information he was getting. He had no pity or judgment in his eyes.

"You find my injuries somewhat repulsive."

"My father lost his arm in WWII...and died."

"The good news is that I lived," he said with a small smile. "I even have some brocade on my neck to remember the experience." He turned his head so she could see the ribbons of scars on his neck. Burns?

She winced. "I...I'm sorry.

"No matter. I'm used to it."

"What you said was very hard to hear," she said to him. What she didn't say was that he had shredded the fabric of her world. Underneath the threads of normalcy, glimpses of another world peeked through—a complex world holding unexplainable political forces that caused ordinary citizens to lose loved ones and livelihoods.

"I imagine you are afraid he died for nothing." He tilted his head toward Rebecca.

"You think?" His conclusion was correct but intrusive to her ears, and she scowled back at him. "Pretty hard to be proud of a husband who served in a war that people in the news say is morally wrong."

"That's politics you're reading. At least you're trying to be informed."

Billy straightened his back and looked off into the park across the street. "Let me give you some insight into the soldiers' perspective. See those woods at the edge of the park?"

Rebecca turned to where he was pointing.

"Imagine you're on patrol. You have to cross the park, you're looking for VC that are taking over the village. You're pretty sure they are waiting for you beyond the trees. You can't hear them, you can't see them, and the villagers won't tell you because they would be tortured and killed for warning you."

Rebecca looked at the late fall scene, the empty teeter-totters, the swing sets, and the mostly bare-branched trees in the woods. Cardinals chirped, dogs barked in the distance, and a soft wind rustled the dried leaves of the oak trees who hadn't given up their leaves. It was impossible for her to insert danger into that serene setting.

"Each man has clicked off the safety on his rifle. Each man is alert with the rustling he thinks he hears and with moving shadows he thinks he sees between the trees. He follows the silent hand signals from his platoon leader. In the back of his mind, rising above the terror he may feel, he knows what he's supposed to do, he's been trained to know it, and the pride in doing it well is almost stronger than the fear."

Rebecca turned back to Billy. "I don't know what you're getting at."

"Politics don't matter in the field at the other end of the barrel. Doing your job matters. Your husband was teaching those soldiers how to do their jobs. Doesn't sound like a wasted life to me. Beats getting flattened by a bus on the way to a bar."

"But the war--"

"Fuck the war, pardon my French." Billy closed his eyes and drew in a deep breath. "My job now is to stop the flow of young men from American streets to the bloody battles in jungles and rice paddies." The wheels on his chair squeaked as he rolled a little closer.

Irene sat still, silent, her eyes going back and forth to Rebecca and to Billy.

Billy's eyes were black opals, his mouth tight. "Come next week to a small gathering here in Columbus. Meet some of my friends. They'll let you talk about your husband and help you find a way to honor him while not standing by as more men are sent to that hell hole for politicians' rhetoric."

Irene and Rebecca exchanged looks. Irene shrugged her shoulders. Rebecca straightened hers. "Okay. Since I'm at war about the war, I need to know more. I'll go.

Damn it, Adam, look what you've gotten me into.

28

Irene and Rebecca stood on the wooden porch of a once stately home on High Street in Columbus. The weather had turned warm for December, and they wore sweaters that were more than enough for the spring like temperature.

The large Victorian home sported turned posts with curved paint chips pulling away with the weight of many years' coatings, now urban white with an industrial coating of black dust. A sofa sat on the porch waiting for some brave soul to sit down in spite of the springs peeking through the once proud early American plaid.

"So, meeting with these people will help me understand what Adam died for? Like that protest meeting you took me to? That didn't go so well."

"Does the scowl on your face indicate your distaste for student housing, darlin'?"

"This is a student's house?" Rebecca fingered the peeling paint on the door.

"Student housing. As in several students live here. They are the only ones who have the time for protests." Irene laughed. "And of course, Vietnam Vets who haven't gotten their groove back, bless their hearts."

"I'm still not sure why I'm here."

"You are the most intelligent, yet naive, adult I know." She lightly bumped Rebecca's hip with hers and smiled. "But you are genuine, and that's why I like you."

Irene knocked on the door. Rebecca examined the porch they were standing on and noticed an empty carton of Carling Black Label beer sitting underneath the stained-glass front window, now held in place with duct tape. She was out of place, a church secretary, standing on a porch littered with beer cans. Not that she was against beer, or students, but her small-town squeamishness reared its narrow and snobbish head. There she was, in a Villager skirt, Peter Pan collared blouse, and black flats. She pulled off her madras headband and stuffed it in her purse.

A twentyish person in bell bottoms, macramé vest, and a head band circling long, dark (but clean) hair opened the heavy carved door. But he (or was he a she?) looked behind Irene and Rebecca as a Volkswagen van pulled up. Two similarly dressed people, more identifiable as boys, jumped out, opened the back of the van, lifted Billy Walters, wheelchair and all, out onto the sidewalk. More bell-bottomed folks came to the door, focused on Billy's arrival. Several bounded down the steps, and five in all hoisted him up the stairs, slapping each other's backs when Billy was able to roll into the house. Almost as an afterthought, the last person at the door turned to Rebecca then focused on Irene.

"Glad you decided to come." She, having breasts it appeared, gave Rebecca a once over. "Brought a recruit, eh?" she said to Irene. She held out her hand to Rebecca. "I'm Sandy."

"This is Rebecca," Irene said. "I told her y'all could help her understand what's goin' on."

Rebecca held out her hand and hoped that the young woman couldn't see the discomfort she was struggling to hide. Sandy had a firm handshake and looked directly at them both. Solid kid. This might be okay.

Sandy stepped aside, and they walked into a dark entrance, a rag rug covering a wooden floor that must have been gorgeous fifty years ago. A strange odor, like new mown hay, permeated the air.

"I smell incense," Rebecca whispered to Irene.

"That's not incense, honey bunch. It's marijuana. All the kids these days smoke it. You're okay with that, aren't you?"

"I...I suppose. Been curious about it."

"Your friend isn't a cop, is she?" Sandy asked Irene.

"Oh heavens, no."

"She thinks I'm a cop?" Rebecca asked in a low voice, but Irene didn't answer and instead gave her a little push toward the living room on the right. From the corner of her eye she saw Irene exchange a look with Sandy, who had a half formed smile.

They entered a large room outlined with old, soft tufted cushions. Draped from the ceiling was a silk parachute that hung over the room like a patio umbrella. Peace signs were painted on the walls along with butterflies, flowers, and random multi-colored polka dots. Students slouched on the sofas and pillows in various postures of relaxation. A sweet smelling haze enveloped them.

They found two unoccupied seats. Rebecca sat on a hard-backed chair, held her purse protectively on her lap, legs crossed at the ankles. They were invisible to the gathering of young, self-focused people. Slowly the students became aware of the two women, and each muttered a "hey" or a "far out" or a "peace" accompanied by two fingers in a victory sign.

Billy Walters rolled up. "Hey. Good to see you."

He motioned to Sandy, "Bring them each a beer, Sweetheart."

"I don't know how staying at a drug fest will help me understand what Adam died for," Rebecca whispered, still holding on to Irene.

Billy cocked his head and said, "If you stick around, I think you'll find at least some of what you are looking for."

Sandy left the room and came back with two lukewarm bottles of beer. Rebecca sat down, grabbed the beer, and thankful to have something to do, drank heavily. The beer warmed her insides, and it didn't take long for a buzz to build. Irene left to find a bathroom, the likes of which Rebecca didn't want to picture.

Billy glanced at Rebecca's delicately crossed ankles. "I don't mean to be rude, but the demeanor doesn't quite fit the occasion."

Rebecca folded her arms. "I didn't think you were into behavior rules."

"Uh, oh, folded arms." He laughed. "There's nothing that can offend me. I've been shot at, spit on, and I lost all pride in the VA hospital." He held on to the arms of his wheelchair and shifted his weight. "I was a lot like your husband. I enlisted to help the boys who had to go. Sometimes I'm not sure who was luckier, me or guys like your husband."

"Excuse me?" Rebecca clutched her arms more tightly. She considered Adam as a Billy and shuddered to think that she could be repulsed by burn scars on his neck, turned off by his withered legs. How would he get to the bathroom? What if my sweet and easy-going husband had turned into a bitter veteran striking out at any hapless effort to help him? What if he came back with "fuck" as adverb, adjective, and verb, like she was hearing in this pot-infused room? She looked at the front door, guessing how many steps it would take to get out of the place.

"You're picturing your husband being like me, aren't you?"

His comment brought her back to Billy and his wheelchair. He expected truth, she knew, but he had not earned access to such personal thoughts.

"How did I know? I've seen the horror in your face on countless women. Here." He pulled down the neckline on his shirt and leaned forward. "Go ahead. Get it over with. Touch the scars."

Rebecca sat uneasily into the vertical hardness of her chair. The room tilted a little from the effects of swiftly guzzled beer. "I couldn't."

"I'd rather you know it than fear it. Please. You'll do both of us a favor."

His scars repulsed her, and she was embarrassed for not wanting to touch a wounded man's scars. Rebecca inhaled a deep breath of pot-filled air and let its chemicals infuse her with courage. "Okay."

She extended her hand, and Billy's toughness evaporated in the narrow space between his scars and her. The room and its noisy inhabitants floated away as she approached the ravages of a war. Ribbons of pale mounded skin snaked from his left clavicle to his earlobe, and they formed a network of cording atop patches of tightly pulled skin that radiated from normal tissue. Her index and middle fingers caressed the largest mound, shiny and smooth to the touch.

"It feels like a butterfly landed on my neck," Billy said, his face still turned away to expose his wounds.

Rebecca sat forward in the chair and allowed a third finger to join the exploration. "What happened?" she asked softly and withdrew her hand.

Billy pulled his shirt back to his neck and turned. "Not many people ask. Usually they're afraid of what I'll say."

"I know my husband died from a gunshot, but I don't know what happened to other people. For some reason it's important for me to know."

"It happened during my second tour of duty. Was goin' to be a career Marine, you know. I was leading a platoon of ARVNs, you know what that means, don't you, the South Vietnamese soldiers?" He kept going without waiting for an answer, "...leading them through the jungle, looking for tunnels, you know, when one of the men picked up a grenade that he thought I had dropped." Billy closed his eyes and shook his head, he became eerily still. He shivered and began again. "Damn kid. Knew better than to pick up anything. I couldn't train the impulsiveness out of him, I guess."

Rebecca shuddered. Her own impulsivity got her into trouble but nothing like being blown up. "Then what?"

"Then what?" he repeated. "Shrapnel got me in the spine." He slapped his silent legs, "Hot shrapnel lay on my neck because I couldn't move to brush it off. So here I am, thirty-five and a repulsive looking warrior trying to stop the war that scarred me."

"Do you live at home?" Rebecca asked, thinking of what Irene had told her about his father, the Patton-like cop who disapproved of his son's avocation.

"Nah...my pop can't stand the long hair, let alone my nightmares that wake him in the night. Like I said, something that your husband avoided."

She glanced at the people reclining at various angles on the sofas in the room. "So where are the people who are going to help me understand what Adam died for?"

"Keep your eyes and ears open. Plain living and learning is a lot like patrol in the jungle—if you're alert to both threats and opportunities, you're more n'likely going to survive."

Irene returned from the bathroom and sat down. She looked at Billy and at her friend. "Such a serious conversation. What are y'all talking about."

"Way too serious subject," Billy answered. His eyes caught Rebecca's. "But one that I enjoyed." And he rolled away.

"Did he tell you about his war experience?"

"Only his wounds. Adam could have come home like that." Rebecca watched Billy cross the room on his wheels. "Billy is a pretty interesting human being."

Irene didn't acknowledge what Rebecca said. Her eyes had a glassy overlay that accentuated her widened pupils. "Do you want to leave now?" she asked.

"Not really. But I want you to stay with me."

"I'll be right back." And she disappeared again.

"Irene?" No answer.

Left alone and feeling helpless, she refocused on the folks around her who had contented smiles and unseeing eyes. The air was getting smokier. A hand with one of those hand-wrapped cigarettes appeared in front of her face.

"Join the party, darlin.' "

29

Rebecca looked up and saw the owner of the joint was an attractive man. A spark of recognition kindled but died.

In the haze of the room, the stranger's dark features accented his white teeth, made all the more attractive by his smile, a little crooked and very charming. He was shorter than Adam but had broad, strong shoulders. His thick dark hair invited fingering, but Rebecca resisted the sensation. Memories of what it was like to be excited in a man's presence teased her.

"I don't smoke," Rebecca managed to say, still staring at his teeth.

He sat down next to her and said, "Don't inhale. Let the smoke travel around your pretty mouth."

"And who are you that I should entrust this experience to?" she asked.

"Robert Norris."

Another faint bell of recognition rang. She took the joint from his hand, letting herself touch his fingers, and enjoyed the jolt of contact. Adam intruded into the scene, but she pushed him away with an image of Lan. Rebecca held the mysterious smoke inches from her nose, parted her lips and waved the joint back and forth in front of her mouth.

"Nothing's happening." Anticipating another touch, she handed the joint back to Robert. Their touch jolted her again.

"It doesn't happen all at once, like so much else." He inhaled deeply on the joint and handed it back. "Try again. Let the smoke roll around in your mouth."

She did as he instructed and fought the urge to cough. Another try and she succeeded to accept the smoky intrusion. A couple of passes later, Rebecca yielded to the urge to inhale, and she sensed she was melting into the chair. The grain of wood underneath her thighs was so pronounced she imagined the pattern. The universe enfolded her, and when she looked again at Robert, his features were more than three dimensional, they became imbued with such detail that she could have journeyed through his pores and into his soul.

She lost all sense of time as they passed the joint back and forth, but when she looked at her watch, whose ticking had taken on symphonic quality, it was only twenty past noon. *Who's naive now, huh, Irene?*

Robert grabbed her arm and said, "Let's get some fresh air, Rebecca."

She jerked her head toward him. "How did you know my name?"

"I heard your friend say your name."

"Oh."

They made their way to the back door and through the crowd of people in the narrow hall and past a beer-guzzling contest in the kitchen. Robert placed his hand on the small of her back, and gently guided her. They descended wooden stairs to a back yard full of dead lawn turf and green crab grass. They walked to the corner of the yard. "Can't have my back to the crowd," he said. Rebecca sat in a broken down lawn chair that had, she hoped, enough webbing to hold her. Robert sat next to her in his own precarious chair and nearly fell out. Rebecca laughed so hard she had to rub the hurt from her cheeks. She tried to catch her breath, failing because she heard Robert snort from his own laughing conniption.

She was soon spent from so much laughing. She leaned back and reveled in the quiet rustling of a huge maple tree, resplendent with a few remaining red and orange jewels.

After a time, Rebecca looked at Robert and his pores had returned to normal, and when she glanced at the tree, the leaves were only late fall drab leaves. A scene from the Sir Lancelot restaurant came to her mind. She sat up. "I think I've seen you before, at a restaurant in Liberty. What were you doing there?"

"Uh, checking out the town," Robert said. He tapped the side of the beer can. "You know, meeting you was an added bonus to this party. You are everything Adam said you were." Robert's face tightened, and he closed his eyes. "Fuck."

Rebecca jumped out of the chair and stood over him. "What? How do you know Adam?" Minutes passed as she watched his mouth twist into a frown, and in slow motion she heard him utter, "We were in the same squad. I was with him when he died."

"You liar! Why did you pretend you didn't know me? How did you know I would be here?" Rebecca paced back and forth a couple of times, rubbing her hands and dodging the drunken partygoers who were making their way into the back yard. She glared at him. "Why?"

Robert looked away and rubbed his mouth and his eyes. "It's complicated." He put his beer down.

"Try me."

"Sit down, please." He motioned to the chair. "About a month ago I came to your house, to introduce myself and tell you how Adam died." He cleared his throat. "Just got back, you know. I'm a civilian again. Divorced. My best buddy said he'd take care of my wife—and he did. Well, anyway, back to you. I sat in the car and rehearsed what I was going to say. I was a little concerned how you would react. It's the right thing to do, to check on a buddy's widow, for him, you know, but it's hard."

"Go on."

"You came out the door, and my first thought was how jealous I was of Adam." He looked down.

Rebecca sat a little straighter. "Jealous? How does this have anything to do with Adam?"

Robert kept his head down, talking to the grass. "I was so struck by your looks and how you carried yourself. You had an inviting presence about you. And I felt guilty."

She wanted to scream, but Rebecca forced herself to ask calmly, "What about Adam?"

"I honestly couldn't go up to you, I was so flustered." He grabbed his beer but didn't drink it, rubbing the rim of the can with his forefinger. "I felt like a junior high kid. So, I decided to back off until I could get myself together. Pretty bad for a forty-year-old, eh?" He took a swig and wiped his mouth with his forearm. He shook his head and avoided eye contact with her. "I saw you at the YMCA and guessed you might be here today."

"Are you anti-war?"

"Struggling with the answer to that question."

"What about Adam?" she asked again, measuring each word.

"Oh. I promised Adam, actually we promised each other if one didn't go home alive, we would make sure the wife would get her insurance policy."

"Insurance policy?"

He scanned the yard, leaned forward and whispered, "You don't understand. Adam and I found some gold bars, thin little things, in an abandoned AVN headquarters, you know, North Vietnamese. We're not allowed to bring contraband back into the U.S., so we hid them."

"I'm surprised Adam would do something like that."

Robert chuckled. "Well, I had to do a little fast talkin' to get him to see my way. Leave the gold for the gooks to buy supplies? Turn them in? To whom?"

"Gold bars? Where are they?"

"In a small wooden box...in the personal effects that you received."

"I saw that little box. There were only stamps in there."

"That's what we intended. When Adam died, I went to his quarters and put both our shares of the gold bars in a hidden compartment...underneath the stamps."

"Of course, I was sick when I heard that Adam's effects were stolen."

"Oh my God." Rebecca sat down and put her head in her hands. Speaking through her fingers she said, "The whole town knew I had the footlocker. I was getting ready to look through Adam's things. The box was visible and a topic of conversation with anyone who visited me." She raised her head. "You knew about the robbery too?"

"As you said, word gets around." Robert took a swig of his beer.

"I went through Adam's effects when the police found the locker. There was nothing missing that I could tell."

"You got it back?" Robert jumped out of his chair. "Let's look at what you have. I'll take you to Liberty." He grabbed her hand.

Rebecca recoiled a bit at his insistence. "But I rode here with Irene. I can't leave her here."

"Yes, you can. She's a big girl and can find her way back." Robert put his hands on her shoulders, so she had to look at him. He did a quick scan of the yard. "It's better that she, or anyone else, not know about the gold yet. Right now, we need to see that box."

Irene came into the back yard, and Robert trotted over to her. Rebecca watched his animated talk, his gesture toward her, and Irene's smile. Irene winked at Rebecca and waved goodbye.

She wondered if she could trust Robert. A red flag jabbed at her judgment. When Robert returned, she asked, "I'm supposed to get in a car with you and drive to Liberty?"

He dropped his hands and looked perplexed. "I dunno. I'm Robert, a friend of your husband's. It's no big deal."

She hesitated. She still hadn't learned anything about Adam. "Before I go anywhere, there's something I need to ask you. The truth. Promise."

"What?" The impatience in his voice made her uncomfortable. His tone was exactly like her mother's whenever she asked one too many questions.

Rebecca swallowed hard. "There was a photo of a Vietnamese woman in Adam's things, a woman called Lan Nyguen. She had written 'Love Always' on it. Do you know who she is?"

"Lan...oh, her." His face brightened. "Now there's an interesting story. I'll tell you in the car."

"But..."

He took Rebecca by the hand and headed for the door. A car backfired in the distance, and his grip tightened. Looking up at him she saw a set jaw.

"Are you okay?"

"Loud noises. Gift of combat," he said, looking toward the street.

Finding out about Lan was worth a gamble on a strange man she didn't know much about. Her mind raced with the possibilities—the sister of an ARVN and she was overly affectionate? A love-struck Vietnamese woman besot with a handsome "numbah-one GI?" "Oh, Adam, please don't let her be a lover," Rebecca whispered to him somewhere up above where people talk to the dead, or God, or both. She hurried to match Robert's pace as they headed through the house and out the front door.

Stern warnings about strangers played in Rebecca's head. They had kept her safe during childhood, and her mother's sterner warnings during high school had scared, and scarred, her. At fourteen years old, she was sure she could get pregnant from sitting in a car that a boy had been wanking in.

Wanking wasn't her concern that night in Columbus. Adam and Lan were. Robert had barely climbed into the driver's seat of the Corvette when she asked, "What do you know about Lan?"

"Aren't you going to say something about the great car?" he asked, patting the steering wheel.

Seemed like a pretty expensive ride for a vet, yet at his command Rebecca did a five second inventory of the red leather seats, red carpet, red steering wheel, chrome trim on the red dashboard and seat back. A lot of red. Like sitting in a ketchup bottle. "Nice car. Now tell me about Lan."

"You are a woman on a mission." He turned the keys, and the engine came to life. He patted the dashboard with affection.

He glanced at Rebecca. "That photo upset you, eh?"

"No kidding. Wouldn't it upset you if you found a photo of another man with your wife, with his arm around her, and 'Love' inscribed on it?"

"I did and not too long ago." He depressed the clutch, shifted into reverse, and smoothly backed out of the parking place. He was skillful—the action was smooth. "This is a mighty fine car, don't you think?" he asked.

"Wait a minute!" Rebecca rotated her body to face Robert squarely. "This isn't about your damn car. Have you no idea how important this is to me?" Her eyes were stinging, and she had clenched her fists.

He pulled back in, turned off the engine, and angled his body toward her. "Well, ain't you the little tiger?"

That's when Rebecca slapped him.

30

The slap sounded like the spontaneous crack of a window that could no longer handle the bitter cold of a January night. Rebecca had never slapped anyone before, and all the anger and angst she had bottled provided the tension in the loaded spring of her hand. Robert froze, his hand on his cheek.

"Oh my God, I'm so sorry!" Rebecca put her hand over her mouth, partly out of shame and partly to sooth the burning skin on her palm.

Robert's eyes took on a quality of hardened steel, his jaws clenched, and his hands stiffened. She braced for a hit. He extended his neck and rotated his head a little to the left and back. He closed his eyes and took a deep breath. When his eyes opened, they were back to normal and his face was no longer tightened into an angry mask.

"I want to hear about Adam," Rebecca said, choking back sobs.

"Sorry. I'm a big self-centered idiot," Robert said. He leaned back in the seat and turned his head. "And you want to know about Lan. The gold can wait a few more minutes. And you'll be relieved."

"How is that?"

"Adam was a great guy, always thinking of others. We were bar hopping one night, not drinking that much, when we saw a woman and a young girl begging outside of a hotel, a nice hotel. Not an unusual scene but there was something about the young mother that was very compelling.

"Something lay in the woman's lap, and we saw it move, the edge of the blanket lifted. We watched as a hotel employee came out and shooed away the little family."

He took on a family? Wouldn't adopt here, but there?

"Adam halted, almost on a dime, they say, and told me, 'If Rebecca were with me, she would tell me to stop and help.' We took a step closer, and there was a baby in that bundle, nearly newborn to my eyes. Looking at the baby we saw her face was pinched with hunger. Such dark circles under her eyes. Adam whispered to me, 'That little girl is part American.' I looked and could see that her hair was brown and curly, her skin a little darker."

Rebecca shook her head, imagining what was in Adam's mind as he considered the impoverished family. Did that hungry little girl touch some paternal part of his heart?

"What did you do?"

"To be honest, we didn't want to touch them. They were pretty dirty." Robert grimaced. "But Adam and I looked at each other, pulled out our wallets and asked the hotel person, 'Have a room for us tonight?'"

Rebecca recoiled. "You used her as a prostitute?"

Robert laughed. "That's what the hotel guy thought too. 'No boom-boom here,' he said. We assured him we were paying for the mother and children. No boom-boom. He wasn't convinced. We added more money to the offering, and boom-boom was no longer a problem. He gestured to follow him into the hotel."

"What did the woman think?"

"She looked real stern at us and said, 'No boom-boom.' She clutched the baby more tightly and pulled the other child closer to her."

Robert continued to paint the picture of how they got the little family up to a room, with a private bath no less, and while the mother was bathing herself and the kids, Adam went out to get some new clothes. When they came out of the bath all clean, they again wore their dirty rags The mother burst into tears when she saw new garments on the bed.

"Oh my," said Rebecca.

"After that, we had a nice little dinner in the room with them. Adam and I put more money in the mother's hand and left."

"But the photo?"

"Turns out that the mother was quite persistent and got herself hired as a laundress in the hotel. Adam came back a few days later and the hotel manager took their photo. Adam gave him an address where he could send the picture."

Rebecca expelled the air she had nearly been holding while Robert told the story. "End of story. Curtain center," she said.

"I wish." Robert grew sober. "The woman was killed by a Viet Cong attack on the hotel, for aiding American soldiers. The children were sent to an orphanage."

"Oh no, do you have any idea where they were sent?"

"No idea. Adam was crushed. He acted like he had lost his own sister. I'm surprised he didn't tell you about it. He died a couple of weeks afterward."

"I guess that's it. We'll never know, will we?" Rebecca's whirling emotions fought each other. On one hand she was ecstatic that Lan was not a lover. On the other hand, her heart ached for those little children, their mother an undeserving victim of an NVA bomb.

"The story may still not be over." Grinning, he said, "Remember the orphanage has Adam's address. When the war is over, you never know…" He straightened and put the car in gear again. "Let's go back to Liberty where things make a little more sense. We have some gold prospecting to do."

So relieved that Lan was not a lover, Rebecca let herself be enveloped by the leather seats, their crimson hue less important than their comfort. She sensed Adam's arms emerge from the seat and hold her. "I need to readjust my anger toward Adam back to love," Rebecca said.

Robert glanced over. "Even with your suspicions, I doubt you ever stopped loving him."

"I thought of something else. The poem. You were the one who wrote a poem about hiding something in a box! And the concertina wire. They were both strange. Sorry."

He paused. "Not many people understand my poetry. A Marine poet—seems strange, doesn't it?"

"Well, yes. Maybe a way of dealing with all the tragedy you saw?"

They sat in silence as they drove by harvested corn fields on either side of the interstate. Corn fields—so far from the jungles of Vietnam, so quiet compared to the bombing that shook the Southeast Asian earth. If Adam had lived, would his paternal instincts have survived the flight over the Pacific back to Liberty, Ohio? Would he have been more open to adoption? The truth pulled at her like an undertow. She would never know.

Did Adam send home some gold? Small solace for empty arms. Rebecca settled even more into the Corvette's leather seats and consoled herself with a goal—recovering those gold bars.

"Are we there yet?" she asked Robert.

"The last marker said twenty-three miles. You asked me the same thing at twenty-four miles. And when we left, we had thirty-five miles to go."

The wheels on the car turned half the speed of Rebecca's mind. Looking out the window, she hoped to be distracted by the city and the rural landscape, but the early winter darkening fields couldn't compete with the tumult she felt. Always, the footlocker. Now there was a box within that. And she was trapped inside a bright red bachelor mobile. Her life seemed like it was either a container she's trying to get into or one she's trying to get out of.

But gold? The idea of gold brought images of what she could buy. A new color TV came to mind. So shallow, yet so human. *How loving Adam was to think of my future. And how petty I had been for doubting him. I want so much to run to his arms and ask for his forgiveness, but I can only hope that he somehow knows.* With familiar sadness, Rebecca wondered how strong Adam's premonition of his death was, or whether he was reacting as most do in war, "Will I make it home?"

She shook her head. "Tell me more about this gold."

"The night that we found the gold, we hatched a plan to smuggle it home—his to help you, and mine to help my wife. We later found out that the gold, actually thin sheets of gold leaf, were manufactured by a Kim Thanh, and are supposed to be nearly pure. They were used by war refugees as a way of taking their savings out of the country. Some poor NVA had to run away without his savings."

"How much do you think they're worth?"

"I don't know, but we had twenty of them, all in this little box, ready to be divided between me and Adam."

"Why were they in Adam's footlocker and not yours also?"

"I'm a more controversial sort. MPs would take a closer look at mine."

Rebecca settled into the mobile ketchup bottle, and she had to admit it was sinfully comfortable. The smell and softness of leather enveloped her, and she was no longer riding in ketchup but in an honest-to-goodness luxury auto.

Using her skirt edge, she rubbed her fingerprints off the chrome trim on the arm rest. *I soiled Adam's reputation with my negative thoughts. And the war. Had I become against the war because my husband joined up and died or because the war had placed so many in a hell hole of death?*

She turned to Robert. "I can't tell you how relieved I am to know the truth. I wasted so much energy on hating him, and her. I'm ashamed I jumped to conclusions."

They were off the interstate, and Robert concentrated on negotiating a sharp curve on a country road. "I think you reacted as anyone would. Adam should have told you what happened." He drummed his fingers on the steering wheel. "I have my own confession to make." He made a quick glance her way. "I'm embarrassed that I made such a big deal about my car. Kinda of self-centered, huh?"

"Uh, yeah."

"Humor me a little. I have an excuse."

"Because you are a male?"

"No, listen. When I was in the boonies, eating cold beans out of a C-rat, I distracted myself with thoughts of what I would do when I got back to the World."

"The world?"

"That's what we called the U.S."

"Oh, that's right. Adam used that term in his letters."

"Anyway, I tried thinking about my wife, the beer I would drink, but nothing distracted me as much as the thought of owning a bright red Corvette Sting Ray.

She grinned at Robert. "Well, it is bright red."

He continued. "The murky swamp became bearable, and the smell of unwashed soldiers faded while I pictured myself in my shiny new car. So you see, this car means I survived, I..." his voice caught.

His story stirred in her a maternal reaction to his pain and a sexual reaction to his willingness to be vulnerable. She put her hand on his knee. Embarrassed, she took it away.

A car passed on the left and pulled in too close to Robert's car. Robert leaned on the horn, stepped on the gas, and sped past the offending car. Robert honked again as he came along the car and flipped his middle finger at the driver. Robert's face was scrunched into a twisted mask of angry flesh. Once past the car, he relaxed, and his face softened into a normal human expression.

"What was that about?" Rebecca was still clinging to the door handle.

He turned to her and grinned. "Man stuff."

And I'm taking this man to my house?

31

Rebecca gave the last "turn here," and Robert said, "I know, I know. Remember I've been here, hoping to catch a glimpse of you." Robert pulled the car over in front of her house. "Funny you live on Elm."

"Have for a long time. Four o seven. Why?"

"Know the Jacksons?"

"Old Man Jackson and his wife? Some. Why do you ask?"

"Family acquaintances."

They walked into the kitchen as the rooster clock crowed six.

Robert rubbed the ears of a tail-wagging Clipper, and his gesture was achingly familiar to Rebecca. After Adam died, Clipper had been Rebecca's reason to wake up. Those brown eyes looked deep into hers every day and required nothing but a pat on the head, a bowl of food and water, and a place to poop and pee. It was the simplest of relationships, and the richest of relationships—one that she missed sharing with Adam. Alone, she could laugh at Clipper turning in circles to chase his tail, but to be able to laugh jointly again with another person would widen the world's loving arms.

Robert was looking at her with a soft smile. He stood very close, and she heard the soft swoosh of both their breaths. She wanted so much to be held by a man, to know she mattered to someone.

He made a slight move toward her and stopped. "I'm sorry. I shouldn't have done that." He continued to look at her with a combination of softness and indecision.

Rebecca took a step back and bumped into a chair. Robert caught her as she stumbled.

Rebecca's face burned with embarrassment, and she righted herself. "That was stupid."

"Maybe we should get back to the task at hand," Robert said.

They both cleared their throats and stared at the locker like it was a prop for *Mission Impossible*.

"Is there a tape recorder to tell us what to do?" Robert asked.

"How did you know what I was thinking?"

"I watch a lot of television. I'm a bachelor, you know." He gestured toward the prized object on the floor. "Hurry up. Show me what's in there."

"Đừng nóng."

Robert's head jerked back as though he had been slapped. His eyes narrowed. "Don't you ever speak gook to me," he snarled, his face dark with anger. All the tenderness she had witnessed a moment ago disappeared, and she felt a stab of fear and anger.

"I only said 'cool it.' Adam taught me a lot of phrases in his letters."

"I don't give a shit what Adam taught you. I heard enough of that in 'Nam." His eyes returned to the locker.

"Ookay."

With more force than needed, she flipped the latch to the locker, opened it, and dug through the contents. At the bottom, unvalued until that moment, sat the wooden stamp box. She pulled it out through the items like retrieving a branch from a pile of limbs and leaves. All else fell away noisily as she removed the small container.

Rebecca handed it to Robert, and he immediately opened the hinged lid and dumped the stamps on the table. "Got a small knife?" She handed him one from the kitchen drawer.

"This is the box in the poem, isn't it?"

"Finally made the connection, eh?" With knife in hand, he put the point between the edge and a barely discernible crack in the bottom of the box. "I don't want to puncture the gold leaves. They're covered with pretty ornate markings. I'm sure that is part of their value."

When she saw him put more force on the point, Rebecca said, "Be careful." He gave her a look that said, "Đừng nóng."

His prodding was in slow motion, inserting the point a hair's thickness at a time. With the "pop" of the lid, they both jumped. Robert's triumphant smile quickly froze into a frown.

"What's wrong?"

He held the box upside down, and the wooden partition of the hidden compartment clanged onto the floor. "Nothing's there." He sat down at the table. "Shit. I don't get it."

"It's gone?" Rebecca sat down. For a few hours she had an inheritance from Adam, proof that he was thinking of her future. She wondered if Robert had made it all up.

"What a waste," he said.

"Shouldn't we call the police?"

Robert looked at her with an open mouth. "You can't call the police about stolen material that's been stolen, can you?"

"Oh, that's right, I'm sorry."

"Nothing to be sorry about. You say that a lot, you know." He looked again at the empty box. Shaking it again.

"I do? I'm sor...," she caught herself.

Robert took out other items from the locker, throwing them on the table. "Nothing."

He stood, his features soft again. "I'll call you. Here's my number in case you find out anything else." He wrote his phone number on an unopened letter she had sitting on the kitchen counter. He gave Clipper's ears a tousle and his belly a short rub. "See ya, boy." Out he went, and Clipper wagged his tail, utterly tuned into Robert's attention.

The contents of the locker lay in disarray. The box's wooden partition on the floor gloated as though it were saying, "Fooled ya." The knife teetered on the edge of the table where Robert had flung it when the partition popped.

What in the world happened? Robert's attention had aroused her. But his change in demeanor was confusing, and his apparent brush-off hurt her feelings. Damn. She'd been made a fool.

Clipper came over to her, whined, and wagged his tail.

"Go!" She pointed to the door, her face tight with anger.

He slunk away, looking back at a person he didn't recognize.

She wiped everything off the table with a large sweep of her arm. Everything clattered to the floor, and a last-minute decision to save the falling items caused her to lose her balance and fall. Damn. The coolness of the linoleum was comforting, and she lay on the floor and let the pleasant temperature soothe her fevered mood. She turned her head and spotted the pouch with Adam's dog tag. She grabbed it, took out the tag, and hugged it to her cheek where her tears fell. Clipper, loyal Clipper, came and licked her salty face.

Shit. What am I doing on the floor? The kitchen light invaded Rebecca's eyelids. She looked at the clock and saw it was four in the morning. She remembered. The gold was gone. Robert was gone. She lay on the floor in a blob of self-pity.

First, I lost Adam to the war. But it was to be only a year. Then I lost him to battle. But there was the gold that Adam saved for me so he would always, somehow, be taking care of me. Oh, wait a minute, it's gone, too. I had a friend Robert who seemed to like me, but he left in a hurry when he found out there was no gold. Loss, hope, loss, hope, loss.

She rubbed her eyes. She was utterly defeated by continuous loss. Was there anywhere she could find hope that would not disappear?

Clipper was spooned into her body, and he sprang up with Rebecca's unsuccessful effort to stand. Her back was stiff, and her face hurt. When she finally stood up, something fell from her cheek and clanged onto the linoleum. It was Adam's dog tag. She staggered to the mirror by the kitchen door and saw the damages of her night on the floor—red eyes, the Jackie hairdo stringy and shapeless, and a dog tag branded on her left cheek. She lifted a hand to tenderly outline its mark. Closing her eyes, she imagined Adam's hand on top of hers. *Enough!* She rubbed the sharp outline into a crimson blotch.

Another glance at the clock reminded her of the hour. She was torn between going to bed and pulling the sheets between her and her disappointment, or staying up. She rolled her neck, the joints making a cacophony of cracking. Going to bed won.

Clipper whined and wagged his tail, his eyes staring at her. The clock read ten. "Okay, Clipper. Let me at least brush my hair." He was dancing at the door.

Once outside, Clipper ran to the first bush, and in contrast to Rebecca's dour mood, peed gleefully. People drove by, encapsulated in their own worlds, unaware of the ups and downs she experienced the previous night. *Why can't I get a break? Would it have been so hard for Fate to allow me a little solace from finding the gold?*

They headed for a park where Clipper could be off leash. He ran to the other dogs, who all alternated between the head-down and butt up play posture and the ritual of tail sniffing. A late Indian Summer warmed the air, and Rebecca sat under a maple tree. A few leaves stubbornly clung to the branches. Fluffy clouds hid the sun, and she burrowed into her scarf. Was she being stubborn like those leaves, denying the inevitable? The sadness pulled her face downward.

I found out that Adam was not having an affair. I should be happy. It was almost easier when I was angry at him. Now all I have is grief. She had no other emotion to dilute the acid bath in which her heart sat.

A crow landed on the topmost of the maple tree, and he stared and mocked Rebeca with a raspy crawk that sounded like one of those wooden chalk holders used in grade school music classes. The crow was dusty black from beak to tail.

She looked back up at the bird. He was still staring at her. Crawk!

"What are you trying to tell me, Mr. Crow?" His ebony eyes bore down. She remembered what her fourth grade teacher told the class about crows. To her relief, the birds weren't signs of bad things to come. They are intelligent and full of mystery. They were a symbol of change, most likely for the better. Her nine-year-old brain had wrestled with what she would do if she found a crow's feather. Would she keep it for good luck or recoil from it?

"Ok, Mr. Crow. If I need to change, how should I change?" The crow didn't answer.

A young mother approached with a baby carriage, and distracted Rebecca. She could hear the child's cooing, and the mother responded with high pitched baby talk.

"You so handsome! My wittle baby boy."

The mother sat down on a nearby bench, looked up, and smiled at Rebecca.

The baby had rosy cheeks, and was blond and blue-eyed like Rebecca had imagined her child would be. From the stroller she heard an orchestra of cooing and infant gibberish.

"Hello, sweetie," Rebecca said. The angelic babe uttered more unintelligible music. The softness of his skin was almost palpable to her hands. Baby powder sweetness emanated from the child.

Clipper whined from his leashed position at the bench.

"Hello. You are?"

"Rebecca Benson. I love this park, I come here almost every day with my dog."

"Say, are you the cop's wife? ."

"Yes, I am."

"May I hold him?"

"I...I suppose. I'm Jeanne, by the way," and she held out her hand to shake, a warm and trusting hand.

With yearning hands, Rebecca withdrew the baby from his blanketed nest in the buggy. She held him close, and he melted into her hug. She gently pressed the baby harder against her.

Crawk! Rebecca jumped. She looked toward the sound and watched the crow flap his wings and call out again.

She put the baby back into his buggy and tucked the blanket around him. His little face registered confusion. She sat back on the bench. Though she understood more about Adam's refusal to have children, she continued to want a family.

Jeanne observed her as a mother might. "Are you all right? You look a little pale."

"I'm fine," Rebecca said and managed a smile. "I was thinking about the 'could have beens' in my life. I've always wanted children but couldn't."

"I'm sorry," Jeanne said.

Rebecca gestured toward the trees. "The last leaves of the season. I was thinking how futile it is for them to try to stay on the trees."

Jeanne said nothing.

"They have to fall sometime," said Rebecca.

"Uh, sure."

"My Uncle Ralph used to say, 'don't waste your time on could've beens.' "

"It sounds like you are having a hard time."

"I guess I'll get going. Thank you for letting me hold your baby."

"You're welcome. Good luck to you."

Rebecca headed toward the wooded path. "Come, Clipper." She pulled on his leash. The crow followed them a little way and flew off until he became a black dot in the sky. Rebecca envied him. He had no "could've beens." And up where he was, he could see the whole scene—people, animals, and foliage. No wonder he was wise.

They walked along the wooded path toward her house,, and she kicked the crinkly leaves underfoot.

She stopped her leaf kicking and sat on another bench. The canopy of trees cocooned her and gave permission to hide her face in Clipper's fur and mourn in private.

PART THREE

When you have decided what you believe, what you feel must be done, have the courage to stand alone and be counted.

Eleanor Roosevelt

32

Looking out the window from her desk at the church, Rebecca observed a young couple walking hand in hand. Instead of feeling happy for the lovers, she felt sad for herself.

She shuffled the papers she was supposed to file and mulled over her attraction to Robert, his relationship with Adam, and his sudden departure. When Robert was around, it felt like Adam was nearby. Is that what her attraction to Robert was about? Yet, when she thought of him, her heart seemed a little less sad. Teenagery. She resisted the urge to call him.

Restless and not ready to go home after work at the church, she thought she ought to go to the library. Perhaps reading some newspaper stories about Vietnam would provide some intellectual distraction.

She hunched over a wooden table in the back corner of the library. She held the newest *New York Times*. Turning a page, she spotted a report about protests multiplying around the country. What would it be like, she thought, to be so public, so rebellious? She pictured herself in the newspaper photo, imagining the excitement of joining an enthusiastic crowd, sharing their passionate view of the war, and showing the world how she felt. An unnamed anxiety crept over her. She would be recognized by someone who would tell everybody in Liberty. She closed the newspaper.

As she did every evening, Rebecca lit the candle next to Adam's photo and whispered "I love you" as she fingered his face. She retired early not wanting to be awake in the lonely house. Sleep was a cocoon from her relentless self-doubts. As usual she slept ten hours, only to be awakened at seven AM when Clipper needed to go out.

Her thoughts about Robert darkened as the holidays approached and wondered why she hadn't heard from him. It was wrong to be interested in him anyway, she told herself. It was Adam she missed.

She appreciated that friends tried to involve her in holiday traditions, but she couldn't generate any interest or enthusiasm. The Christmas decorations stayed in the darkened basement whose gloom matched her own. She spent Christmas dinner with her mother and pretended to be in holiday spirit.

Early in January, the phone rang, and she reluctantly picked it up, anticipating yet another activity to find an excuse to decline.

"Hi. I'm glad you're home." Robert's voice had a lilt, a come-on-down invitation in it.

Rebecca willed her heart to stop beating so hard. She shouldn't be glad to hear from a man who had ignored her, or, she shouldn't have feelings for anyone yet.

"Want to watch the ice-skaters down at the park?"

"I'm surprised to hear from you. Why now? It's been how long? I don't know whether to hang up on you or hear you out."

A pause. Robert said, "I guess I deserve that. I was, uh, in the hospital for a while."

"Oh no, are you OK?"

"Uh, sure, only some war injuries that haven't healed."

"I didn't notice any scars or anything."

"Not all scars are visible, you know."

Thinking that Robert's scars were perhaps in an intimate area, Rebecca chuckled. "That's all you need to tell me."

"Good, now back to going to the park."

They sat on the bleachers, installed for the temporary ice rink. They laughed at the stumbling and falling skaters. "Wow! That one took a hard fall," said Robert, pointing to a young man who was sheepishly trying to get up from the ice.

"I can feel his pain. I'm glad you suggested watching the ice-skaters and not going ice-skating. I never got the gist of it."

"Not much ice in 'Nam. But I will say this cold feels good compared to humid jungles." He pulled his hood onto his head and helped Rebecca adjust her woolen scarf.

"Speaking of 'Nam," Rebecca stopped. "I mean, well...I don't know."

"You want to ask me how Adam died, don't you?"

"Yes," she said in a low voice.

Looking at the families laughing and squealing as they skated, he said, "It was very quick." He looked back at her. "He loved you very much, you know."

"Did he talk about me?"

Robert laughed. "Oh, did he. I think I fell in love with you by listening to Adam's incessant praise."

Robert's eyes took on a tenderness that gave her goosebumps. She hoped he couldn't see the flush in her heated face.

"Adam is here, with us," she said quickly. "His presence."

"Someday you will have to go on and make another life for yourself."

Rebecca panicked. "How?"

"Adam would want you to be happy."

"He hasn't been gone a year yet. I can't be thinking of those things."

"You can think of those things whenever you're ready. There's no calendar for grieving."

Rebecca's thoughts jumbled with hope, guilt, and attraction. She shifted on the bench. "I didn't want him to go. He didn't have to."

"He did have to. He was one of those principled guys whose job was to support his country." He leaned on his elbows toward her. "Don't you understand that?"

She sat in silence, hoping Robert would change the subject.

"At least he stepped up," Robert said. These namby-pamby protestors are only trying to save their own asses."

"Maybe it's a war not worth dying for."

Robert's face hardened. "Tell that to the parents who received only a torso in the casket that came home."

"Do you have to remind me that Adam was unviewable?" she managed to choke out.

Her remark didn't register with him, and he continued. "I have a baby brother who recently finished boot camp. I'm really pissed he did that. He ships out soon."

"You must be worried."

"Worried?" He looked at her, nonplussed._"I didn't want him to go, I told him to go to college, but no. He had to do it. Now I think he's not so sure he did the right thing. And I said to him..." --Robert leaned closer to Rebecca, and his lips turned into a half snarl. " '--Boy, you've signed up and you better follow through. I don't want no snivelin' coward in my family.' "

He sat back and put his hands behind his head. "Let's talk about something else."

"Please."

"My wife left me for another man while I was gone. But you stayed true, didn't you?"

Rebecca cocked her head and wondered where the conversation was going. "Of course."

"The more I know you, the more I like you. Admire you, actually. And you're fun."

Rebecca stayed still on the bleacher. She wasn't sure she should be enjoying his compliments.

"Tell you what. Adam said you were enthusiastic in the kitchen. I would love a home cooked meal. How 'bout it?"

Rebecca smiled. "I would love a reason to cook. Friday? And you can tell me more about Adam."

Neither smiling nor frowning, Robert looked at her. "Sure."

Rebecca reasoned that a home cooked meal should be filling, not fancy. Simple table setting, no flowers. Just friends sharing a meal. Maybe a turkey, like the

Thanksgivings she shared with Adam. She felt alive, womanly, wanting to please a man with food.

She spent the next two days buying food, standing in long lines at the meat market, and surprising her friends who saw her. Always teasing, her friends.

"You're cooking? Did you have to ask directions to the meat counter?"

"Stop the lights! Are those potatoes in ya' cart? Did you know you have t' peel, boil, and mash those things?"

Reverend Kaskell eyed her cart at the check-out line and said, "Do we need a prayer for your guests?"

She fooled them all. By Friday morning, the house smelled like a home should on Thanksgiving Day. When she closed her eyes, she was back in her mother's kitchen, hanging near the oven, inhaling the aroma of a crisping turkey. "Is it ready? Is it ready?"

A pumpkin pie sat on the counter, the cranberry relish sat in a bowl still having the shape of the can it slid out of, and the potatoes were boiling on the stove. The canned green beans were warming in a pot. Clipper stayed on his mat, head down, watching her every move.

When she served a perfectly prepared turkey, Robert applauded.

"Wow, this is a pleasure, indeed." He raised his glass of wine to her.

Rebecca watched Robert dig into his food—knife in one hand, fork in another. "You must not have had a home-cooked meal in quite a while."

"Let's say hospital food is not that appetizing. This is, as Tony the Tiger says, 'grrrrreat!' "

Startled, she asked, "You must have been in the hospital a long time!"

Robert lost his smile and looked down. "Yeh, thanks to Uncle Sam. Say," he said looking up, "how about passing me some more of those potatoes."

To Rebecca's relief, the conversation went back to light subjects: embarrassing high school moments and social faux pas of their young adult years. After dessert and coffee, she poured more wine, and they retreated to the living room. Only a few lamps were on, and she felt mellow in the shadows that gave a soft and ethereal glow to the room, maybe too mellow.

"Let me get more light in here." She reached toward a lamp to turn it on, but Robert brushed her hand away from the switch.

They both sat on the sofa, but he motioned for her to move from the end of the sofa to the middle.

"We know each other too well to sit so far apart."

"Well, I guess," Rebecca said, and she moved to the spot next to Robert. His nearness was both comfortable and unsettling. She turned her face toward him. She lifted her ching. A million seconds passed while Rebecca took in the closeness of his lips. Her breathing quickened. Robert put one hand under her chin to raise it closer to him, and he leaned forward to kiss her.

Robert slowly moved back and took her hand. "That was wonderful. Are you OK? I don't want you to do something you don't want to do."

"I haven't felt like this in a long, long time."

Robert smiled. "Shall we try it again?"

She leaned toward him. He rewarded her with a soft kiss, and he ran his fingers lightly through her hair. She heard him softly moan, and she lifted herself toward him.

"Such a woman," he said, his words coming from deep in his throat. "You must have been a beautiful baby!"

His words broke the spell she was in, and Rebecca pulled back. "Did Adam ever talk about wanting kids, especially after helping out the orphans?"

Robert raised his hands in frustration. "I thought we were enjoying us. Do you always have to bring up Adam? He's gone. I'm here."

"I'm sorry, maybe I'm not ready for this." She felt tears forming.

A car outside the house backfired, and Robert dove to the floor, covering his neck with his hands.

Rebecca looked at him, crouching. "That was only a car."

He leaped up and brushed off his pants. "You don't understand a god-damned thing, do you?" His face was red, the veins on his neck bulged.

"What are you talking about?" Rebecca stood and stared at him.

"You have no idea what it's like to be in the jungle..."

"It seems a little dramatic to me. You came home alive," she interrupted. "Be grateful, at least."

He glared at her, his face pale, his pupils wide. He breathed through his mouth as though he couldn't get enough air. She saw beads of sweat on his face.

"Robert, are you okay?" She looked at him in alarm. He looked around the room as though he didn't know where he was.

He didn't answer. He grabbed his coat from the front hall hook and stormed out into the frozen night. When the door closed under Robert's fury, the house shook.

Rebecca, her mouth open, tried to process what she had witnessed. He frightened her with his strange and threatening behavior. She had an immediate sense of loss, guilt, and fear. She had offended her only connection to Adam. She didn't help him, she hurt him. But, diving to the floor?

She returned to the dining room and with shaking hands she cleared the table. She admitted to herself that maybe she didn't understand, herself or Robert.

33

Finishing the dishes, Rebecca still could not make sense of Robert's overreaction to her comment. The swirl of the soapy dishcloth over each plate mimicked her recall of the nice conversation and some tantalizing kisses. Who could have thought the romantic moment would dissolve into drama? A car backfired and Robert dove to the floor. The noise could have sounded like gunfire. She recalled the car backfire they heard coming from the party. His hand had tightened. "Loud noises. Gift of combat," he had said. The car they heard tonight was closer, louder. She watched the sink drain of bubbles and cloudy water, and she concluded her friendship with Robert may also have drained away.

Winter passed, and spring arrived in spite of her disinterest. Robert disappeared again, and she gave up the hope that they would be friends. More importantly, she realized, she lost opportunities to learn more about Adam.

She saw Mr. Jackson in his driveway one morning, and she signaled to him that she'd like to talk.

"How are you doing, Missy?" asked the grandfatherly Mr. Jackson. "Haven't seen much of ya, but people don't see much of me, either," he chuckled.

"Wonder if I can ask your opinion of something, but I'm kind of embarrassed. Don't want to bother you."

"Shoot," he said.

"Well, that's kind of the problem. I have a friend who served in Vietnam, and he's, well, kind of.."

"Robert." He nodded. "I've seen him at your house a couple of times. What about him?"

Taken aback, she asked, "How well do you know him?"

"He's our daughter's ex-husband."

"Oh my gosh."

"Don't see him much. He came back from the war kind of messed up. He always was kind of tightly wound, if you know what I mean. Wrote some weird poetry and all."

"I've read some."

He paused. "I'll come out and say it, I hope you're not getting involved with him. Takes a lot to motivate a woman to divorce her husband, but that's what our daughter needed to do. He was making her life miserable. While he was in Vietnam, our daughter realized her life was better without him."

Rebecca took a step back. "Oh, he's only a friend. He served with Adam. He seems nice enough, but he has a quick temper, and he acts really frightened when he hears loud noises. I'm afraid I didn't handle it so well."

"Yeah, we call it 'shell-shocked.' " He shook his head. "Some guys never get over it. Like they have devils inside ready to jump out. Saw it in the Great War too." He shook his head. "Such a shame." He looked at her and patted her arm. "You be careful, Missy."

One morning in April, Rebecca and Clipper headed to the park and for a change she decided to sit on a low mossy wall. She wanted to clear her head and have no more drama. The anniversary of Adam's death passed with little fanfare other than for her to realize she no longer had thoughts of "a year ago this happened" or "a year ago Adam and I did..." It was a huge relief and still another loss. What was to take the place of that inner conversation?

Overhead she heard the cry of the crow. She glanced up, but what she saw in the distance was a young Marine in dress khakis coming toward her. She strained to read his face. What did Adam tell her once? "They are three types of Marines these days, Becky. They are either on their way to Vietnam, in Vietnam, or coming back from Vietnam."

Did this one have the brightness and eagerness of the newly trained who was ready to take his place in the fight? She looked more closely as he approached. Did he have the thousand-year fatigue in his eyes from the wear and tear of battle? Maybe he had hidden devils as Robert did, ready to jump out at every noise mimicking battle? Or perhaps he had a depth of sadness from reporting to another family about the loss of their loved one.

The Marine drew near, and his face had neither eagerness nor fatigue.

"Excuse me, ma'am?" He stopped in front of her, his head lowered to meet Rebecca's eyes. "I'm a little lost."

The sun struck and bounced off the shiny brass embellishments on his uniform. A good Marine.

"Yes?"

He touched the brim of his hat, barely moving the crisply pressed uniform. He stood stiffly as a new Marine would. His face looked too smooth and full to have recently come back from a war.

"You're in your dress khakis. A special occasion?"

"Yes, Ma'am. I'm getting ready to ship out, and I'm visiting family."

Clipper came over and sniffed the young man's ankles and shoes. His tail wagged. The Marine bent down and patted him.

"What's his name?"

"Clipper."

"My name's Timmy, er...Tim Norris." He looked up and smiled.

"Oh, I know some Norrises. So, you're shipping out. Trying to impress someone?" she teased. It had been a long time since she had had the energy to tease.

"Yes, ma'am. To both." He lost some of his stiffness and shifted from one foot to the other. "Can you tell me where Elm Street is?"

"Why, Elm Street is where I live. Whom are you looking for?"

"Just a friend."

"I would think a young man would know where his friends lived." She regretted her remark, which came out as more of a rebuke.

"It's a long story, ma'am." His gaze dropped. A slight blush reddened his face.

"Yes, I understand long stories. I do." A few leaves left over from last fall drifted in slow motion around the base of the wall.

"Whom are you looking for?" she asked again.

"Thank you, Ma'am, but if you point me in the right direction, I'll get on my way."

Rebecca pointed to a street outside the park. "That direction."

He tipped his hat and turned toward the direction she signaled.

So, the young man was on his way to war. Innocent, proud, strong. Fear for him rippled through Rebecca. She thought of Billy in his wheelchair, Robert so psychologically broken, Adam, un-viewable in his casket, her widow's flag at home.

Clipper and Rebecca walked home.

In the hallway, she hung up her coat and fed Clipper. "You liked that nice young man, didn't you?"

She turned on the radio and heard her favorite song of the day, Good Lovin' by the Young Rascals. The music transformed Rebecca. Alive again for a moment, she gyrated around the kitchen, bobbing her head to the beat of the music, lapsing into the Mashed Potato she had seen on American Band Stand. A few times she bent to pat a confused Clipper when she "peeled" the invisible potatoes. Poor thing. His eyes followed every gesture of her hands as though they had treats in them. "All I need is that good lovin." She sang while slapping the countertop. The music was too fast for the Mashed Potato. In spite of loving the free spirit of the music, she slowed her gyrations to catch her breath.

There was a knock at the front door. Breathing hard, she turned off the radio, went to the door, and looked through the door's peephole. There was the Marine she had seen in the park.

She opened the door, and before her was a very surprised young man.

"You live here?" he asked.

"Did you get lost again?"

He looked at a small sheet of paper in his hand. "I'm trying to visit them," he said, pointing to Jackson's house across the street, "but they don't seem to be home. Would you by any chance know when they'll be back?"

"Jacksons?"

"Yeah."

"You know them how?" she asked. "Excuse me for being a little protective of them."

"Oh, well, Mr. Jackson is my brother's former father-in-law, and he was also my former Scout leader."

"You look like you might have been an Eagle Scout, is that right?"

"Yes, ma'am."

"Wait a minute, do you have a brother named Robert?"

"Yes, ma'am."

"No kidding. I'm Rebecca Benson."

His face registered surprise, and he took a step back.

The world of secrets flung another arrow at her. What seemed to be too much of a coincidence was another reminder that hiding won't protect anyone from heat-seeking truth. Robert wasn't only Adam's buddy, he was also this young man's brother and Mr. Jackson's former son-in-law. He was the little brother Robert talked about.

"You're welcome to come and wait a spell. They shouldn't be gone long." This Marine looked legit, friendly, she thought.

"You're sure the dog won't mind?" he smiled and pointed to Clipper, who was wagging his tail and had that "pet me, pet me" look.

"My guard dog?" They both smiled. She stepped aside to let him in. A spring breeze followed the young man into the living room. "Sit anywhere, and I'll bring you a Coke."

She went into the kitchen to get the Cokes from the refrigerator, came back in, and sat on the sofa.

"I haven't seen you before today. Do you visit Mr. Jackson often?"

"Since I'm shipping out, I wanted to see 'im. He's a real war hero, you know." He took a swig of his Coke. "I have really good memories of 'im when I was in scouting, but I've never been to his house. He helped me a lot. I'm kind of fond of 'im, although my dad isn't. I want to see 'im, before I leave, in case, you know…"

"Don't say that, you'll be fine," she said with a flick of her hand.

"I guess I kind of went on and on, didn't I?"

He cleared his throat a couple of times, and he rubbed his knees and thighs with his hands, back and forth.

He inhaled deeply and adjusted his posture to face her. He opened his mouth, closed his mouth, and squared his shoulders. He looked at Rebeca directly. "My brother was in Vietnam, and he wrote me about you."

"Your brother? About me?"

"Yes, Robert Norris. He was a buddy of your husband."

"What did your brother write about me?"

"I'm not sure what to say." Timmy shifted in his chair; his eyes darted around the room. He looked out the window for signs of his grandparents. "He wrote me about your husband's death."

She gripped the arm of the sofa and leaned forward. "What did he say?"

"It's a lot of detail, soldier talk, you know. And my brother was trying to convince me to not to go Vietnam, so he told me the worst," he stammered. "I'm sorry I brought it up."

"If I could read the letter, I could somehow be with him, in his final moments. I want to know everything I can."

Rebecca knew she had the upper hand, an adult making a request of a young man.

"You would be doing me, and my husband, a good thing. I so wish I could have held him when he died. It would be a way to connect with him." Rebecca's voice cracked a little.

Timmy rubbed his knees again, back and forth, back and forth. "Most of his letters are back home, on the farm. I took a bus to see Mr. Jackson. Staying at a local motel."

Rebecca saw movement over at Jackson's and went to the window to see if they had returned. How could she maneuver a visit to Robert's?

"The Jacksons just pulled in. Why don't you tell me where you're staying, I'll pick you up in the morning and drive you back home. I know your brother pretty well; I don't think he would mind. You live on a farm, correct?"

Timmy stood up. "I can always accept a free ride home. It's a deal." He looked relieved.

"Great, I could use a country drive."

Rebecca leaned against the door she closed behind Timmy. The damn war. He was so fresh, so vulnerable, so untouched by battle.

And maybe she was going to learn more about Adam's last hours.

34

Rebecca drove the next morning to pick up Timmy at his motel. She was wide awake in spite of tossing and turning last night. In a few hours she was going to read about Adam in Robert's letters. When Timmy told her his brother Robert had written him the details of Adam's death in an ambush, that's all she could think about. Sure, the letter from his commanding officer gave details in military words, but an eye witness would be more intimate, more revealing.

One voice said, "You'll be sorry. You'll have that image in your head for the rest of your life." Another voice said, "But it's a way of knowing how he died." The winner of that inner argument was knowing, rather than not knowing. Maybe to bring closure to that gaping wound of grief.

A beeping horn stopped her ruminating, and she heard it trail off as it passed by her on the left. She looked at the road only to see that she was a little over the center line. Keep your eyes on the road, she told herself.

Robert had discouraged his brother from joining up. How did his parents feel? Adam had told her he had seen so many fathers push sons toward the military to "grow into a man," while the mothers' hearts were filled with terror. But he understood, "that's what men do—step up to the plate."

Her hands tightened on the wheel. Can't a boy become a man without fighting? Can't parents show their sons other ways to be a man? She sighed with confusion.

She pulled into the parking lot of the motel, an on-the-edge-of-town establishment that reminded her of The Bates Motel in *Psycho*—low ranch style L-shaped building, fronted by a wooden porch. She was hesitant to count the doors. If there had been twelve, like the movie, she might have bolted.

Timmy came out the door of the last room, Room 10, and he was dressed in blue slacks and one of those two-tone blue sweaters with a vertical front panel and rib-knit cuffs. And penny loafers. The buzz haircut gave away his military status.

"Hey, good looking!" he said as he threw his bag into the back seat and jumped into the car. He had a big grin that matched his animated figure, so different than his Marine bearing yesterday.

"Good looking? I like that," Rebecca said then laughed. "What brought about this happy heart?"

He turned to her while he was buckling his seat belt. "I looked out the window and saw your dynamite car. Who would have thought that I'd be riding in a Chevy Impala SS? A sport coupe, no less." He grinned as he looked at the interior, smoothing his hands over the white vinyl seats and chrome trim. "If this were red, it'd be perfect. A woman your age..." He gave her a sheepish look. "Sorry."

The "good looking" was for the car. *What is it with men and cars..*

"My husband gave it to me as a consolation prize when he decided to go to Vietnam. He was a police officer, you know, and appreciated horsepower, or whatever they call it. I named her Susie Q."

"Susie Q?" He looked at her with wide eyes. "That's not what I'd name a car like this."

"What would you name this car?"

He smiled. "Men don't name their cars."

"Oh, I see. Tell me. How did the visit with the Jackson's go?"

"I'm really glad I made the effort. Mr. Jackson is very proud of me." Timmy's face fell a little.

"What's wrong?"

Timmy's face snapped back to friendly and happy. "Oh, nothing."

Rebecca pulled onto the road.

"I've never taken this car over fifty-five miles per hour."

"No? You live an exciting life, don't you?" He grinned. "Try it a little."

She gently pressed on the accelerator until the speed gauge registered sixty.

"A little more."

Never had Rebecca paid attention to the sounds of an engine. After hearing its horsepower, she enjoyed the hum of the pistons that Timmy had explained.

Adam never told her about these things. A slow car in front and a clear left lane gave her the opportunity to try a little more aggression than her usual, dainty passing. She turned on the blinker and pulled left of the sluggish Ford sedan.

She pressed down on the accelerator and the car took off with a force that nearly made her lips curl back from her teeth. "Yeehaa!" she yelled.

Rebecca passed the Ford so fast she approached a hill before pulling back in her lane. Her varied and colorful life passed through her consciousness. When the hill came and went without an approaching car, she was able to breathe again. She slowed and pulled over. The Ford putted by and the driver honked his horn and shook his fist at her.

Timmy was gripping the door handle, his eyes as big as dinner plates. "That was close," he managed to say. The color returned to his face.

She shook from the enormity of what could have happened. "I'm so sorry."

"I hadn't considered that I might die before I got to Vietnam." He turned to her. "Is that what they mean by 'waking a sleeping giant?' As in, don't show a woman how to drive a sports car?"

"Oh no, Timmy. I wasn't thinking, I was stupid. Power in the wrong hands can end badly. That's me."

They smiled weakly at each other. After checking for any coming traffic, Rebecca pulled out onto the road and drove bucolically, like the Sunday drivers that everyone tries to pass.

"I appreciate that you are willing to share your letters with me," Rebecca said to break the awkward silence. "It means a lot."

"The letters? Is that why you're driving me back?"

"You look disappointed. I'm sorry. I'm desperate for anything about Adam."

"Are you sure you want to know what happened?"

"I have to, that's all."

Timmy looked ahead. "I'm not sure it's a good idea. I don't know how Robert will react when he sees you—or feel about me sharing the letters. But you do seem intent on closing chapters and all. Maybe I could just slip them to you."

Rebecca nodded.

"Besides, you have a great car, although you did give it a girly name."

Rebecca laughed. "Thanks for the endorsement."

Timmy was quiet again, and Rebecca was grateful. His comment about dying in Vietnam renewed her anger about the war.

Her curiosity returned. "How do you feel about going to Vietnam? Maybe that's a stupid question."

Staring straight ahead, he answered, "Not stupid at all since I can't quite decide how I feel. How did your husband feel? He volunteered, right?"

Her hands tightened on the wheel. "He felt it was his duty."

"Did you feel the same?"

"No." They rode in silence for a few miles. She sensed the questions Timmy wanted to ask, but she wasn't going to encourage him. The questions hung over her like perched birds that were waiting for the right moment to drop their shit.

"I'd really like to know."

The first plop of shit hit.

"It's complicated."

"Try me," Timmy said.

She didn't know what to say. She had heard many stories about mothers who cried and clung to their sons as they went off to war, trying to convince them to not go because they had a sixth sense that their sons were going to die. Other mothers steeled themselves and their jaws as they told their sons they would be fine. Most fathers swelled with pride and fear as they slapped their sons' backs and told them they were now men and should make their country proud. But whether they came back on foot or in a box seemed to have nothing to do with their send-off. At least that's what Rebecca told herself whenever she was tempted to replay her goodbye to Adam.

"I'd rather hear how you feel. You're the one who's shipping off." She kept her eyes on the road.

"I'm torn."

"How's that?" Rebecca stole a glance at his expression. He was looking out the window, his playfulness gone.

"I joined the Marines to avoid the Army draft. Bad grades my first quarter in college. I had the silly idea that class attendance was optional. Ha!"

"How did your parents react?"

"Disappointed. Dad was proud I joined the Marines. Mom was beside herself, yelling and crying at my dad for encouraging me to go to my death."

"I can understand that."

"My brother was furious. He's not doing so well, you know. He can't sleep. He jumps at any loud noise. He's always arguing about something. He told me he helped you go through your husband's personal effects. Too bad about the gold."

"Yeah."

"I understand it's a pretty well organized ring that bootlegs or confiscates bootlegged valuables. Yeah, you'll never see it."

"I have to admit I was surprised that Adam would be involved with something like that."

"My brother convinced him it would be a way to take care of you if something happened. I don't think he would have packed it himself."

"Were the two of them going to split it then? Why not pack some in your brother's locker?"

"Adam was the more trustworthy one. Given his spotty conduct, Robert's stuff would be, actually was, scrutinized pretty closely."

"That's what he told me. I just wanted confirmation. By the way, how's he doing?" Rebecca asked.

"When I graduated from boot camp he wrote me a kind of scary letter. He seemed to be going off the deep end."

"Scary in what way?"

"Let me read it to you. I carry it with me for some stupid reason. Maybe because I'm doubting my choice to join the Marines. I can't decide what Robert is trying to tell me. So I read it over 'n over." Timmy pulled a raggedy piece of paper from his wallet. "Just to warn you, my brother writes kind of flowery. Writes poetry too." He cleared his throat and read.

Hey, Timmy, guess I can't call you little brother anymore, having gotten through boot camp and all. I should probably let you grow up and call you Tim.

The flashbacks are worse than ever. I hope you don't mind that I tell you these things. Have no one else to talk to. I nearly cut off my finger slicing carrots when I heard a helicopter flying overhead the other day. The whomp, whomp sound took me right back to those medevacs, coming to pick up bodies. The cut-up carrot, the knife in my hand, my blood. Oh God, Timmy, the smell of blood and piss and rotting flesh was all around me. I was back there, Benson's body covered with that tarp...

Rebecca gasped.

Tim stopped and put the letter in his lap. "Are you sure you want me to go on? Can you drive okay and listen to this?"

"Y...yes."

Tim pulled the letter back for reading.

I was back there, I saw Benson's body covered with that tarp, and the other men, some dead and the rest moaning. The blood smells metallic and mixed with the helicopter fuel.... I hope you never experience it. At least Benson never felt anything, didn't suffer.

Rebecca sighed and said, "Thank God."

I'm back in the World, but I've really never left Vietnam, Timmy. The enemy is the lack of an enemy, and I see him everywhere. And hear him everywhere. A car backfires, and I duck. I almost threw up during the fireworks on July Fourth. I ran from the park and went home, closed all the windows, laid in bed with three pillows over my head, rocking until I finally fell asleep.

I thought I was doing some good by signing up. Courage turned out to be naiveté. Every gook I killed was revenge for my friends, and I got medals for it. Maybe the guys that run to Canada have more courage. I don't know, I'm not sure what courage is anymore. All I know is that I don't have it.

Don't mind me, Timmy. I'll be fine. Keep this between us though. I don't want to worry Ma.

Rebecca was silent, thinking about the time Robert ducked to the floor in her living room. She had made fun of him. And Adam, dead with a tarp over him.

"I'm so sorry, Timmy, I had no idea what your brother was going through," Rebecca said. "I made fun of his reacting to a car's backfire."

"It's hard for people to understand. He spent some months in a VA psychiatric ward over the holidays. He's been staying on the farm since then. Ma hovers over him like a hawk."

"Your brother told me he was in the hospital, but he was vague about it."

"Anyway, back to your question. You can see why I might be questioning whether I did the right thing in signing up. One moment my brother gives me the hoorah song about courage, the next moment he's hinting about Canada. He'll rant on about cry babies who can't face a man's job. In boot camp a few would question the war, and we were encouraged, shall we say, to beat that thought out of them."

"The Marines are tough…"

"I figure if I could get through boot camp, I could handle anything. I made a commitment, but why did Robert write me about all that if he didn't want me to consider options?"

"You'd be willing to go to Canada?" Rebecca couldn't hide her surprise. "Running? A Marine running from duty?"

"It's a bad war. Vietnamese people and Americans are dying for no good reason." He sat forward toward her. "You said you're against the war. Why can't I be against the war? Do I go anyway? Kill people I don't want to kill? It takes about six weeks for grunts in country to realize they are only pawns."

He sat back. "I don't want to go to Vietnam."

"Nobody wants to go to Vietnam. You sound pretty normal to me." Rebecca watched the road as a truck passed by.

"No, you don't understand. I'm NOT going to Vietnam."

Rebecca chanced a look at Timmy, keeping a sideways eye on the road. "Did you make that decision like, right now? I thought you were on the fence."

"Talking about it out loud made me realize what I want to do."

"You mean you are going to ignore orders? That's desertion."

"I know."

She took a hand from the wheel and pushed some hair behind an ear. "But running to Canada? I assume that's what you're going to do. You'd be leaving everything, everyone behind."

"Well, which do you think takes more courage—fight in a war you know is bad, and maybe die for nothing, or leave everything, including family and country behind, to avoid being part of the madness?"

Rebecca's knuckles ached from gripping the steering wheel. Timmy had thrown a cold bucket of reality on her. He had a choice, he had options for taking a stand against the war. But desertion? She tried to picture Adam's reaction. He would pace the kitchen, slam a hand down on the table, cry out, "How dare you shirk your duty?"

She drove on autopilot. Nothing existed outside that car. She couldn't hear the birds, the crickets, see the bluest of summer skies or smell the fields in their fullest green glory. The scenery flew by unnoticed.

"You can't abandon your country, or your fellow Marines. Is that the legacy you want to leave? To run from your duty? You signed up."

Beside her, silent, was Tim, cheek muscles twitching, mouth tightly set. "Being a little judgmental, aren't you?"

"I'm sorry. I've never talked to anyone who has or planned on going to Canada. Have you thought about applying for that status they call conscientious objector?"

"CO doesn't mean 'conscientious objector' to the Marines. They are the first two letters of 'coward.' By the way, turn on County Road 56."

Up ahead Rebecca saw the turn-off, and she eased Susie Q onto the dirt road.

"It's the first farmhouse on the right," Timmy said. "I'm sorry you won't meet my parents. They are visiting family in Toledo."

She pulled into the gravel driveway alongside a pristine white clapboard farmhouse surrounded by geraniums and white daisies. Cornfields grew behind, beside, and across the road. Just as she had pictured a farm to be. She parked the car, and they got out.

"Something's not right. Usually the dogs come and greet me," said Timmy, "I think I see them cowering under the porch."

"Robert, I'm home," he called to the back door.

No answer. Timmy opened the side screen door and stepped aside to let Rebecca in. "Goes straight to the kitchen."

With Timmy behind her, she entered. Robert sat on a chair, pushing the barrel of a shotgun under his chin, the butt on the floor, his thumb on the trigger.

35

"Robert, Robert, what are you doing?"

"Get out of here."

Rebecca stood aside and let Timmy go forward. He took a tentative step toward his brother, and Robert jammed the shotgun tighter against his chin.

"No, don't, Robert! What's happening?"

Robert cried. "I can't get the war out of my head." His eyes wild, he glanced around the room, doubt crossed his face.

Rebecca whispered to herself, Adam, Adam, tell me what to do. Her heart pounding, she stepped forward with her palms facing Robert. "Adam wouldn't want you to do this."

"Why him and not me? At least he had something to come home to."

His hold on the shotgun loosened but tightened again when Timmy took another step. "Don't stop me."

"You had us to come home, to me and Ma and Pa," Timmy said.

"They're old, and you're going to war and not coming back. I know it. Why did you have to go and join the fucking Marines? I told you not to," Robert said between sobs. "What use am I to anybody?"

"No one knows why you were spared," Rebecca said, not sure where the words were coming from—maybe Adam? "But you were spared, and you came home. And with all your arms and legs. Your family is here to help you come all the way home."

"I can't get the pictures out of my head, so much blood, body parts blown yards away. And I did it too." Robert closed his eyes and grimaced. ""I blew heads away. Damn gooks." He looked at Timmy. "Don't go, don't become what I've become."

Timmy stood as though he were nailed to the floor. His face ashen, his hands to his side, fingers twitching. He fell on his knees. "You're my big brother, you can't do this."

Robert gritted his teeth and shoved the shotgun farther into his neck, his skin beginning to enfold the steel.

"I saw those demonstrators in Washington, holding up their baby killer signs. They were describing me. Every time I close my eyes, I see what I did." Robert's face was wet with his tears.

Rebecca shouted, "How dare you!"

Timmy and Robert looked at Rebecca in surprise, and her next words came from somewhere outside of her.

"Adam gave his life, and you're going to waste yours? Do you want to throw that final grenade into the lives of the people who love you?" Her body felt on fire. "It will explode again and again in their hearts." She walked softly toward Robert, his face registering disbelief. She forced herself to not look at the shotgun pressing into his neck. She laid her hand on his forearm. Dropping her voice, she said, "You matter to a lot of people regardless of what you think you've become. Please don't."

"Yeah? Watch this."

The click of the safety thundered in Rebecca's ears. She grabbed Timmy, helped him up off the floor and pulled him out of the kitchen, out the back door.

"Robert. Robert!" Timmy's hands reached back to his brother.

"I don't want you to see this," she said to Timmy. He fought her grasp, but she persisted, and they stumbled down the steps. They clung to each other and waited. Right or wrong, she didn't know what else to do. "Please don't, please don't," Rebecca prayed.

The windows shook from the shotgun blast, and the noise exploded their ears. Rebecca couldn't hold back her sobs—sobs for Adam who died and didn't want to, sobs for Robert because he had lost his will to fight his inner enemies, sobs for Timmy who had to watch his big brother morph into a wounded child. And she sobbed for herself, who couldn't escape the claws of an awful war that grabbed at soldiers whether they were in the jungle or back home.

Through her tears she looked up at Timmy, who was staring at the kitchen steps. There stood Robert, shotgun hanging loosely from his right hand. "I'm a failure at this too," Robert sobbed.

Timmy stood and ran to him. He grabbed the firearm, emptied the shotgun, and threw the remaining shells into a bed of daisies. He hugged his brother. Brother held on to brother while time stopped. When the world started to spin again, each looked at the other with the deepest exchange of understanding that could possibly be transmitted between two siblings.

They walked into the house, the screen door slamming.

Rebecca stood frozen. Her body was exhausted by the drama she had witnessed and by the words that she had spoken, whether they were really her words at all.

She looked around and saw an old tire swing that hung from a much older oak tree that shaded the kitchen side of the house. She climbed into the ring and with a push of her toes swung back and forth, not thinking at all, yet aware of the air brushing past her. It was right to give the brothers some time.

Not sure it was real at first, she felt Adam's hands gently push her from behind, giving her momentum to go forward and backward into his presence. Forward momentum had its limit, and she swung backward to Adam's reassuring touch on her back. Real or not, it didn't matter. Her heartbeat slowed. The rhythmic movement through the breeze cocooned her from the tortuous past ten minutes. Two fat farm dogs emerged from under the porch, waddled over and lay at the base of the tree beside her.

Soon she heard the sirens of an ambulance and a police car coming down the lane. Two medical drivers and two policemen sprinted into the house. Rebecca waited.

The screen door screeched again, and Robert came out escorted by a police officer and one of the ambulance attendants. They gently put him in the back of the police car and left. The ambulance followed.

Timmy stood on the porch and gestured for her to follow him. He had some envelopes in his hand.

Rebecca slowed her swinging and climbed out of the tire. A tender touch gently pushed her a step toward Timmy.

"He's in good hands. He'll get some help."

Rebecca nodded.

"You said you want to read Robert's letters about Adam."

The hole in the ceiling of the kitchen was too much of a reminder of Robert's pain. Timmy made them both a cup of tea and went into the living room where Rebecca sat. The rising steam of the tea provided a kind of comfort, even for a warm summer day.

Timmy placed an opened envelope before her. The paper was thin military issue, the address was to Timothy Norris. With steady hands she pulled out the two pages of handwriting.

March 15, 1966
Tay Ninh Province, South Vietnam
Hey little brother, you're always asking what it's like here. I'll tell you, but don't let on to Ma. This was one of my saddest days.

Our platoon of ARVNs (the South Vietnamese soldiers) made as little sound as possible as we made our way across the dikes of the rice paddy, parallel to a tree line on the left. Fifty yards. Only fifty yards to the village we were to search and clear. I'll tell ya, even though we were surrounded by flooded rice paddies (which stink, by the way) my mouth was as dry as our farm in August. The men, spread out as they had been trained, scanned the edges of the woods, turning this way and that to see what couldn't be seen, rifles poised but safeties on. Like when we go hunting, eh, Timmy? My buddy and fellow advisor, Gunnery Sergeant Adam Benson stayed beside the Vietnamese commander who directed the ARVN soldiers with silent hand signals. I watched carefully, taking direction from Benson.

They say you don't hear the round that hits you, only the ones that hit someone else. I heard a bullet sing and slice its way from the tree line. I saw Benson spin and crumple. When I reached him, his eyes were already vacant, looking toward nothing. The back of his head was gone. I could have prayed but it would have been useless— another goddamn waste.

Rebecca put the letter down on the table. The urge to vomit was so strong, she leaped up and ran to the kitchen sink. A few dry heaves later, and tears falling where vomit should have fallen, she hung onto the sink, leaning on her elbows. Finally, she stood.

"Are you sure you want to go on?" Timmy asked.

"You're right, he didn't feel anything, did he?"

"I wouldn't think so," he said.

"I think the worst is over." She walked back to the table, sat down, and picked up the letter with shaking hands.

36

Rebecca glanced at Timmy. He nodded.

I looked toward the woods where the shot came and saw the slightest movement of a human form. I yelled, "đi đi," and the men scrambled to the adjacent tree line. To Benson I whispered, "I'll be back." The ambush erupted in front and to the side of us, making the mud and paddy water dance in bursts of filthy spray. We made it to the tree line and returned fire. After fifteen minutes the only sounds were coming from our rifles. Then all was quiet, and we were able to retrieve Benson and the five other casualties.

The heat and sun are not good to the dead, but I insisted that extra care be taken when wrapping Benson in a tarp. More un-viewables. Their families will be haunted by what they imagine is in the metal coffins they would receive.

I couldn't help but think of Benson's wife who wanted her husband home and a future with kids. Now she would have neither. Never met her, but Benson told me plenty. He'd light up like a firefly talking about her quirkiness, her questioning mind.

Rebecca looked up and smiled at Timmy. "I'm glad he liked my quirkiness."

What the hell are we doing here? Timmy, you stay in school and avoid this god damned war.

Your brother Robert

She folded the letter, taking care to follow the folds to make it fit into the envelope. She looked up at Timmy, blurry through the tears in her eyes. He handed her a tissue and presented another letter.

"You need to read this too. It will help you understand Robert's craziness about Adam's box of personal effects. Are you up for it?"

Adam was near. Rebecca felt his hands ever so gently on her shoulders.

"Yes." She grabbed the cup of tea and drank, letting the warmth comfort her throat. "May I have more, please?"

Timmy brought more tea.

She took a deep breath.

March 16, 1966
Tay Ninh Province, South Vietnam
Timmy, here's the rest of the story...
Back in camp I went into the tent I shared with Benson and headed for his cot. Knowing that I would never see Benson again on that cot was like getting hit in the gut. A photo of his wife sat on the crate beside the bed, and a small wooden box held his wedding ring and a small field Bible. He never wore his wedding ring into the field, fearing that a land mine would pulverize him and the ring. "Something has to go home in one piece," he told me. Kind of scary, huh?

I opened his locker to a pile of folded uniforms, underwear, and stuff (Benson kept his area cleaner than a momma cat). I was trying really hard not to cry, Benson being such a good buddy. The guys here all hide behind the words "it don't matter." It did make me smile when I saw the unopened bottle of hot sauce. We use that to make C-rats palatable, if possible. You think Spam is bad?

She stopped reading to say to Timmy, "I sent him hot sauce every week." She went back to the letter.

What I was looking for was hidden in some Fruit of the Loom socks, ultra-white, telling me they had never been worn and probably never would have been. Socks make jungle rot worse. The folks back home don't get it. Maybe it's good they don't, I dunno. But I figure you're old enough to understand.

I felt the gold bars in the first pair where Benson told me they would be. Now these aren't Fort Knox kind of bars, they are paper-thin sheets of gold, easy to transport. We found them in an abandoned hooch, guy must have been in a hurry...saw us coming, Ha! Benson and I had made a pact to provide for our wives this way—for whoever did not make it. Anyway, since my wife skipped out on me, my gold bars will go to you, and you use them to make sure Ma has what she needs. I hid them in a hidden compartment at the bottom of a small, wooden box where the guys in personal effects would not find them.

Lt. Attwell, an officer from Mortuary Service, showed up at the entrance of the tent. He came to collect Benson's things, but I was able to close the box before we exchanged salutes. That was close. I'm pretty sure he didn't see me hide the gold.

Going "humping" (out in the field) for a few weeks, so you may not hear from me as often.

STAY IN SCHOOL, little brother.

Rebecca laid the letter down and fixed her gaze on the calendar towel hanging on the wall next to the refrigerator. "Adam was thinking of me all along, wasn't he?" she said to Timmy but talking to the calendar.

"Yes."

"I'm exhausted and need to go home. Thank you for showing me the letters. I think I understand things a little better, as hard as it was." She gave Timmy a hug. "Are you going to be alright?"

"Yeah, have a lot a' thinking to do."

"Me too," Rebecca replied. "I'm glad you called the police. Your brother needed help." She paused. "What are you going to do now?"

"I don't know. That's what the heavy thinking has to do with. When Ma and Pa come home, I need to tell them what happened. See ya around, I guess."

"Please stay in touch. Let me know what you do." She gave Timmy a half smile and a hug.

She walked out the kitchen to the outside. As she neared her car, the tire swing moved ever so gently back and forth like a friendly wave. One of the dogs, sound asleep on his side, twitched his paws as though he were running after a long-sought prize.

Rebecca pulled out of the driveway and drove slowly back into town. Poor Timmy. What was the difference between courage and judging cowardice? What was it that

Billy once said? "I always felt that anyone dodging the draft meant that someone else's number would come up. I didn't want anyone else to take the hit for me."

And Robert? Was that cowardice? The lack of courage to face the life that was in front of him? Or was it out of his control?

She drove down Main Street whose stores were flying their flags, onto Vine Street where homes had American flags cut from the newspaper and taped to their front doors. An occasional house had a small fabric flag hanging from a front window, rectangular with a red border and a blue start in the center, indicating the dwellers had a son or daughter serving in the military. One house had two blue star flags. One of the stars was covered by a smaller gold star—a service member had died. Sadness seemed to hang over the modest house, branded by the small star of sacrifice. She had one of those flags but had never placed it on her window. It would a perpetual reminder of loss, to be seen every time she came home. *Maybe I need to rethink that.*

She parked the car in front of the house, turned the motor off, and didn't move. She slid her fingers along the smooth plastic of the steering wheel, smooth on top, wavy with finger grips underneath. Up and around the shiny hardness, up and around, using the repetitive motion to clear her head. Each lap of her fingers on the wheel brought to mind the Vietnam soldiers she had met and come to know: Robert, mentally haunted and damaged by what he saw in the jungle; Billy, physically damaged but mentally driven to make some sense of the hell he experienced; and now Timmy, torn between his allegiance to his fellow soldiers or by his personal convictions that tell him this war wasn't worth dying for. And of course, Adam, ever-loyal-to-his-country Adam.

Her fingers stopped their revolutions at about two o'clock on the steering wheel. "Adam," she pleaded aloud, "where do I go from here?" She watched a crow perched on top of the roof. Even the crow was silent.

She went into the house and retrieved the gold starred flag from the closet where she had tossed it. She held it to her heart and walked to the kitchen to get some tape. In the living room, she carefully hung the memorial flag on the picture window.

37

Summer changed into days heavy with heat and humidity. Rebecca retreated into a clamshell of no decisions and no conclusions. She peeked out from time to time. She watched the news, went to DAR meetings with Ruth, attended occasional protest meetings with Irene in Columbus, and half-heartedly conducted her secretary tasks at the church. Occasional visits with Aunt Debra gave Rebecca an outlet for her grief about Robert's attempted suicide. She listened to the patriotic rhetoric of the townspeople who scoffed at antiwar professors leading their students down the hellish road to Communism.

Rebecca continued to collect information and observations like a squirrel preparing for fall, but she didn't know what to do with the bounty she was gathering. Instead of burying acorns to be eaten throughout the coming winter like a squirrel did, she put her bounty in some remote corner of her mind. Each meeting she attended ended with an exit to muggy air that produced a sticky sweat that ran down her face, pooled in the cups of her bra, and moistened the backs of her knees and the crooks of her elbows. Those were the only concrete sensations she had.

In the evenings she took a daiquiri out to the back porch and sipped the drink while she read Timmy Norris' letters from Vietnam. He called her "Auntie Becky." He decided against going to Canada, and the U.S. Marine

Corps made the rest of his decisions. And though his
letters bragged to Rebecca that he was doing fine, she
read a different story between the lines. He was sick most
of the time, and he focused on the job ahead of him, which
was to stay alive and help his buddies stay alive.
Whenever one of the information nuggets she had stored
away would try to sneak into her consciousness, especially
if it rang an alarm of danger for Timmy, she pushed it
back into its storage bin.

Her one small comfort was the memorial flag hanging
in the front window. Adam had been brave, Adam died
doing what he believed in. And she loved him. The flag
represented Adam, but not her. She wasn't sure what her
flag would look like.

On one of those humid evenings, when even the frozen
daiquiri didn't cool her, Rebecca fanned herself with an
unfolded newspaper she hadn't yet read. She closed her
eyes, flapped the paper back and forth, feeling the push of
the sultry air, getting little relief. She opened her eyes to
open the paper to make a bigger fan. On the front page of
the newspaper, above the fold, was the photo of Timmy
Norris and the headline "Local Marine Killed in Action."
All the grief she had pushed down made its painful thrust
into her heart.

Rebecca saw the tears at the Liberty Cemetery fall easily
from the people who attended Timmy's funeral. Timmy,
hailed as a hometown hero, drew a large crowd of
townspeople who stood shoulder to shoulder around the
funereal tent and at a depth of five gravestone rows back.

Rebecca watched as Robert Norris arrived with his
parents—father stoic in his World War Two uniform, the

mother barely controlling her sobs, and Robert. He was as gray as the granite that announced the short life of Timothy Norris. In contrast to his father's formal military dress, Robert wore the jungle fatigues he wore in Vietnam, and he had a black ribbon across his medals. He stared straight ahead.

The Jacksons also came to honor the boy Mr. Jackson molded into an Eagle Scout. Ol' Man Jackson wore his WWI uniform, which hung on his frail frame. Mrs. Jackson held on to her husband's arm as though she might fall to the ground if she didn't have his support. Mr. Jackson caught Rebecca's eye and gave her a saddened nod.

A taxi pulled up, and Rebecca saw the driver get Billy's wheelchair from the trunk and help him get into his chair. Billy churned his wheelchair through the fine graveled path to the funeral tent. He, like Robert, wore his old fatigues. He was not wearing his Vets Against the War vest.

Rebecca gritted her teeth and clenched her fists to not bolt from the too familiar scene. Flashes of memories assaulted her as she stood unhearing and mute during the prayers: her father's cotton arm billowing from his uniform, her father smiling at her, Adam looking so handsome, Adam turning to see Rebecca's back before he got on the plane, Billy in his wheelchair, Robert with the gun to his throat. And Timmy, smiling so bravely in spite of his fear and doubt.

She was surprised and delighted to see Aunt Debra at the funeral. Aunt Debra was one of the first people she relied on after Timmy's death. She had become a rock of support.

She steeled herself for the firing of the guns during the twenty-one-gun salute. The booms she heard made her jump, and a moment of panic traveled through her. When the folded flag was handed to Timmy's mother, the air around Rebecca thinned, and she fought to stay upright. Her heart pounded to the rhythm of a bass drummer, growing bolder and harder as she watched the anguish in Mrs. Norris' face. TA-dum, TA-dum. Did she see anger behind those mother tears?

When she was able to breathe again, a familiar mass of emotion rose, and she wanted to scream "Don't you see? Don't you see we all had a part in Timmy's death? We killed him." Rebecca took a deep breath before the anger burst its ugly contents onto the people around her, but it left a bitter taste in her mouth as it retreated back into its hiding place.

At the end of the service, Billy rolled up to her and said, "Hell of a waste, don't you think?"

"I need to talk to you," Rebecca said. "Someplace private."

Rebecca and Billy sat in one of the meeting rooms of the church that owned the cemetery. Easy for Billy to access, private for their conversation. Before she sat down, she pulled a box of tissues from a shelf and placed it on the table. She gave Billy a thin smile. "For me, not you."

Billy took her hand into his hands. "What's going on?"

The compassion in Billy's warrior's hands comforted her. Hands that held a rifle, hands that threw grenades, hands that groped the burning wounds on his own body, hands that had become hands of healing for her. She opened her mouth to explain her emotions, but nothing came out. Her eyes filled. Her struggle to not cry and the fight to get out the words she wanted to say created an internal warfare. And she was losing.

Billy rolled his chair beside her, took her in his arms, and asked, "What can I do to help?" He stroked her hair and held her with the softness and confidence of someone who knew exactly what she was feeling.

Rebecca let it all go. Her confusion. Her grief. Her helplessness. Her loneliness. Once the dam of emotions breeched, she had no control, and didn't want any, anymore. She held onto Billy as though she were trying not to let go of the edge of a cliff. She didn't care how loud she cried or how Billy reacted.

When she was spent of tears, Billy handed her a clump of tissues. It took several to blow her nose and dry her eyes, and a small pile of used tissues sat on the table as evidence of her overwhelming emotions.

"I must have needed that," Rebecca said with a sheepish look and a final sniff.

"You did, and I'm glad I was here. I didn't have anyone to share my grief. No one would let me have any. I'm happy you trust me."

Rebecca looked at him. "I'm tired of hiding from the war, I'm tired of learning about the war. I'm sick of feeling so helpless, but I don't know what to do. My friends, people around me, even Adam once, claim they are patriotic, but say I'm not because I question things." She gestured toward Billy. "The people you hang with say they are the patriots." She sniffed again and used another tissue to wipe her nose.

"A lot of people confuse patriotism with blind loyalty." Billy folded his hands and took a deep breath.

"What is it then? Was Adam 'blind?'"

Billy leaned forward, put his elbows on the table, and looked directly into Rebecca's eyes.

"Your Adam was patriotic in the fullest sense. He thought he was helping preserve what our country was built upon. If he had had the information you have, he would be confused, I bet." Billy leaned back. "But even smart, good-meaning people get mislead by folks who have more to gain by siding with the government. You gotta be open to ideas that are counter to how you're usually thinking."

"I don't know how to think, except that Timmy's death has pushed me to be part of ending a war, rather than standing by."

Billy looked at her sideways and tried to read what she really meant. "Are you ready to do more than go to meetings and read more articles that all say the same thing?"

"What do you mean?"

"I mean, become one of us. Put Timmy in your mind. Use your anger to be active rather than stewing in a pot of bitter feelings."

She looked at him, her head tilted, her arms folded. "So, you think I'm stewing?"

Billy pried her hands from the defensive posture she clung to. "Yes. Help us make a difference. Honor Timmy and your husband and all the other young boys that will be dragged to 'Nam because our government won't own up to what it really knows and does."

"Protests make people mad. They don't seem to be helping."

"Bit by bit," Billy said, "protests move us forward, gather supporters with each pamphlet, each placard, each body."

"Rebecca Benson a protestor?" She shook her head and rolled her eyes. "Wouldn't the folks in Liberty be shocked?"

"Precisely," Billy said.

38

Rebecca strolled alone along the sidewalk and pondered how her decision to support the anti-war effort was going to affect her life.

And what form of protest to take? Images came to her from licking envelopes to handing out pamphlets to standing in the street shouting at people who shouted back. Her heartbeat went from normal to nervous as she considered the increasingly public, and risky, choices.

Reputation in a small town like Liberty was as sacrosanct as going to church on Easter. If you didn't attend services on that day of Christian days, you weren't a Christian. If a person spoke against the government, you weren't American. God and country. The young boys who ran to Canada—did their choices make any difference to the war makers? Certainly, to their families.

Rebecca pulled back the imaginary curtains that hid what she feared, and the faces of Rebecca's accusers floated in front of her, brows furrowed and index fingers pointing at her. Ruth Middleton, pin wearing bastion of the DAR, Annie, tending to the wounded in Vietnam. Robert, wearing his nightmares on his sleeve. The bridge ladies, clucking about the long-haired kids who had nothing better to do than cause trouble in the streets. Her mother, speaking and living patriotism in honor of her own husband and of her daughter's husband.

In the park, she found her favorite bench and sat. In her mental house of fear, she turned from the accusers toward her supporters, her cheerleaders, her new friends. They sat comfortably and stood easily in the imaginary gathering. Their smiles were warm and encouraging. They looked directly into her eyes, no averted gazes like the accusers. Irene in her madras. Billy in his wheelchair, sure in his purpose. Timmy in his uniform, giving her a thumbs up. The young people and veterans at the meetings she had attended.

She couldn't picture Adam in either setting. She shut her eyes, and as hard as she strained to bring Adam into either scene, he refused to enter. Rebecca opened her eyes to view reality—the trunks and swaying green leaves of large trees that had been silently watching hundreds of people walk, sit, and chat through the decades, probably centuries. They were still standing. The people were not.

She pulled out a newspaper from her coat and read the headlines: "Westmoreland asks for more troops." More boys, more death. She looked up to see a couple of women from the bridge club walking towards her. Rebecca smiled. The ladies gave thin-lipped responses and moved on. One said to the other in a loud whisper, "Imagine, her husband was a Marine, and she's into all that anti-war malarkey."

So that's what it's like. Friendship is based on having the same opinions. The whispered comment she heard cut her more deeply than honestly hurled words of criticism. She'd rather be called a Commie.

Rebecca came home to Clipper's happy greeting. "I need to revisit Adam, to hear Adam's voice, in the footlocker," she said to Clipper. She gave him a quick pat and headed for the footlocker she had stashed in the newly decorated, unused bedroom she had never returned to. She sat on the floor, opened the lid, and shuffled through the contents. *Where are you Adam? Can you speak to me? Would you hate me if I publicly came out against the war you so proudly fought in?*

She set aside things that didn't speak to her, the envelope of coins, the socks, the box that had no gold. She stopped when she saw the blood-stained watch. She held it in her hand and wondered whether that blood was spilled for a good reason. Adam would think so. She placed it in a separate pile. Next she saw the Zippo lighter with UUUU crudely carved into the scratched chrome. She needed to ask Billy about that.

She looked at the books *Armageddon* by Leon Uris and *The Good Soldier Švejk*. She set them aside with the lighter and the watch. She fondled the wedding ring on the chain she wore. After taking it off, she looked at it with new understanding. She held the ring in her hand and inspected it with the eye of an x-ray technician. What secrets did the gold have within its metallic composition? Is Adam's energy still locked in the band? Stumbling with the catch, she put it back on her neck. *It's home again.* Nothing else spoke to her, and she put all but the set aside items back into the footlocker.

First item, call Billy.

"Well, that was a common carving on those lighters. It means 'the unwilling, led by the unqualified, doing the unnecessary for the ungrateful.' Interesting that he would have that. A change of heart, maybe?"

"Maybe. I don't know."

Rebecca hung up the phone and continued to examine the pile for possible evidence of Adam's state of mind. Looking at the inside flap of *Armageddon* she read that the book was about the Berlin airlift after World War II. "Captain Sean O'Sullivan faces profound moral choices..."

She lay the book down only to be nuzzled and licked by Clipper. "Go lie down, you silly dog."

She picked up *The Good Soldier Švejk*. On the cover she saw that it was about the Czechs, participating in a conflict they didn't understand on behalf of an Austrian emperor to which they had no loyalty.

She recalled the Vietnam vets, the long-haired men, and Joan Baez-y women holding up placards and chanting at the anti-war meetings. *Eighteen today, dead tomorrow; I don't give a damn for Uncle Sam, I'm not going to Vietnam.* She thought of the "patriotic" citizens outside with their placards "America-love it or leave it."

Maybe Billy was right. Maybe Adam had been having a change of mind. Why wouldn't he say something in his letters? Pride? Didn't want to admit he was wrong? Both volumes had the look of reading material that had been passed around to quite a few hands. The books had stains and rips on their covers, the pages were tattered, and some were loose.

The light coming in the bedroom window faded and threatened to leave Rebecca in the dark. She realized that she hadn't had lunch or dinner—her appetite had yielded to the task in front of her. She had neither the time nor the urge to put anything in her stomach.

"Here, boy." With Clipper in her lap, Rebecca reached over and turned on a light and continued to scrutinize the momentous pile in front of her, willing it to talk to her.

"Why is it so hard to do what I need to do, Clipper? I've never been in a war, but I think people's opinions are my enemy." She buried her fingers into his soft fur and let the heat from his body travel up her hand. She hugged him. "I suppose it doesn't matter whether Adam would approve or not. He's not here, but I am. I don't want any more Adams or young boys like Timmy to die."

She took *The Good Soldier Švejk* to bed with her. With Clipper pressed up against her legs, Rebecca opened the first page and read. The last words she absorbed before she fell into that welcome abyss of sleep were "Preparations for the slaughter of mankind have always been made in the name of God or some supposed higher being which men have devised and created in their own imagination."

39

Billy was the first to arrive at Rebecca's gathering to prepare materials for a Cleveland protest, Rebecca's first. A pot of chili simmered on the stove for later sustenance.

"That's a mysterious item you have in your hand," she remarked as Billy lay a small Woolworth's bag on the table.

"Go on, open it. It's for you."

"You shouldn't have," she laughed.

"It's for your snack time, when you get a craving. I had to get here a little early so you wouldn't have to share it with anyone."

"Oh." She peered into the bag and saw familiar cellophane wrapping. "Oh my goodness! Chuckles!"

Billy beamed as she took out the Chuckles package. Unwrapping it, she asked, "How perfect! No one has ever bought me Chuckles even though people know I'm crazy about them. Not even for Easter."

"I like them too, you know, but I hope we don't have to fight over our favorite flavors."

"You couldn't possibly like the same ones I do. People tend to give away my favorite, fortunate for me."

"Try me," Billy said. He cocked his head.

She pulled out the black licorice Chuckle and posed with it near her protruding tongue.

"No way." He shook his head. "I guess we'll have to divide it." He grabbed it from her and took a bite.

"Pretty equal bite," she said.

The doorbell rang, and the chatter of several people was heard on the front stoop.

"Let's greet them with black teeth," Billy said.

"My kind of guy."

Chatter bounced back and forth between war news, family happenings, and what was to be expected at the protest. The gathering of people stood around Rebecca's dining room table, supplied with markers, posters, duct tape, and pamphlets.

Rebecca looked at the congregation: Ruth, converted to the anti-war scene because of a nephew's death; Betsy, also from the DAR, because she decided the purpose of patriotism was to make her government accountable; Irene, her madras wearing, pot smoking buddy who supported her questioning; Billy, the guy who had been there, and helped her work through Adam's viewpoint. They and five more made an assembly line of citizens creating the tools of their trade—large signs to carry at the next protest to be held in Cleveland, Ohio.

"I want to thank everyone for coming. And a big welcome to Adam's aunt Debra, who came all the way from Zanesville." Rebecca pointed to Debra and gave a thumbs up." As you know, I've had a hard time coming to this point." She heard a light laugh and smiled. "We all have the same goal, fighting against a war that's fighting the wrong things. But, we should always be mindful of the needs of those who are called to service, whether by the government or by their own volition."

The group applauded, and they got to work.

"I'm a little nervous, but we have to make a stand somehow," said Irene as she drew in big letters 'Support our military, bring our boys home.'

"There will be protestors and anti-protestors. Both will be angry," Billy said.

"You've made a big decision, Rebecca," Irene said. "You seem so sure of what you're doing. What made you take the leap?"

"Oh gosh." Rebecca gazed up at the ceiling. "Anti-war or anti this war? It was a combination of things, I suppose. Timmy's death, Robert's regrets, and...anything that was not reported by the government. And I've decided that Adam, had he come home, would have been like you, Billy," she nodded toward him. "But I have to admit, if he hadn't changed his opinions, we would have had some pretty big arguments." She smiled to think she was able to joke about Adam.

"Have you heard from Annie?" Irene asked.

Rebecca shook her head. "Poor Annie. She serves as a triage nurse, and though she's gotten pretty good at it, the decisions she has to make are really difficult. Most importantly, she feels she's making a contribution." Rebecca finished a sign and passed it down to Aunt Debra, whose job was to staple it solidly to a pole.

"Sure hope the guys in 'Nam don't think we're against them. It makes me nervous to be lumped into the same group as the idiots who are going way overboard, calling vets 'baby-killers,'" Ruth said.

"Me, too," Rebecca said.

The group fell silent a few minutes, each person focused on his or her task—deciding which slogan to write, getting the next piece of poster board. Rebecca stole several glances at Billy, hoping he would say something. He didn't.

"What can we expect when we get to Cleveland, Billy?" Rebecca asked.

"Yes, the elephant in the room is what we're all in for," Ruth said. Everyone looked at Billy, the only one in the group who had been in a major protest.

He kept his head down, concentrating on putting poster boards back to back. "Things are heating up. Folks are tired of punks and hippies causing trouble. Police are getting more forceful. Don't do anything aggressive. Just hold up the damn signs." He kept working, his eyes on his task.

"Look at what happened in Alabama. Cracking people's heads open," Rebecca said.

Billy looked up. "We've talked in the meetings about possible violence. This ain't no picnic. You all realize that, don't you?" He gave everyone a hard stare. "Those crowds aren't Viet Cong, waiting in a line of trees to ambush you. They are going to be in your face." Rebecca felt a shiver.

"You do look troubled, Billy," she said. She looked at him. His experiences didn't make him bitter but wiser and more determined. That's how she always thought her father would have been, if he had lived long enough to witness other wars.

"You staring at me?" Billy asked her with a laugh.

Her face burned. "I was thinking how remarkable it is that you aren't bitter and angry like Robert is."

"Oh, I'm angry alright, but I'm using that anger. Using it smart, using it to, shall we say, enlighten those sons o' bitches in Washington."

"Have you been reading about Martin Luther King, Jr.?" Irene asked. "He said he refused to accept that nations have to slide down a militaristic stairwell into hell, or something like that. Pretty powerful words, I think."

"I hope his opinion has some impact on Washington," someone else answered.

"It's already made an impact on the FBI," Ruth said. "That's not what our country is about."

"All I know is," said someone opening a pack of markers, "I sat on my bum thinking how I hated this war, then I saw you fine folks making a stand. I knew I had good folks to stand with."

The doorbell rang, and everyone jumped. Rebecca opened the door to the mailman, who was holding a mangled letter—crumpled, taped in spots.

For Rebecca the world froze. She recognized the military stationary, her address in Adam's handwriting. She put a hand on the door jamb to steady herself and put her other hand out to receive the letter.

"Sorry, Mrs. Benson," the mailman said. "Letters fall into cracks and get found by the darndest circumstances, cleaning ladies even." He turned and went down the few steps to the sidewalk.

Billy rolled up to her. "What's wrong?"

Still leaning against the door, she said, "It's a letter from Adam."

The chatter stopped in the room. Billy looked toward everyone and gave a nod toward the door. He took Rebecca's hand and gently led her to the sofa. He positioned his wheelchair so he sat in front of her.

The workers filed out except for Irene, who stopped to give her a hug. "I've turned off the stove for you. The chili needs to cool for a while. Call me when you're ready." She gave Billy an approving nod. The door closed behind them all.

"Do you want me to leave while you read the letter?" Billy asked.

Rebecca looked up at him and shook her head. Carefully and with shaking hands, she opened the envelope.

"Oh my God," she said. "This was written on the day he died."

Billy closed his eyes and gave Rebecca the privacy she needed to read Adam's last words.

"No, Billy, I want you to read it...out loud. Please. I can't."

Billy reached for the letter and took a deep breath.

Dear Becky, I hope this finds you well, darling. I'm heading out on patrol today with Robert. The guys we're training are getting better and even learning to clean their weapons properly!

I love you so much, and we've always promised to be honest with each other, right? For some reason, I have to apologize for something that's been on my mind.

Billy looked at Rebecca. "You sure you want me to read this?"

"Yes," she said in an almost indiscernible voice.

The day I left for training was not our best day, and I was angry that you were not more supportive. I'm so sorry, darling, that I didn't turn and blow you a kiss when I boarded the plane. You chose to ignore that in your letters.

You could have been so hurt, and I was too ashamed to bring it up. Yet you chose to love me even with that spiteful thing I did. In your letters you have been more supportive and loving than I could have imagined.

Rebecca put a hand to her mouth.
"You alright?"
"Yes, go ahead."

Some guys' wives and girlfriends have broken up with them for lesser troubles. I'm sorry, darling, that my patriotic fervor took precedence over our marriage. At the time, I really thought I was doing the right thing, and in the end, you supported me in the best of all possible ways...you kept loving me.

Rebecca gasped. "Oh my god."

I have another confession. The more I see of this war, the more I realize that we don't belong here. All we're doing is killing people, bombing farmland, destroying their forests. And for what? Yeh, I'm against Communism, but I'm not sure the people have the will to fight. You can't imagine the damage we're doing with the bombing. Not many talk about it, but I see the same opinions in the thousand yard stares of the men who return from the jungles and hamlets. But I have a job to do. I have only a few months left, and I'll make dang sure the South Vietnamese soldiers I train will be the best trained ever. They have the right to protect their way of life.

Something else. Robert and I helped out a young family living on the streets. The mother died from shell-fire near the hotel where she worked, and her kids were sent to an orphanage. If something happens to me (which it won't), could you find it in your heart to try to find them? Maybe just be sure they are OK? Her name was Lan Nguyen. Might be an impossible task. Hoi Duc Anh is the name of the orphanage.

I love you. Soon we'll be able to kiss all we want!
Adam xxxxxxxxooooooooxxxxxx

Rebecca sat still for a moment, felt her face reddening and swelling from emerging tears.

Billy pulled on her hand. "I can't sit beside you, but I can hold you on my lap. Let me help."

Rebecca moved onto his lap and let Billy wrap his strong arms around her. She yielded to his comfort, and Billy's silent tears joined hers as she cried into his shirt collar. The comforter and the comforted held on to each other as the room darkened with the approaching evening.

Passing by flag-draped houses, the mailman continued his special deliveries down Elm Street. The few elm trees left stood tall and proud, far from the rice paddies and jungles where Adam Benson, Timothy Norris, and other unlucky souls lost their lives. Streetlights popped on and illuminated the elm leaves, casting faint but growing shadows on the sidewalk. Mr. Jackson came out of his house and lowered the flag in the front yard. A dog barked in the distance, and another barked his response.

The majestic elms could not know their lives would be shortened by a disease imported from Asia. The good citizens of Liberty, Ohio, had not known their lives would be changed by an Asian country they didn't know about a couple of years ago. They didn't know proud flags would be burned in protest or that increasing numbers of body bags would be flown back from southeast Asia to American soil. They didn't know their assumptions about what it means to be American would be challenged and changed.

The rustling leaves of the American elms and the snapping of the American flags covered the whispers about a war that would confuse and ignite the hearts of the All-American Town. Few were listening, yet.

Acknowledgements

Two key sources for military and police procedures were my cousin Jack "Skip" Stephenson, USMC Vietnam 1968-69 and my brother Walter "Buz" Rudin, USMC Reserves and former police officer. Other former military who shared their experiences include: Alvin Simpson, USMC Vietnam 1967-1968; Jack Jackson, U.S. Navy, for ballistic information; John Beam, USMC; Dennis Tavares, USMC Vietnam 1969-70; Col. Alfred H. Elliott III (Ret.) Army Vietnam 1969-71, Jeffrey Emery USMC Vietnam 1967-68; Dick Robertson, US Army, Vietnam; Bruce R. Marshall, U.S. Army Vietnam 1967-68; Col. Hollance Lyon (Ret.) USAF; Col. Linda Lyon (Ret.) USAF; Irene Marley, widow of Major Robert L. Baldwin, killed 31 March 1967 in Laos while attempting to evacuate wounded; Army personnel; Frank Shipton, US Army helicopter pilot, Vietnam 1971-72; Dana Hughes, President and Founder of Vietnam Veterans Wives.

Girlfriends patiently listened to story ideas and contributed some of their own: Charli, Deb, Rita, Carol; Vivian Herman for, well, the more colorful scenes; and several unnamed souls who shared their experiences with marijuana. A big thank you goes to September Fawkes, content editor extraordinaire; beta readers; my children who gave me courage; and the Twin Lakes (MI) Book Club for hosting my book launch. Special thanks to my biggest cheerleader, Elwin Coll, whose sanctuary in the woods of northern Michigan enabled my creative muse.

Discussion Questions

1. What elements of the 60s did *Rebecca Benson's War* reflect?
2. Is Rebecca justified to feel that Adam had betrayed her? Is her reaction appropriate for a woman in 1965?
3. How would you describe Rebecca's relationship with her husband?
4. How would you describe Rebecca's relationship with her best friends Annie and Kathy?
5. Have you ever been in a quandary over an important stand you needed to take? What were the risks?
6. The dog Clipper is a main character in the story. What do you think his role is?
7. The author intended to show the many dimensions of war and how people can react differently. Did you think the author had any bias?
8. The story begins with a contextual zoom into the town of Liberty and ends with a zoom out of the final scene. What do you think this technique tries to communicate?
9. How does Rebecca change?

Author's Notes

In preparing to write a novel about a military widow, I chose the Vietnam War—the conflict of my generation. I read many books and watched numerous movies related to the war in Southeast Asia. My research provoked neither a hawkish attitude nor a dovish posture. Reading about the Vietnam conflict made me more thoughtful about wars and the people who fight in them. The words and images of those I read about or interviewed gave me insight into realities and misunderstandings of a war fought by soldiers who slogged through rice paddies in a foreign land where they could barely discern who was friend or who was foe. Not to be forgotten are those who served in hospitals, equipment repair, journalists, or anyone in supportive roles. And let us honor those wives, mothers, sisters, and girlfriends who waited for her warrior to return, alive. For those who didn't survive, we must shed a collective tear.

I did not serve in Vietnam nor did I lose anyone in the war. Yet I humbly offer a story for sharing and exploring an era in American history that tore families apart, challenged social norms, and shaped media coverage in decades to follow.

The more I learned and listened, the more I encountered the reality of the human condition—the need to survive, to have a purpose, and to measure up. I have unlimited respect for people who serve our country even when they are doubting their purpose.

While the Vietnam cities and battles scenes are actual

locations, *Rebecca Benson's War* is not a factual account of the Vietnam War in 1965-68. Newscasts and quotes are authentic and placed in approximate time sequences. Some may ask, "How can someone write about a war without having experienced that war?" Research. Like other authors who attempt to capture the culture, people, and events of a time period, I read books considered by veterans to be authentic; interviewed soldiers, former Marines, wives of Vietnam veterans, and military personnel. I also watched many movies and television documentaries that would give me insight into the Vietnam War causes and controversies.

While no list is ever complete, I have included a compilation of the most informative media I used:

NON-FICTION

- *A Rumor of War*, Philip Caputo, 2014
- *Achilles in Vietnam*: *Combat Trauma and the Undoing of Character,* Jonathan Shay, 1995
- *Antiwarriors*: *The Vietnam War and the Battle for America's Hearts and Minds*, Melvin Small, 2002 -
- *Dear America*: *Letters Home from Vietnam*, Bernard Edelman, ED,W.W. Norton,1985.
- *Distant Shore: A Memoir*, Alvin Simpson, 2009
- *Grief Denied: A Vietnam Widow's Story,* Pauline Laurent, 1999 -
- *Lonely Girls with Burning Eyes*: *A Wife Recalls Her Husband's Journey Home from Vietnam*, Marian Faye Novak, 1991 -
- *Nam: A Photographic History*, Gregory L. Mattson & Leo J. Daugherty III, Metro Books, 2014
- *Soldiers in Revolt: GI Resistance During the Vietnam War*, David Cortright, Haymarket Books, 2005

- *Vietnam War Almanac: An In-Depth Guide to the Most Controversial Conflict in American History*, James H. Willbanks, Skyhorse Publishing, 2013
- *Vietnam Zippos*, Sherry Buchanan, Asia Ink, 2007
- *Warriors of the Sea: Marines of the Second Indochina War*. CSM Michael Martin, Turner Publishing, 2001

FICTION

- *Born on the Fourth of July,* Ron Kovic, 1976
- *Fields of Fire,* James Webb, 2008
- *Matterhorn: A Novel of the Vietnam War*, Karl Malantes, 2011 -
- *The Things They Carried,* Tim O'Brien, 1990
- *The Thirteenth Valley*, John M. Del Vecchio, 1982

FILM

- *Apocalypse Now*, Francis Ford Coppola, director
- *Born on the 4th of July*, Oliver Stone, director
- *(The) Camden 28*, (documentary) Anthony Giacchino
- *Coming Home*, Hal Ashby, director
- *Friendly Fire*, David Greene, director
- *Full Metal Jacket*, Stanley Kubrick, director
- *Gardens of Stone*, Francis Ford Coppola, director
- *Good Morning, Vietnam*, Barry Levinson, director
- *(The) Killing Fields*, Roland Jofe, director
- *Platoon*, Oliver Stone, director
- *(The) Vietnam War* (documentary), Ken Burns, director
- *We Were Soldiers*, Randall Wallace, director

Made in the USA
Coppell, TX
26 September 2021

63049397R10176